THE WIENER ACROSS THE WAY

COCKY KINGMANS
BOOK TWO

AMY AWARD

THE WIENER ACROSS THE WAY

What happens when the sunshiny pop princess and the grumpy football player discover there's more to their fake romance than inspiration for a new love song?

Kelsey Best is America's pop sweetheart and anyone who says they don't like her music is a liar and needs to be punched in the nads. And I'll do it too, because I'm the guy the NFL dubbed the meanest player in the league. Great for my career on the field, not so much for my reputation off it.

So I'm shocked as hell when Kelsey's team sends my agent a wild idea – they want a showmance between us. She's looking to dodge the media frenzy after her breakup with Hollywood's latest heartthrob, and I apparently fit the bill as her perfect distraction. My agent is convinced this fake dating stunt is the key to fixing my image. The whole world is going to hate me when we fake break up. And what happens when I fall for her? She's going to create a blank space in my heart, and I don't think I'm going to be able to shake it off.

This plus-size curvy girl romance has a burnt cinnamon roll hero with a mean protective streak and a baddie plus-size pop star who is on the verge of burn out. But a Bridgertons-meets-American-Football family you'll wish you were a part of will make sure they get their happy ever after.

CONTENT NOTE

This is a book of fluff. (Fluff that I worked really hard on and am extremely proud of.) It's meant for escapism and laughs. We need fluff; it's the insulation from the harsh world around us.

I think it's important to have fat representation in the media, and I do that by showing fat women getting happy ever afters without ever having to lose weight.

However, that doesn't mean there won't be any conflict or angst.

While it was really important to me to write a story with a confident plus-size - fat - curvy heroine whose inner strength and love for herself doesn't waver, I will always put pieces of myself into every one of my curvy girl FMCs, and I'm still working on my own journey of self love - aren't we all?

That means that the heroine does face some

external fatphobia in this book. It's not the main storyline, but it sneaks in.

There is also talk about loss of a parent in the past. Our Cocky Kingmans were raised by a single father.

What I can promise you though is that my books will always hold a space that is free of violence against women including sexual assault. That just doesn't exist in the world I create in my mind.

And finally, I love to write about funny animals and pets. No pets will ever be harmed or die in any of my books.

I like to cry at touching Super Bowl commercials and Broadway musicals about witches who defy gravity, not in my romances.

wink

Also, I full well known I've taken liberties with how the music industry works, and yes, I did a crap ton of research, and have made the choices I wanted anyway.

IT'S MY WORLD, I DO WHAT I WANT

*Knocks glass off the counter.

I'm just sayin' suspend a little disbelief, so you can swoon, and giggle, and kick your feet.

For all the women who've never been skinny dipping because you weren't skinny.
You can go chunky dunkin' with me and the Kingman boys.

"That's why her hair is so big. It's full of secrets."

— GRETCHEN WEINER, MEAN GIRLS

WIENERS AND GRAY SWEATPANTS

DECLAN

The only time I enjoyed being up at the butt crack of dawn was when I'd pulled an all-nighter between the legs of a lush and gorgeous woman. That was not why I was awake at sunrise today, and that just fucking sucked.

I was in a shitty mood. Which wasn't anything new. I certainly shouldn't be around anyone, including my well-meaning brothers who were probably already knocking on my door this morning to console me.

I was all up in my head and the only way to get out was a brutal workout, like the one I was inflicting on myself this morning at stupid o'clock early. I wanted punishing. Only an asshat like me would come this close to losing the Mustangs our whole damn game yesterday.

Too bad it wasn't snowing like it had a week ago. No, today, the sun was shining down, setting us up for a seventy-five-degree day. Fucking sunshine. Even climbing the steps at Rust Rocks wasn't enough to shake off the funk that had enveloped me. Maybe I'd have half a chance if someone wasn't singing the fluffiest pop. The kind that wormed its way into my brain and took up way too much space.

Damned if I didn't already know every word.

I wouldn't have hit the Rocks this morning if I knew there was going to be a sound check. Although Jules was going to pee her pants when I told her. I may be a professional athlete, but even I got a little starstruck over Kelsey Best.

Nobody needed to know that listening in on the bits of songs she sang testing her equipment out lifted the dark cloud over my grumpy ass just a little.

Security had already kicked everyone else out, but one scowl from me, and they'd left me to my workout. Helped that I'd been coming here for years, they all knew me, and I was generous with tips when they let me in early. And the fact that I'd promised to go after a few more rounds of climbing the steps.

Besides, I was here first. Kelsey and her people had shown up after sunrise, so I wasn't giving up my time just because she was one of the world's most popular singers.

I needed to beat this mood, get above the line, or I'd never find my focus for practice today. It was going to be hell reviewing those tapes, and I had a feeling coach was going to kick my ass.

Sort of like I wanted to kick the ass of whoever decided it would be a good idea to add a yapping dog track to the song Kelsey was singing right now. It was really throwing off the beat.

I hit the top step, gave a good stretch of my neck from one side to the other, took the last swig of my water, tossed it in the trash can, and turned to head back down the almost two hundred steps to the stage area. Hold up. That barking wasn't part of the song. Kelsey just stopped singing and the music track that accompanied her did too. But the yap yap yap was still going strong, and it was coming from all the way up here somewhere.

Who the hell let a dog loose in the amphitheater? And a little yappy one at that? Dumb fuckers. It wasn't safe. Coyotes or mountain lions would have no qualms about making a snack out of someone's pet. I followed the sound of the barking until I saw one of the weirdest things in my ever-living life. A sparkly blue blob was barking like some kind of stuffed animal come to life. Was this a joke?

Either that or I was hallucinating. Must be the lack of oxygen to my brain from going twelve laps up and down the enormous steps.

Except, the barking turned into a low growl, and

that's when I heard the distinctive and scary as shit rattling sound coming from the scrubby trees and rocks on the north side of the path over to the parking lot at the top. The sweater was not yapping at some baby toy. Nope. That was a rattlesnake, and if I didn't do something fast, blue fluffball of fur was going to die.

I crept closer, slower than the concrete-cleated New England Rebels quarterback, and called to the pooch as quietly as I could. "Here doggy, doggy, doggy. Come here you dumb little poop, before you really piss that snake off."

The dog lowered its head and growled some more, but it also wagged its tail. Little bugger had heard me but wasn't willing to give up the fight yet. I didn't know whether it was brave or dumb. But as I inched closer, the same thing could probably be said about me too. "Come on, poochy poo. Someone is going to be really sad if you get poisoned and eaten by that snake."

Doggo still didn't back down, but its tail basically went ballistic, which did not please the rattler. Shit. I started looking around for something I could throw at the snake to distract it so I could make a dash for the pup. But I didn't see a damn thing. The Rust Rocks maintenance crew were on their fucking game. The walkway up here was immaculate.

Kelsey's voice burst through the speakers, but this time it was no sound check. "Has anyone seen Wiener the Pooh?"

If I wasn't afraid either me or the dog were about to

die, I would have snort laughed. She named her dachshund Wiener the Pooh? I had to assume that was who was growling and wagging her tail in front of me right now. I quietly called her name, but it had the same effect as before. More tail wagging.

Okay, time for plan B. I slowly pulled my shirt up and over my head. No, I did not think I was going to dazzle the snake with my abs. That would have worked if Chris or Everett had tried it, I'm sure. I was the bulkiest one of the bunch, and that made me a killer defensive linesman. But not an underwear model.

On the steps below, I heard people calling the dog's name, and for the first time, it distracted her from her prey. Which was a bad thing. I launched my t-shirt at the snake in an attempt to either cover it up or at least block it if it decided to strike. I hit the thing dead on, and while it flopped about under my shirt, I lunged forward to snag up the little dog like a fumbled football.

Like I should have done in the game yesterday.

Little Wiener wiggled like a happy baby and licked my face about a thousand times. I headed toward the steps and called down, "I found her."

Kelsey was already halfway up the steps, and the closer she got, the more I fucking forgot how to breathe. And it wasn't the altitude. She was so much prettier in person than on the screen, and that was saying a lot. I was going to have to hold her squirmy little dog in front of my junk, because my gray sweat-pants were not going to hide the bulge forming there.

Shit.

She was breathing hard by the time I met her a tenth of the way down, and while my mind was completely in the gutter, I was also impressed she hadn't keeled over racing up here like that. The steps at Rust Rocks were a workout for even the fittest, plus, this was the Mile High City baby. What we lacked in oxygen, we made up for with the view.

But even the sunrise over the Flatirons didn't compare to the beauty that was Kelsey Best with rosy-red cheeks.

"Wiener the Pooh, come here you little poop face." She panted and reached for the dog, who she had to practically wrench away while Little Miss Wiggle Worm tried to lick my face some more. "Thank you for finding her, uh, umm—" her eyes went from my face, down, down, down my bare naked and sweaty chest, and paused at the very obvious bulge in the front of my sweatpants, "Why aren't you wearing a shirt? I don't need to call my security, do I?"

There was a quick flash of worry in her eyes, but I took a step back and folded my hands in front of my growing erection to appease her sense of safety and keep me from embarrassing myself any more than my dick and its excitement already had. My reward for that was a sparkling smile that just about knocked me off my feet. "Didn't mean to make you uncomfortable.

My shirt is right over there, and we need to call security up here anyway because there's a cranky-ass rattlesnake underneath of it."

"A what now? Did you say rattlesnake? Holy crapballs." She clutched the dog closer to her and turned, yelling down toward the stage. "Penelope! Get somebody up here ASAP. There's a freaking snake."

Man, oh man, did this girl have a set of lungs on her. She didn't even need a microphone to project from all the way the hell up here down to the stage. Maybe it was the amphitheater, but I doubted I could yell that loud.

Instead of moving further away at the news of that threat, Kelsey stepped closer to me, and fuck if I didn't feel protective of her in that moment. I could absolutely see why her fans were ride or die for her. I was damn near ready to swoop her up like a fricking fairy princess and carry her off to safety right this second.

But I was no knight in shining Under Armour.

"Don't worry, I got you." I moved myself so I blocked the snake under my shirt from her view and got closer to her at the same time. The way she looked up at me had me feeling a hundred feet tall and like I wanted to pull her into my arms and kiss her.

Whoa, whoa, whoa there, Mustang. This was probably all part of her charm and every man on the planet wanted to kiss her. Even the ones who said they hated her and her music. Especially the ones who trolled her posts and made shitty comments about her body.

Yeah, I saw her posts, and the comments. Those guys were dick munches. Kelsey and her thick hips, thighs, and her ass were beyond delicious. God, she was exactly my fucking type.

Shit. If she even glanced down, she was going to think I was a fucking perv. I needed to either keep her eyes up here on mine or distract her in some other way. "Why don't we head back down toward the stage? We'll let the park staff take care of the threat. They're probably trained in rattlesnake wrangling, and I wouldn't want your people to get hurt."

I held one arm out and pointed her toward the stairs, and when she turned, I did the dumbest thing I ever could have. I put my hand on the small of her back to guide her away.

The absolute electric zing from that simple touch went straight to my dick. Jesus, Mary, and Joseph. I had to use every thought of losing football games, the Queen of England, and the effects of global warming on poor polar bears just so I didn't come in my pants like a thirteen-year-old boy.

We proceeded down the steps at about a tenth of the speed I was used to, and I was going to relish every single moment of it. Jules was going to die, come back to life to hear me tell her all over again, and then go catatonic, probably while listening to Kelsey's collected works at full volume, on repeat.

And the boys, well, every single one of them, except

for maybe Chris who was happily engaged to the love of his life, were going to be jealous as shit.

But I was going to need about a hundred and two cold showers after this. And then I'd head to the field and punish myself with those game day films and another brutal workout.

When we approached the stage, a group of people surrounded us, all fawning over Kelsey and her little dog too. For the briefest flash, Kelsey looked up at me and rolled her eyes. I didn't think I was supposed to see that. Then she put on that dazzling smile for them and told them what I'd done.

"I'm telling you all, he sacrificed his whole-ass shirt to save Wiener the Pooh."

As one, every eye turned on me, and I think I understood exactly how Everett felt whenever a new underwear ad came out and his adoring fans went all goo-goo ga-ga over him. How the hell did he deal with that?

I knew how I was dealing with it. The same way I dealt with everything else. I scowled.

I didn't mean to, it was just my... face. Jules called it my resting bitch face. It scared quarterbacks around the world. What it had Kelsey and her crew doing was not what I expected. Half of them giggled like little schoolgirls, and the other half awwed as if my scowl was the cutest fucking thing they'd ever seen.

Okay, that was weird, and I did not know what to do with any of them. I wasn't the Kingman brother women oohed and awwed and fawned over. Did I like this?

Nope. No. Huh-uh. Time to get the dodge out of hell. Not that being in the presence of Kelsey was hell in any way shape or form. I just was not used to having this much attention on me.

Chris was the eldest, everyone's favorite, and the star quarterback. He was the golden child chosen one who soaked up the spotlight like the rays of the sun. I quit competing with him for attention way back in high school when I moved from offense to defense. And that worked fine for me.

I knew I was the best at what I did. So did the rest of the league.

Except for fucking yesterday.

"Okay, ladies, I gotta go. Glad you got your dog back unharmed. Good luck with your shows this week." I carefully backed away, but almost squashed the circle of women behind me. When had they closed ranks? "Excuse me."

"God, such a gentleman," someone cooed.

That was not the term most people used to describe me. Not that I was an asshole to the ladies or anything, but "nice guy" wasn't synonymous with Declan Kingman.

Kelsey and Wiener the Pooh both looked at me like I was the bees' knees. She winked at whoever had said that. "He is quite the gentleman. Can I thank you with some tickets to the show on Friday?"

I was this close to refusing. I didn't need to be paid off for saving a dog. But Jules would probably pee in my Cheerios if she ever found out I had the chance to get my hands on tickets that had sold out in zero-point-two seconds. She'd been begging Dad for months for an advance on her allowance to buy some off one of the resale ticket sights.

The Kingmans might have a combined net worth in the tens of millions, but nobody should be paying five grand for two tickets to a concert. Yeah. Five grand. I wondered if Kelsey even knew people paid that much to see her. She didn't seem like a diva who would roll around in a bed full of money.

Oh, shit. And now I was imagining her rolling around in a bed. No money, no nothing, just naked.

I needed to extract myself from this situation immediately. And go take a cold shower. Or fifteen thousand. "You don't need to do that. But my little sister would probably never speak to me again if I refused the tickets, so I'll just say thank you for the kind offer and yes please."

One of the women surrounding me fanned her face with her hand and said, "Somebody thank this man's mama for raising him right. Whew."

I mentally sent that thanks up to heaven. My mom had raised us right for as long as we had her.

"Kels, ready to finish up the sound check here?" A woman with a stern look, a headset, and a clipboard moved in next to Kelsey. She attached a sparkly blue leash to the collar on Wiener the Pooh and took her out of Kelsey's arms.

The little wiener dog wiggled her way out of Clipboard Commander's grasp and came over immediately to me, trying her best to crawl right up my leg.

"All right everyone, back to work. Come along Miss Queen of Wieners and Mr. Knight in Shining Sweat. Kelsey has a lot to do today. Let's go, people." The group grumbled but moved away, all except Kelsey. Clipboard Commander gave her a raised eyebrow, then turned, and signaled to me to follow her.

"It was nice to meet you, Kelsey."

"You too, Sir Shining. Ooh, no. That just makes me think of that Steven King movie and those creepy twins and the bloody elevator." She made an adorable fucking face that was supposed to be disgusted but was too cute.

I wanted nothing more than to stand here and see what other faces I could get her to make.

"Mr. Half-Naked Man, let's go," Clipboard Commander shouted from halfway across the stage.

Kelsey made that almost invisible eyeroll again. "I'm not calling you that either."

"Declan." I held out my hand ignoring the demands to leave. "Declan Kingman."

She took my hand and the second her skin touched mine, I was a goner. "So not a knight at all, but a king among men."

I almost dropped to one knee and swore my fealty

to her right then and there. I might have too if Wiener the Pooh hadn't come tearing across the stage and jumped up, hitting me right in the junk.

I went down and got a face full of doggie licks.

"Pooh, oh no. Shit. Penelope, you'd better upgrade those tickets to VIP."

*H*ey Besties,

I'm in the Mile High City and ready to hit Rust Rocks on Friday. But whew, how do you Coloradans even breathe up here? Like, where's the oxygen? I'm gonna have a challenging time singing along to the songs. I'm still searching for an oxygen bar. I was promised oxygen.

I don't know how Kelsey's going to do it, but we know our girl. She gets it done for her fans, always.

Who's hoping she tests out a new breakup song on us this weekend?

I heard a rumor that the schmoe drunk dialed her. Dumbass shouldn't have effed up like he did if he still wanted her to talk to him.

All I want for her is a nice guy who will treat her right. I know we all do. She deserves to be happy. Even if we don't get any more break up songs. lol

I'd be down for a good love-story ballad, wouldn't you?

Who's gonna be at the show? If not, you know I'll be live streaming!

Your BFF,

Mz. Besties' Bestie

CHEESY KIND OF LOVE

KELSEY

*D*enver was beautiful. Rust Rocks amphitheater amazed me, and I loved the sound. What I didn't like was how fast the paparazzi had found me. It was like they had tracking chips implanted in my freaking brain or something.

Our sound check wasn't supposed to be until this afternoon, but I'd offered a little bonus to the crew if they'd sneak up here with me. I didn't want to believe that someone on my own team had tipped them off, but the thought had snaked its way into my mind. Ooph. I sure hated the idea though.

I gave Wiener the Pooh a quick kiss on the top of her head right in that super soft spot behind her ear.

There were some days I was fairly sure she was the only one who actually cared about me.

No. Ridiculous. Silly. According to the entertainment publications, FlipFlop, FaceSpace, and that other one that the electric car guy bought, the entire world loved me. And I was grateful for it. They hadn't always. To be fair, there were a lot of unhappy little men who still liked to tell me to eat a salad on every single picture.

Penelope wouldn't let me reply that they should eat a bag of dicks. No matter how badly I wanted to. Luckily I had fans that did that for me.

"Kelsey, the cars are ready. Do you want to do the bait and switch or walk tall?" Pen looked at me expectantly. As if I had a choice. I did what she told me to, because most of the time, she was the only person standing between me and death by a thousand flashes.

"Whatever you think. But I'll be honest, I'm already exhausted so I doubt I'm going to be able to give them my best face." I liked the idea of walking tall, and it gave me an idea for a lyric. I pulled my phone out and quickly made a note. I needed every shred of inspiration if I was going to get the songs for this next album written.

One long, assessing stare later, and she must have agreed the no makeup, awake before of dawn look wasn't good enough for the press. "Bait and switch it is."

She lifted the ever-present headset up and clicked

on her phone. "Grab the wig and head toward the east entrance."

Okay, good. It wasn't that I minded the press. They were an important key to my success. When they were kind. So many of them had been great to me over the years. Well, once I'd proven I was not a one-hit wonder and none of them could hurt me by reporting about what I looked like. But these days it seemed like the only thing they cared about was who I was dating, or rather, who I'd broken up with.

It was hard to find love when your every move was documented. Not that I thought I knew what real love meant anyway. I knew plenty of heartbreak though, and that made for great songs. Grammy winning songs. Multi-platinum record sales songs.

If I couldn't use my own pain to create art, what was it all for anyway?

Penelope and two women on my security team hustled me and Pooh toward the east entrance, and the weight of getting up so early tugged at my steps. I forced myself to be a morning person, but deep down, if I could sleep in until eleven, have brunch in bed, watch a movie or read a book until two in the afternoon, and then start my day, I would.

Every single day.

But that wasn't going to happen in this life.

I slipped on the wig, a simple, chestnut-colored bob that made me look like an entirely different person. It was funny how a slight change in appearance could give me a sliver of freedom. The wig was my invisibility cloak, a brief respite from the eyes always seeking me out. Especially in colder climates where bulky coats hide body shapes.

Because my dog and my thick tushy gave me away every time. Although it helped when I'd finally convinced everyone that we needed to hire more women with bodies like mine to be backup singers and dancers. That had been a harder fought battle than the finale of *The Choicest Voice*.

We navigated through the backstage area, toward the waiting cars, and my phone buzzed in my pocket. It was a text from my agent and manager, no doubt a reminder about some interview or photo shoot. But for a moment, I ignored it.

I glanced back at the amphitheater, the sun casting a golden hue over the rust-colored rocks. It was a place of pure magic, a natural cathedral that had seen the highs and lows of countless artists. I wanted to soak in that energy, to let it infuse me and my music with something raw and real.

I'd always wanted to play here. I'd had to twist the arms of some flies with honey to get the show added to my schedule, and even then, it took the promise to do this music festival gig in Aspen.

"The cars are pulling up now. I've got your decoys heading to their exits too. Be ready to make that mad dash," Pen said, forcing me to give up the peaceful moment.

"Let's do this," I said, more to myself than to her. I nodded, adjusting the wig, and took in a couple of deep lungfuls of air, blowing them out like I was about to run a sprint. Or up the steps like the hunky rescuer of dachshunds. Just thinking about it had my legs feeling like Jell-O.

The steps. Not the hunk.

Or maybe.

No.

I was not looking forward to spotting him in the VIP section of the show later. Nope. Not me. Pooh squirmed in my arms and wiggled her little butt like she knew who I was thinking about. "Woof, woof."

"You're the one with the crush, aren't you, poo poos?" I gave her a little boop on the nose, and then wrapped the oversize shacket around her to hide her presence. She knew the drill and snuggled up right under my arm.

Penelope touched her earpiece and gave me the you're-not-gonna-like-this look. "Ah, shizznit. The bastards figured us out, Kels. Might as well face them now. We've got too much on the schedule today to camp out here for much longer."

Well, didn't that suck a bunch of ducks. "Yep. Fine."

I pulled the wig off and shoved it into a shacket pocket but kept the sunglasses. They didn't need to know I wasn't wearing any makeup. I did give my cheeks a little pinch though, to give them some color.

The cameras liked when my face was rosy and smiling. So that's what I'd give them.

We stepped out into the world of flashing cameras and shouting reporters, and I put on my best smile. One day, I'd find a way to really walk tall, not just faking it for the media.

Pen wasn't kidding when she said we had a full day. We went straight to the studios of one of the local news stations for a press junket that entailed six ten-minute interviews, back to back to promote the tour. Thank goodness they had hair, makeup, and wardrobe ready for me.

Too bad none of the reporters cared a lick about my music or the concert. They sure did care about Jake Jay. The number of times I had to tell them that no, I hadn't seen his latest movie, and no he hadn't drunk dialed me like the rumors said, and no we were never, ever, ever getting back together, was exhausting.

He had drunk dialed me. A lot.

I really needed to block his number.

After escaping the relentless barrage of relationship questions, my screwed-on smile literally ached. All I wanted to do was take Pooh for a quiet walk, away from the cameras, and then crash in our posh hotel in Peachy Creek.

But first we had another press conference. This one for the reporters who hadn't scored the one-on-ones. Two things I knew that got people cranky were feeling left out and being hungry. Same.

While I knew they were all waiting in the studio area, I motioned for Penelope. "Can you arrange for catering to bring them snacks, please? Get them some charcuterie boards. Everyone loves those things."

Well-fed reporters were much kinder to me. Although, god forbid they see me eat.

We recorded the fifteen second spot that would play during prime time for the next couple of days, and I had the makeup artist give me a quick refresh before I psyched myself up one more time to face a sea of reporters. They were all itching to ask about my love life, but I had a different plan.

I walked through the side door to the studio and into a barrage of questions. The snack table was pretty much eviscerated, but I snagged a couple bits of cheese on my way up to the table with the mics. Pooh wagged her little tail as I set her down on the stool set up especially for her next to me. She knew what was coming.

Just as the first reporter geared up to ask me a predictable question about my dating status, I leaned into the microphone with a conspiratorial smile. "Before we start, I just want to say I'm thrilled to announce a new love in my life."

Penelope and my agent, Skeeter, looked at me with giant bug eyes straight out of a sci-fi romance novel. I gave them a conspiratorial eyebrow waggle. They hated when I went rogue. But I knew what I was doing. Time to win the reporters over.

The room went silent, every reporter ready to

pounce on the juicy tidbit. Flashes popped and recorders clicked on, capturing what they thought would be a sensational revelation.

"Yes," I nodded, my smile broadening, "I've fallen head over heels for... cheese."

I reached for the little plate of food on my right and popped a piece into my mouth, and then fed a tiny sliver to Pooh.

There was a moment of stunned silence when I thought I might have just blown it. I rarely talked about food and never ate in front of anyone else. There was just too much harassment from people who thought they knew my body better than I did. But something about today made me say fuck it. Before I could completely overthink it, the room erupted into laughter. Some reporters looked confused or surprised, others amused.

"I mean it," I said, chuckling along with them. "Have you tried the brie here? It's life changing. And don't even get me started on the gouda."

A reporter from a well-known entertainment magazine raised her hand. "Kelsey, are you saying your love life is... cheesy?"

Yes. I got 'em.

"You could definitely say that." I flashed them my best smile, as close to a genuine one as I could give. "Okay, and now that you know my deepest, darkest secret, can we talk about my tour? I promise it's going to be *grate*."

The air quotes and my super dorky joke made them all putty in my hands. And not a one of them said anything about how I was glorifying obesity by eating a piece of cheese. Huh.

The rest of the press conference went better than normal. Reporters asked about my show and the upcoming festival in Aspen, tried to get me to tell them which songs from past albums I'd do, and, of course, my favorite cheese pairings. It was refreshing and, honestly, a lot of fun.

I left the room feeling lighter than I had in days. Who knew a little humor could turn the tide of an interview? Maybe I should start taking my relationships with dairy products more seriously. Although, there would inevitably be the haters who, once again, would tell me to eat a salad.

After a quick appearance at a shopping center, where I sang my first hit, "Book Boyfriend" to thousands of screaming fans who also knew every word and sang along, we finally got to the hotel and I went straight to my room and changed into day jammies.

The luxury and quiet of the place were a stark contrast to the chaos we'd just left. I slumped into one of the plush chairs, my exhaustion manifesting not just in my body but in my soul. Skeeter and Penelope were already waiting in the suite's spacious living area, their expressions a mix of concern and anticipation.

"I'm so done with every single reporter only wanting to talk about who I'm dating—or not dating." I understood the nature of parasocial relationships, but honestly, why did they care so much? "It's like my music doesn't even matter to them anymore."

It used to be about the music.

Skeeter, with her ever-business over emotion demeanor, flipped open her tablet and tip-tapped away at whatever secrets it held within. "Kels, you know how this industry works. Your personal life has always been a big sell. Maybe we should give them something to talk about. A new relationship, perhaps?"

I rolled my eyes. I knew this was coming. "Not another actor. Not for a long time. And not a musician either. I'm so tired of big dick egos but no actual big dicks."

Penelope snorted. When it was just the three of us, and Wiener the Pooh, I could be more myself. I'd die if anyone else ever heard me talk like that. Cute and innocent was the Kelsey Best persona everyone wanted from me. So that's what they got.

Pen held a finger up and made that face she did when she had a really clever idea. "What about Declan Kingman?"

"Who?" The name sounded so familiar, and warm and delicious. "He's not that FlipFlopper who says he's into thick girls but is, like, weird and fetishy about it, is he?"

"No. Ew. The guy who rescued Pooh this morning." She put her hand over her heart and pretended to swoon. But popped right back up. "He's not an actor or musician and I doubt he has a FlipFlop. He's a professional football player, so he knows how to be in the spotlight, but he isn't in the showbiz world."

My legs went all jelly again thinking of our brief encounter. His strong hands gently cradling Pooh, his eyes meeting mine with a mixture of concern and warmth.

"Declan Kingman," I repeated, rolling the name around in my mouth like a new flavor. Mmm.

I pondered that for a moment, the idea of Declan slowly seeping in. A part of me was excited at the thought of seeing him again, but another part dreaded the idea of another public relationship. Not that it would be real or anything. All for show.

"I don't know," I admitted. "I'm not ready to jump into something just for the sake of headlines. And do pro athletes even do these kinds of setups?"

Skeeter nodded, understanding the dilemma. "It doesn't have to be serious. Just a few public appearances, something to get the press off your back about Jake. I can reach out to his agent. Honestly, Kels, it would probably give his career a boost to be seen with you. So it's win-win."

I didn't know diddly squat about football. Except they had cute butts. It was the tight pants. Hugely different from the gray sweatpants that had shown off every one of Mr. Kingman's attributes and then some. He'd tried really hard to hide it, but someone should have told him that was a lost cause, and that most, if not all, of my staff would probably be imagining what that bulge could do when they were alone in bed tonight.

Whew. I picked up my water. Was Denver always this hot this time of year?

"Okay, call his people. But make sure they understand this isn't long term. I'm not pretending to be in some long-distance relationship while we're on the international leg of the tour."

I'd better do some research on football and the guys who played it. And by research I meant scrolling Flip-Flop to see if he did have an account. Surely, he did. Because even if it was a manufactured romance, I could still get some inspiration for some kind of a love song out of it.

Since that's all anyone wanted from me anyway, not an artist seeking truth in her work. Not that I would ever complain. I was lucky and privileged and got to make music for a living instead of working at a desk, or in a restaurant, or any other number of jobs that real people did every day and probably worked a hell of a lot harder than I did.

I supposed if anyone would understand that, it might be a man who played a game for a living.

MEAN DECK KING

DECLAN

*T*he roar of the crowd from yesterday's game is what should be echoing in my head, a muddled mix of cheers and boos. It wasn't. "Book Boyfriend" was drowning out all other thoughts.

I was on the field for practice, trying to focus, but my mind kept drifting back to Kelsey Best. Her laugh, her smile... her dog. I shook my head, chiding myself. Focus, Declan, focus.

Out of nowhere, a football smacked against my helmet.

"Hey, Earth to Declan," Chris called out, waving his arms to get my attention. I rubbed the spot where the ball had hit, glaring at him. Classic Chris. Wasn't the first time I'd been beaned in the head by a ball from my older brother. At least this time I was wearing a helmet.

I jogged over to where my brothers stood, Chris with his quarterback's smirk, Everett tossing a ball up and down, and Hayes stretching his legs.

"What's up?" I tossed the ball back to Chris, but Hayes snagged it right out of the air. The kid was fast.

Chris clapped me on the back, his big shit-eating grin barely containing his excitement. "No one in the world would believe it, but you've been nominated for the league's meanest player."

"Just like Dad back in the day," Hayes added, thumping me on the arm in a brotherly punch.

"Yeah, our not so secret weapon is the Kingman mean machine on defense," Everett chimed in, nodding approvingly.

I blinked. I was just doing my job. Usually pretty damn well. My plays on the field were aggressive, sure, but mean? I glanced at my brothers, their faces alight with what they saw as an honor.

"Who else is on the list?" I had to be on there because I was a legacy for the award. "It better be full of the best goddamned linesmen in the league."

That came out a bit gruffer than I'd intended. It was irritating that I both wanted to win the accolade and I didn't want anything to do with it.

Chris nodded. He got the competitive streak better than any of the rest of us. He and I had been competing since diapers. "It is, man. It definitely is."

"Well, badass, I guess." At least that meant it wasn't completely a fluff title. "Now you shitheads get back to prancing around the field. I've got work to do."

I picked up my helmet and got the hell back to my own drills. I was Declan Kingman, linebacker for the Denver Mustangs, and maybe the league's meanest player, which meant I had to work doubly hard now.

During the next drill, I threw myself into the tackling dummies with a renewed vigor, plowing into them with precision. I was their defensive cornerstone, the one who kept the opponents at bay. Meanest player... I wasn't fucking mean, just focused, determined, and got the job done.

Grumpy on occasion, maybe.

"That's my man." Chris caught my eye after a particularly sharp tackle and threw a super annoying thumbs-up my way. What were we, seven and eight years old? I gave him the bird in return.

After practice I slowly made my way to the locker room, where my brothers were already changing.

"Man, you were on fire out there today." Chris slapped me on the back as I walked up to my locker. "But you're also grumpier than Luke Skycocker when he doesn't get his strawberries. What's eating you?"

I shrugged off his comment, stashing my helmet, and peeling off my uniform. Yeah, I was going to have some bruises. "I'm not grumpy."

Everett eyed me closely. "You've been growling

around since that mistake last game. You need to shake it off."

He and Hayes exchanged a look and then both burst out into the Taylor Swift song "Shake It Off" and did a dance that looked more like they were having seizures than choreography. Eyeroll. Only dudes who scored touchdown after touchdown did dances like that off the cuff.

Hayes stopped gyrating around first and pointed at me. "You're too hard on yourself, dude. You need to calm down. You're being too lou—"

"I will sit on you and make you cry like you're five years old if you start singing and dancing again."

Like any self-respecting man, I loved me some Tay Tay, but she was not the pop star on my mind at the moment. Shit. No. I should not be thinking about Kelsey Best. Again. She was already a distraction I couldn't afford.

"One error doesn't define you, little brother." Chris got all serious and captain of the team with me. "You're the best linebacker we've got."

I appreciated their support, but their words did little to ease the knot in my stomach. I probably just needed to eat.

Everett clapped his hands together. "I know what you need. To get laid. It's been ages since I've seen anyone sneaking out of your house at sunrise. Well, except you. This morning."

Chris laughed, nodding in agreement. "Everett's

right. Look at how having a fucking baller sex life has improved my game this season."

"Oh my god." I tossed my gear into my locker a little more forcefully than necessary. "We know. Trust me, we know exactly how much sex you and your fiancée are having."

"I don't even need an alarm clock anymore," Everett said. "Trixie's louder than her pet rooster in the morning."

"I know." Chris waggled his eyebrows and grinned like... well, a guy getting laid more than seemed humanely possible. That, and he'd finally told the love of his life how he felt about her and they were living a disgustingly cute, and noisy, happy ever after.

I rolled my eyes. "I don't need to get laid, or even a date, and I don't need to lighten up. I'm just being me and the rest of you are being giant man-babies."

Hayes slung his towel around his waist to head to the showers. "Come on, Deck. It might be good for you. You might even smile, but don't break your face."

Maybe they were right. Maybe a night out, away from the field, away from the expectations, was exactly what I needed. I worked hard, and I knew how to play hard too.

I did have concert tickets after all. I was just going to give them to Jules and tell her to invite a friend. But maybe I was going to be her friend.

"Alright, fine, I will go out and blow off some steam," I conceded, closing my locker with a thud. "But don't you even think about setting me up with some-one, Ev. Put your little black book of a phone away right now."

Everett raised his hands, but the screen of his phone was facing me, and there was already a woman's name pulled up in his contacts.

"I swear, if you try some matchmaking scheme, you're going to see who the meanest linebacker is when I squash you into the ground in front of the cheer team."

Everett's grin widened. "Ooh. Do that anyway. Then they'll feel sorry for me, and maybe they'll kiss my boo boo and make it all better."

"Like most of them haven't already kissed your boo boo." I punched him in the nuts but being my closest younger brother, he'd perfected his block for that particular move.

I was ready to hit the showers when fuck if the PR team didn't hit the locker room, phones in hand, prob-ably already recording. They were always wanting us to do some quiz or game or other annoying thing to promote the team on FlipFlop or FaceSpace. I was better on the field than I was on camera.

Of course Everett and Hayes were the first two they flocked too since both had huge social media follow-ings already. I kept my back to them, hoping they'd know better than to try to get me to say anything on camera.

"Hey, Everett, who would you pick as a partner in a

dance off?" They named three popular singers, and I just shook my head.

"Oh, it's got to be—"

"Kelsey Best." Somehow, I just blurted that out. What the fuck was wrong with my mouth? They weren't even talking to me. She wasn't even on their list. But she should be.

Everett, Hayes, and the two PR kids turned to me. I looked back at them and shrugged. "Whatever he was going to say was wrong because the only right answer is Kelsey. She's got all the moves."

I dropped trou and grabbed my towel to hit the showers before they could even think about any follow up questions.

I went straight from practice back to the neighborhood we all lived in. My house was across the way from my childhood home. Well, it was only mostly mine. Chris owned it. I'd buy it from him eventually. When I had a reason to.

After I parked my truck in the driveaway, I jogged across to my dad's house and braced myself for the whirlwind that was my little sister. None of us were worried in the least that she had us all wrapped around her little finger.

She was sprawled out in the living room, surrounded by schoolbooks, and blasting the one and only Kelsey Best. I started singing along, and she looked up, her eyes lighting up with that mischievous spark unique to her.

"Dorklan. What are you doing here on a school night?" She jumped up and gave me a hug that nearly knocked the wind out of me. Thank goodness she wasn't one of those too cool for hugs teenagers. "Running away from your adoring fans?"

I laughed, ruffling her hair. "Not quite. Actually, I have a surprise for you."

Her eyes narrowed suspiciously. "If this is about dating advice, I'm ready. Hit me with your deepest how to get the girl questions."

"No, no," I interrupted, holding up my hands in surrender. "Nothing like that. I happened to get my hands on tickets to Kelsey Best's show on Friday. Thought you might want to come with me."

Her reaction was instantaneous. Her eyes went wide, and she let out a squeal that could probably be heard from the next block. "Are you serious? Kelsey Best? She's my fricking idol. I'm dead. Literally, not literally dead."

I nodded, enjoying the rare moment of seeing her this excited. "Yeah, figured you'd maybe die if I didn't take you with. Either that or I would because you'd kill me if you found out I went without you."

She threw her arms around me again, this time with a force that spoke volumes of her excitement. "Thank you, thank you, thank you. I always said you were the best older brother. Don't tell the others I said so though. I still have to live with Flynn, Garrett, and Isak in the summer."

"Only the best for my little sis," I said, feeling a warmth in my chest that only family could bring.

She pulled away and did a little dance around the coffee table. "We're gonna have so much fun. And just so you know, if any of your adoring fan girls try to crash our night, I'm totally prepared to take them down."

I laughed, knowing full well she could and would. "Why do you think I invited you? You're the only one who'll protect me."

Like, for real. Everett had already texted me the names of three of the ladies on the cheer squad who were ready for a night in my bed and nothing more.

I was just about to leave when Dad walked in from the backyard, carrying some freshly grilled chicken. "Declan, staying for dinner?"

"Hey, Dad," I greeted him, but his attention went straight to Jules, who was still bouncing around with excitement.

"Who spoiled you and with what?" he said, setting the plate down and crossing his arms. He glared at me. "What did you do?"

Jules rolled her eyes but grinned. "He's taking me to the Kelsey Best concert at Rust Rocks on Friday. I can go, right?"

"Did you finish your paper for psych?"

"What does it look like I'm working on?" She indicated her books. "It's not like I'm up for valedictorian or anything."

Was she? Probably. And taking psychology? I didn't even know they offered that in high school. The smarts were strong in this one. Not that any of us were slouches in school. Dad was a stickler for grades.

She pulled on her lip, like she was actually worried he wouldn't let her go. But I'd been on the receiving end of this routine a few times myself. He was a big proponent of work hard, play hard. And I happened to know he thought she worked too hard and didn't play often enough. "So can I go?"

Dad chuckled, but his eyes were serious when they met mine. "You make sure she's safe at that concert, kid. She's my baby girl."

I nodded, understanding the weight of his trust. Moments like these were what grounded me. "I'll look after her, Dad."

Jules gave us both her patented fuck-the-patriarchy glare. "I'm standing right here, you know. I'm not a damsel in distress."

Dad smiled at her, the love for his one and only daughter evident in his eyes. "I know, JuJu Bean. But even a bowl-winning quarterback makes sure he's got protection when he's out of the pocket."

Jules made a moue face but accepted his response. Then she dragged me into the kitchen to help her set the table. I certainly wasn't saying no to my dad's barbecued wings and a nice spinach salad. Not since what I had waiting at home was a protein shake, three plain chicken breasts, and another protein shake.

We sat and loaded up our plates. "How'd you even get these tickets anyway? They sold out in like two-point-two seconds. Where are our seats? We're all the way at the back, aren't we? Wait, did you get them off a scalper? Ew."

"Take a breath and a bite. Jeez." I shoved a huge bite of salad into my mouth just to make her wait until I finished chewing.

She flicked a cherry tomato off her plate at me. Which I caught and also popped into my mouth.

"You're the worst. The best, but also the worst. Tell me."

"I did not get them off a scalper. They were a gift, and only the best for us. We're VIP seats baby."

Her eyes went wide, and she stopped mid-bite of wing. "Your agent is so much better than Chris's at getting you cool shizz."

Alexis had worked some miracles in her time. I still had my fingers crossed she could get me that shoe deal.

"Imagine if we got to actually meet Kelsey? Oh my gawd. You should make a Bestie bracelet and put your number on it and give it to her. Like, what if you two went out? She's single right now, you know?" Jules made waggly matchmaker eyes at me that were identical to the ones that Ev had given me earlier. She continued to go on and on about how she was going to make a whole bunch of Bestie bracelets to trade at the show and how she'd make some for me if I wanted.

I'd go, I'd sing along, and I might even dance, but I

wasn't an actual Bestie. Even if I did have all her albums on my car jams playlist.

"I heard about the nomination," Dad said, his voice even. "Meanest player, huh? That was me back in the day too."

It was the part of the 'How I Met Your Father' story my mom had liked to tell the most. He'd gotten that same nomination the season the two of them met. She'd always called him her growly bear.

I shrugged, unsure how to respond. "It's just a title. Doesn't mean anything."

Dad nodded, understanding. "It doesn't. And it doesn't define who you are off the field either."

I pretended not to care and took another wing. "I know."

But did anyone else?

INSTASNAP POST

*H*ey Besties,

It's cheesepocalypse. Like... I popped into a grocery store here in Denver, thinking, hey, if Kelsey says she's having a love affair with brie, I can at least try the weird gooey stuff.

They. Were. Sold. Out.

Not just of brie either. Every cheese. Even cheese sticks.

That's the power of Besties.

I guess we like cheese now, so dairy farmers of America, you're welcome. (But be good to your cows, or we'll come for you.) Also... who else needs to stock up on those lactose pills? Just me? Beware, that's probs the next thing to sell out. Uh-oh. This could cause a bigger TP shortage than Coronapocalypse.

Luckily for me, the room service at the hotel still

had a stash, and for today, I'm going to be like Kelsey and eat what I want, not what I think I should.

And anyone who tells me to have a salad instead can eat a bag of dicks.

I'm still crossing my fingers that our girl Kelsey will find real love with someone who treats her right and isn't made out of dairy. Is there anyone out there like that? She deserves someone who will worship her like I'm currently worshipping a nice piece of nutty and buttery sheep's milk cheese. Because we fancy.

Two more sleeps until the next show. Who'll be on my livestream?

See ya there, Besties!

Your BFF,

Mz. Besties' Bestie

I LIKE BIG SACKS AND I CANNOT LIE

KELSEY

*F*uck cheese.

No. Sigh. Cheese didn't deserve that. Cheese was delicious, cheese wasn't the villain here.

But neither was I.

While I was doing my cool down after my morning workout, I scrolled through the comments on my phone, each one a little sting.

"I was just trying to be funny," I sighed, locking the screen, and looking up at Penelope, who was busy organizing my schedule.

Penelope was on the treadmill next to me and glanced over, her expression a mix of sympathy and resolve, and then stole my phone. "Kelsey, you know how it is with the media. They twist everything. But your fans, they get you."

I huffed but was also glad she'd made me stop doom scrolling. It was bad for my mental health. I nodded, trying to shake off the negativity. "It's just frustrating, Pen. I thought by now even the hater dudes would buy into that I'm about body positivity, about loving yourself. Not about making my cheesy jokes about how I need to go on a diet and the size of my butt."

She stopped her treadmill and turned to me. "Your fans do understand. And honestly, I thought it was funny. Who doesn't love cheese? Cheese haters are the worst. Only slightly less worse than concern trolls."

I chuckled despite the frustration. "Right. Maybe I should release a song about it. Brie my lover. No, no wait. It's not you, it's Brie."

Penelope laughed, her eyes twinkling, but shook her head at my horrible lyrics. "Your incredible ability to turn anything into a song that tells a story is why people love you. Just keep doing that."

I slowed the speed of my treadmill, really ready for this work out to be over. "You think it's not a setback then? This whole cheese debacle?"

"Absolutely not," Penelope assured me. "If anything, it shows how real you are. You're not just a pop star with nothing in your head. You're a person who can have a laugh and stand up for what you believe in."

I didn't know if declaring my love for cheese in front

of a bunch of reporters did all that, but her words bolstered me anyway, reminding me of why I did all this in the first place. "I do know how to laugh. Most of the time."

I didn't used to need someone else to confirm that I was okay on a daily basis. But thank god for Pen. She was good at making sure I was, well, not going crazy.

Penelope jumped off the treadmill as soon as the timer went off ending the cool down, tablet in hand, ready to tackle the next item on our endless to-do list. Sometimes I wondered where in the world she got her Energizer bunny energy. I used to have that.

I was tired and it wasn't the workout. Which I hadn't wanted to do but did anyway because my stage shows were physically intense. So if I didn't work out pretty much every day, I'd suffer under the spotlight. Which wasn't fair to my fans. They deserved the best show I could give them.

"Look, for every negative comment, there are a thousand positive ones." She showed me an InstaSnap post by one of my fans, a Mz. Besties' Bestie. It was the pic of me from one of the news articles. The one where I was literally biting into that piece of cheese. There were a lot of comments. A lot. "Your message about self-love and acceptance resonates more than you know."

The warmth of her encouragement did give me some mental energy. "You're right. Let's focus on the good. And maybe start brainstorming that cheese song, huh?"

I thanked the hotel staff who'd closed the gym for the hour I scheduled to be in here and then we headed back up to the suite. In the elevator I tapped my lip thoughtfully, pretending like this had just occurred to me and hadn't been on my mind for two whole days. "Hey, Pen, did we hear back from... um, that football player? Declan Kingman, was it?"

Penelope raised an eyebrow, a knowing smile tugging at the corner of her mouth. "Oh, interested in Mr. Meanest Player, are we?"

I rolled my eyes and pressed my lips together to hide my smile. She and I had done some research on my potential faux beau. We'd found out about this meanest player in the league nomination when we googled him. Seemed weird because he was definitely not mean to me. I understood a PR thing when I saw one. "No, no, it's not like that. Just, you know, professional curiosity. He did save my dog, after all. And he's... well, he's not hard on the eyes."

Penelope chuckled, flipping through her phone. "Well, if you must know, we haven't heard back yet. But I'll chase it up. It's not every day we pair you up with someone who's actually taller than you, right?"

I laughed, trying to brush off the flutter in my stomach. "Right? It's just practical, really. I mean, it's not often I meet someone who I can wear high heels around. But I could have worn the Wonder Woman style costume from the "Borrow My Strength" video and he still would have been taller than me."

I'd felt almost small next to him. Which was not something I ever felt around pretty much anyone else.

I wasn't that tall. For a Viking warrior princess maybe. Not even six feet like everyone said. But I still wouldn't have been as tall as Declan Kingman if I'd been in high heels. Which I never wore around any of the other men I dated.

The two of us did a couple of steps to the choreography to "Borrow My Strength". There had been like a million FlipFlops made for that segment of the song. We tumbled out of the elevator when it got to our floor and were in a fit of giggles.

That was the kind of thing I didn't do enough of these days.

"You look stunning next to anyone, Amazonian or not. But yes, Declan Kingman does have a certain presence." Penelope winked at me, her teasing light and playful.

I nodded and tried to keep my smile at a lower voltage. Declan Kingman was more than just tall and built, and did I mention his muscles? He had an aura about him, something intriguing beyond his rugged exterior, drool-worthy frame. But I couldn't let myself get too caught up in that. This was meant to be showmance, nothing more. I didn't need anything more right now.

"Anyway," I said, steering the conversation back to safer waters, "let me know as soon as you hear from his team. It's important we get the ball rolling on this if we're going to pull it off convincingly."

"Of course, Kels," Penelope replied, already back at her ever-present tablet, typing away. "I'll keep you updated. Maybe this fake dating will be more than you expect."

As Penelope was about to leave, my phone buzzed with a text. I glanced at the screen, my heart skipping a beat. It was from the world's worst ex, Jake. Our breakup had been way too public, and now he was being all sneaky and quiet, messaging me on the downlow and calling at weird times.

Penelope noticed the change in my expression. "Everything okay, Kels?"

I hesitated, the message burning in my mind. "It's Jake. He's... he's asking to meet up. Says he wants to talk."

That was never just it with him. I was always left wondering what the hell Jake actually wanted anyway. At least this time it wasn't a drunk dial in the middle of the night.

Penelope frowned, glaring at my phone. "You don't have to see him, or talk to him, or text him back you know. Especially not after how things ended."

I sighed, a knot forming in my stomach. "I know. It's just... complicated. I... thought he was the one, and then everything in the press..."

We hadn't even dated that long, but he'd won me and my heart over with a lot of what I recognized now was just a bunch of love bombing. If any romance had ever been fake, it was ours. Although, not on my end.

Penelope placed a reassuring hand on my arm. "You don't owe him anything."

I nodded, feeling a mix of apprehension and resolve. I'd missed so many red flags with Jake, and I knew there were some great lyrics that would come out of that, but they just stayed out of reach in my mind. "You're right about that."

I tucked my phone away, trying to push off the unease from even thinking about how I'd felt so damn duped.

I forced a smile, the idea of being in a real fake relationship suddenly more appealing. "If the football hottie agrees, at least that's one relationship I know is just for show."

"Right. That will be, um, good. Okay, you've got one promo to film this afternoon, but I've rearranged some other stuff that the crew can take care of without you needing to be there, which means, I've got two full hours for you and your guitar and a pen and paper on the books."

That was more than I could possibly ask for these days, and somehow the thought of it was a rock in my stomach. One covered in acid. I absolutely needed the quiet time to work on the songs for the next album. There was no pushing the date to get into the studio a second time. Not if I was going to work with the producer the label had pulled strings to get.

"That's great. Thanks."

Wiener the Pooh waited for me in the bedroom,

curled up next to the pillows on the big plush bed. "I'm hitting the shower, poo poo. Then we can have a snack and go for a little walk, huh?"

She stretched and yawned and went right back to sleep. I wasn't jealous of my dog. Not even a little. Not even a lot.

I popped into the fancy hot rain glass box and stayed in for longer than I should, hoping for that mythical shower inspiration. I even tried to hum a few lines, but the acoustics in here were funky. What I wouldn't give for the bathroom at my parents' house right now.

After I toweled off and put on my favorite day jammies, I stared at my guitar. If I was going to get any song writing done, I guess I'd have to actually pick it up. Strumming a few chords didn't do much except wake up Pooh, who trotted over to the corner of the bed closest to me and wagged her tail. She loved when I sang to her.

I hoped for a spark, a hint of a melody to break through the fog. But each note echoed back empty, bouncing off the walls of my suite, mocking my efforts. The lyrics refused to come, each scribbled word a dead end. Even Pooh curled back up and fell asleep. I was that unentertaining.

I set the guitar aside. A distraction, that's what I needed. Instead of typing in a meditation or pulling up my schedule, which used to motivate me but now just gave me anxiety, I maybe, perhaps, kind of typed in

Declan Kingman, to the Google search bar. The first things to pop up were football game videos. Some were from news sites, but I knew the better highlights would be fan made.

I clicked on one by a user called MustangCowgirl and watched, entranced. There was Declan, filling up the screen, commanding, powerful. He tackled the crap out of some guy, over and over. At first, I thought it was the same clip repeated, but I looked at the description, and apparently, he'd done something called sacking the quarterback some record number of times. One commenter called KingmanPrincess said he'd turned the guy into oatmeal.

I clicked on another montage and watched him basically catch a guy running with the ball and smash him into the ground in a dance of raw power. I found myself leaning in, eyes tracing his movements. Even when he was off the field, helmet off, waiting for his turn to play again, the focus in his eyes, that unyielding determination, it was mesmerizing.

Watching him pummel big dudes into the ground was so fricking sexy.

A laugh escaped me, light and unexpected. I was supposed to be working on lyrics, and here I was, getting lost in football highlights. I knew next to nothing about sports, but even I could tell he was really good. And I was... really turned on.

Oh my god. Like... I might need to take another shower.

My notebook lay open, forgotten, as I watched him. One play after another, he dominated the field, a king in his realm. I reached for my pen, an idea flickering, something about bad blood. But it sputtered and died as quickly as it formed.

The alarm on my phone dinged warning me that I had fifteen minutes before I had to get ready to leave for the promo shoot. I clicked the laptop shut and the room was silent, save for the faint hum of the city outside and Wiener the Pooh's cute little snores. I sank back into the chair, eyes closing, Declan's powerful form still imprinted on my mind.

I'd just spent almost two hours watching his absolute raw masculinity and power. And now I had fifteen minutes.

That was plenty of time. I wasn't going to need more than three. I grabbed the little pink silk pouch that stored my vibrator and headed straight back into that shower.

SHOWMANCE?

DECLAN

*A*fter a long day reviewing plays from last week's game and watching even more tapes of our previous matchups with the Tycoons to prep for our upcoming Monday night game against them, I was more exhausted than if it had been a workout day. The last thing I wanted to do was talk to anyone. I just needed a long, hot shower and maybe a beer.

But that wasn't going to happen because my phone pinged with a message from my agent.

> Call me ASAP. Kelsey Best's people want a meeting with you. WTF did you do?

Shit. Had I somehow offended Kelsey or some of her people the other day?

> Gimme two mins to get home.

If I was about to get my ass reamed, I wanted the sanctity of my own space to take the blow in. I swear to god that I didn't do anything wrong. But I also would swear up one goal post and down the other that I wasn't mean, and yet the whole-ass league thought I was.

The second I shut the door behind me, I called Alexis at the De le Rein Agency. She picked up immediately, and I didn't even get to say hello before she went straight in on me.

"Deck, we have got to improve your image." She'd laid into me before about my image, it was part of why I hired her. She didn't pull any punches with me and wasn't afraid of me either. But I'd rarely heard her sound both resigned and irritated with me. "Do you hear me? I'm not screwing around anymore. Your grumpy-ass facade is costing us both a lot of money."

I leaned against the door, taking a deep breath. "I hear you, Alexis, but what exactly do you suggest? It's not like I'm going to turn into Mr. Charisma overnight."

I hadn't been a jack ass to Kelsey or her people though. How the hell was I in trouble with them? All I did was save her dog and maybe get a little bit of a stiffy. Which I had done my absolute best to hide.

"No, but you could at least talk when a camera is pointed at you. Just a few words would do."

Damn. This was about the PR team and the filming they'd done the other day in the locker room. I had said something. More than I normally did.

So I was going to get my ass chewed for several things on this call. I needed a beer for that. I made my way into the kitchen and pulled a Fat Tire out. Good thing I'd already had my protein.

"I hate talking to the cameras. It's not like they don't already know who I am."

"Nobody wants to do a deal with a player who never says a word to the press. You wouldn't even get airtime if you weren't such a phenomenal player."

I was a good player, dammit. Why did it matter what I had to say? "It's always the same inane questions that they already know the answer to."

Except that dance off question wasn't.

Alexis sighed, her tone softening. "That nomination for meanest player is great for the team, but it isn't helping off the field, and now this potential shoe deal is in danger. I know you're not actually mean, Deck, but they're hesitant when your image is negative. Perception is everything."

I was only mean when I needed to be. Like when I was sacking quarterbacks or smashing tight ends into the ground. I pinched the bridge of my nose, and then took a swig, frustration mounting. "So what's the plan? Smile more in interviews I don't give?"

That comment for the PR team was a one-time thing.

This wasn't about the money. Sure it would pad my bank account and hers. But I already made plenty. However, the Kingmans were football royalty, and no way I was letting my brothers down by not continually competing with them to be the best... at everything. It's how we all thrived, and I knew that just as well as the rest of them.

Chris upped the ante with that car commercial, but this shoe thing was actually a bigger deal. Half the athletes in the world would be wearing shoes with my name on them. Including all of my brothers. We'd been working on this for almost a year. They knew who I was when we started though, and it pissed me off they were pussyfooting now.

"Actually," she began, her voice perking up with a note of excitement, "I have good news. An opportunity that could turn this all around."

I rarely liked what she had in store for me when her tone went all perky like this. "I'm listening."

"It's about Kelsey Best." Alexis let that hang in the air. "Her team reached out. They have a proposition."

"Kelsey's people have a proposition for me?" Wait, so I wasn't in trouble? I was confused. Why would her people want anything from me? Maybe they wanted me to dog sit? I did like that little wiener dog. "I already got the tickets for the show on Friday."

"Oh, interesting. They're trying to court you. That's good news for us."

"What?" There was no way my dog rescuing and her offer of tickets to her show was a set up. I saw how worried she was about her dog. That wasn't fake. I didn't think there was anything fake about Kelsey. It was one of the reasons I liked her. But this was all sounding suspicious. Just because she seemed legitimate, it didn't mean her people were. This was showbiz after all. "You'd better tell me what this proposition is."

"Her team wants to set you two up on a date, or two, or... well, a showmance between the two of you."

A date. With Kelsey Best?

What the fuck was a showmance?

"Just for a little while. It's perfect timing, Deck. Being seen with her will soften your image. She's beloved by the media, and they're hoping to take the heat off her recent breakup. It's a win-win. There's no way Swoosh will be anything but pee their pants excited to sign this deal once they see the two of you together."

"Hold up. You want me to fake date the most popular singer in the world?"

I didn't say the part about it being so I could get a shoe deal. I was already shaking my head. I wasn't fucking mean, and I wasn't a fucking liar either. "You're kidding, right?"

I was speechless. A fake romance, once all for show, with Kelsey Best? This was the sort of thing you read about in tabloids, not something that happened in real life. "They've got the wrong guy."

The wrong Kingman. This had Everett written all over it. He was the one who charmed the pants off people left and right. He was a perfect match for her.

"No joke, and if I'm honest, it took me a bit by surprise too," Alexis replied. "But this could be a game changer for you. Clean up your image, get the press on your side without having to say a word, and secure that shoe deal. All you have to do is attend a few high-profile events with Kelsey, maybe a couple of cozy-looking dinners. The press eats this stuff up."

The idea was stupid and absurd. So why the hell was I considering saying yes? It had absolutely nothing to do with the benefits Alexis prattled off.

"Think about it, Deck," Alexis urged. "This could be exactly what you need right now. Plus, it's not like spending time with Kelsey Best is going to be a hard-ship. She seems like a genuinely lovely woman, and she's been through hell in the media."

"She has?"

Fucking press. I'd kill them. Who the fuck said anything bad about someone who brought such sunshine into the world?

"Yes. I'd ask what rock you've been hiding under, but I know the answer starts with an F and ends in ball. Maybe ask Jules about it. She's a smart cookie."

I was definitely asking Jules.

It was ludicrous. But knowing the media were assholes to her kind of made me want to do this, just so I could protect her from that kind of bullshit. Who would blame me for punching out a reporter if it was because they were being a dick to Kelsey?

A showmance with Kelsey Best. I hated lying liars. And this was completely deceptive.

"You don't have very long to decide. They want to know before her show on Friday, preferably sooner than that if at all possible."

I gave her a grunt as a reply, which she took as my goodbye.

"I'll call you tomorrow after practice. Do not piss anyone off between now and then, got it?"

After we disconnected, I stood in the quiet of my kitchen, just leaning against the counter, and finished my beer. A showmance with Kelsey Best? It was like a plot straight out of some cheesy romantic comedy, not my life.

I didn't get even a quiet minute to think about what the hell I was going to do before my front door flew open and Chris, Trixie, Jules, Everett, and Hayes practically fell into my house. I needed to remember to take Chris's spare key away from him.

"What?" I narrowed my eyes at the bunch of them and did my best meanest player in the league impression.

Jules's laughter filled the room. "I maybe accidentally spilled the beans about the Kelsey Best concert tickets."

Hayes scoffed and jumped up to sit on the counter. "Good try, Bratty McBratterson. You didn't maybe accidentally spill anything. You couldn't wait to tell everyone on the planet you were going to the concert."

"Look who's a secret Bestie," Chris teased, plopping down on the couch.

His fiancée Trixie sat down on his lap and gave him a pinch. "You're one to talk. I've seen your morning run playlist."

"I will have you know, there is just as much Tay and Bey on that list as there is Kels."

Chris could have Barney the Dinosaur on his playlist and Trixie would still think he was the bees' knees. They were disgustingly cute and absolute couple goals.

Everett grinned, "Come on, Declan, confess. You've got all her albums, don't you? If I go upstairs, am I going to see her poster hanging on your bedroom wall?"

I rolled my eyes. "Shut it."

Hayes looked genuinely impressed. "It's cool, man. Kelsey Best is awesome. But don't you have extra tickets for your favorite little brother too?"

"No." I was not giving up my ticket.

"C'mon. I've had a crush on her since I was, like, twelve." He batted his eyelashes at me. That probably worked on every girl he'd ever met. Kid was way too good-looking. "She'd go for a younger man, right?"

I was going to fulfill my earlier threat from practice today to sit on him in a minute. "No."

"I'm not that much younger."

"Stop thinking about her that way."

He looked at me all innocent-like. "What way?"

I crossed my arms and gave him my best older brother stare down. "You know."

"Do I?"

Nobody got to think about her as anything but a woman with the voice of an angel. Except me. "The way that's gonna hurt when I punch you in the dick."

Everett gave me one of his damn all-knowing side-eyes. "Feeling a little proprietary over Kelsey Best there, my man. She's belongs to the world, and I think you'd have a lot of fans to fight you for her."

Hayes raised his hand. "Including me."

"You're not the ones she... invited to the concert, are you?" Ooh. I'd almost fucked up and told them about the showmance. They were going to eat me alive if they found that out.

"I thought you got the tickets from Alexis," Jules said.

I sighed. Fuck. This is why I didn't lie and didn't keep secrets. In a family of seven brothers and the nosiest little sister on the planet, it didn't ever work out. Might as well just admit it all now because they'd find out sooner rather than later anyway. "I... met

Kelsey Best the other morning when I was doing the steps at the Rocks. She gave me the tickets."

"She... gave you... tickets to her show?" Hayes and Jules exchanged glances. Then Hayes narrowed his eyes at me. "Why? What the hell did you do to her?"

Why did everyone think I'd done something horrible? Hayes hadn't said that, but his tone sure as shit implied, I'd held her dog for ransom in exchange for tickets. "I saved her dog from a rattlesnake."

Jules gasped and her hands shot to cover her mouth. "You saved Wiener the Pooh?"

I still found that name to be hilarious. Like, did she have other dogs at home named Alison Wienerland, or Mary Queen of Wieners? I could just imagine her rolling on the ground with a million little wiener dog puppies, giggling and letting them kiss her and lick her... and this fantasy was going to get me in trouble.

Because I wanted to be a wiener dog right about now.

"What else are you not telling us?" Everett asked.

See? No secrets. Zero. None. So there was no way I could pull off a fake relationship with a pop star. I was going to have to say no.

Unless... no. Maybe? No.

"Nothing. If you dickheads want to go to the Kelsey Best concert, get your own damn tickets. Now get out of my house." I pointed to the door, and for the first time in my entire life, my siblings actually did what I asked.

That was sus.

All except for Jules. "Even me, your adoring little sister, to whom you can tell anything?"

"Don't you have homework?" I pointed toward the door again.

She didn't budge. "Yeah. My assignment is finding out what secrets my older brother is keeping from the rest of us."

Shit. She'd probably get an A plus on that.

LIVE AT RUST ROCKS

KELSEY

The opening band finished their set, and I was definitely inviting them back. I liked their sound and their attitude. It was so easy to get jaded in this business, especially when you'd been putting in the work and just hadn't yet been blessed by the fates or Loki, or whoever it was that doled out the good luck in the world.

The backstage area buzzed with energy, and I tried to absorb some of it, giving the ladies each a smile and a wave or a thumbs-up as they came off the stage. But my mind and body felt like I was wading through molasses. I stretched my arms, trying to shake off the fatigue clinging to me like a second skin.

I was blaming the altitude. Which was only going to

get worse when we headed into the mountains for the music festival. At least the show in Aspen wasn't just me, but a whole line up of different artists. I needed that little break. Although, I'd never admit that out loud to anyone.

Penelope nudged me and nodded toward the VIP section in the front, stage right. It was filled with the small group of people I'd do a meet and greet with after the show.

"Look who's here," she whispered.

She didn't have to be any more specific. Declan Kingman was hard to miss, towering over the other people. And his focus was fixed on me. No, silly. I was hidden off stage where the fans couldn't see me yet, but I could see them. But it sure felt like he was looking right at me. A flutter of nervous butterflies danced in my stomach.

It wasn't stage nerves. My days on *The Choicest Voice* had ground those out of me. Not to mention ten years of constant touring since then. This was just another concert and another night of work for me.

"He still hasn't given his answer about the show-mance." Penelope sounded a little irritated about that.

"Who is that with him?" A bright-eyed and excited young woman was with him. She kept grabbing his arm and bouncing, clearly trying to get a look back-stage. She wasn't quite as tall as I was, but she was soft and curvy. At least he wasn't here with some stick-thin cheerleader type. I'd been worried he was going to say he didn't want to do this fake dating thing because I wasn't his type.

That little sparkle in his eyes, and the massive hard-on that nobody missed in his gray sweatpants the other day, even though he'd tried his best to hide it from us, said otherwise. "Maybe she's the reason he doesn't want to agree to our proposal."

I gave a little jerk of my chin to indicate the girl. She seemed young for him to me. He probably had all kinds of women knocking down his door. A guy like that didn't need his agent to set him up on a date.

"Oh. No." Penelope shook her head and tapped on her tablet. "I already did some Google Fu. That's Jules Kingman, his little sister."

Okay. It was cute as all get out that he brought his younger sister to the concert. Those tingly nerves in my belly went a bit tinglier.

Pen pulled up a picture filled with a whole army of handsome giants, including Declan and the girl. That's their family? Who hit them with the supermodel stick? Every single one of the men in that picture was ridiculously good-looking. And built, and had those same sparkling eyes. Like... swoon.

But there was something special about Declan. His smile wasn't as big as the rest of them, and he somehow looked as though he was everyone else's bodyguard or something. I'd let him guard my body.

Oh god. That thought needed to go straight back to

the naughty corner of my mind where it had popped out of.

I pitied the man who ever tried to date their sister. All those brothers would be quite the gauntlet to get through to what I'm sure was the family princess. But she was already quite the knockout herself. She had a look that was oddly familiar to me. I wondered if maybe she'd done some modeling.

"Maybe give him a little wave, blow a kiss during the show?" Penelope demonstrated said wave and kiss followed by an eyebrow waggle and a wink. "Start the rumor mill?"

Too contrived, even for showbiz, and the idea unsettled me. Plus, if he didn't want to do this thing, I didn't want to force his hand because of the media making assumptions about us. That's what always got me into trouble.

"Hmm. I'll think about it." I already knew I wouldn't. I tapped my lip and then shook my head. "Okay, I thought about it. Nope. Don't like it. Let's just see what happens, huh?"

No more time for Pen's machinations, or my fantasies about seeing what I could do to put a smile on Declan's face. It was showtime.

The lights dimmed, and I stepped onto the stage, the crowd's roar filling my ears. I let the magic of this amazing outdoor amphitheater setting seep into me, and then I launched into my first set, my voice hitting every note of this kick-off upbeat song. I always started off with something fun and boppy to get the crowd going to the same happy place the music took me.

The band, my dancers, the backup singers, and I rolled through the songs from the latest album, really getting the crowd going. This was the fun and easy part, when we were all hyped and raring to go.

After we did the new songs, I took a minute to introduce my people, because they all deserved accolades too. They worked just as hard as I did.

The show was going well, all according to plan, and the crowd's energy fueled me, pushing back the fatigue that shadowed me at the beginning of the night. Riding this wave of confidence, I decided it was the perfect moment for something new. My people knew to expect these kinds of moments and were ready when I paused before our next scheduled song and stepped up to the mic. I gave one little strum of my guitar and shot the crowd a smile, waiting for the cheers to calm down.

"Okay, Besties," I said into the microphone, my voice steady and bright. "I've been working on something fresh, and I'd love to share it with you. Bear with me, it's still a work in progress."

The audience cheered. This was often the part of the show that fans got excited about because I tried to make each night special for them with something different. I strummed the first chords of the new song, the lyrics bubbling from me like the head of a gentle stream.

"Under the spotlight, where shadows fall, echoes of

a warrior, standing tall. In your eyes, a silent call, a dance of strength, that captivates us all."

I gave a couple more strums of the chords that resonated, but the words I'd thought I could continue blurred, and the melody slipped through my fingers like water.

I reached for the lines, but they floated just out of reach. The music faltered, and I let out a light, self-deprecating laugh. "Well, it seems the rest of that song is still a bit of a mystery, even to me."

I joked and the audience's laughter joined mine. The crowd responded with a warm, forgiving cheer, but I should have kept that song under wraps a bit longer. My mistake.

"I guess it's back to the drawing board for that one," I gave one last chord, still thinking the song was there for me to reach out and grab. But it stayed hidden in the night around us. "That's the beauty of live music, right?"

I moved on to the next song, the hiccup in the performance already fading into the background. It was moments like these, raw and real, that made me love performing, even when the tank was running on empty.

After the set, I had a short break for a costume change, and I retreated backstage for a quick drink of water and into the tiny dressing area. The adrenaline rush from the performance was wearing off, leaving me more aware of each step.

In the privacy of the little dressing room tent thing, I leaned against the stand that had a snack and more water, allowing myself a moment of rest away from prying eyes. The last thing I needed was the press to catch any picture of me looking tired and blame my size. Been there, done that, got the 2xl t-shirt.

I slipped out of my stage outfit, the sequins and lights replaced by something more comfortable, yet still dazzling, for the second half of the show. The cool fabric against my skin was a small relief, but it did little to give me the boost of energy I needed.

Maybe I needed to increase my cardio workout. I put that on my mental checklist to have Penelope arrange for me for the rest of the tour. If I pushed through, everything would be fine.

Pen peeked in, her eyes scanning the countdown timer on her tablet. I was pushing the edges of the dance performance my people were doing that gave me the short moments I needed to swap costumes and refuel. I did not like the look she was giving me. "You're doing great out there, Kels. But you sure you don't want to take a quick break? Maybe skip the next song for some water and a breather?"

I waved her off with a tired smile. "I'm fine, Pen. The crowd's amazing tonight. I can't let them down."

She hesitated, clearly not convinced, but nodded. "Okay, but I'm gonna get you some caffeine for your next change over."

Uh-oh. I wasn't a big caffeine person in the first

place. Made me feel too jittery and not actually energized, but I'd drink it in a pinch. Like when I had back-
to-back shows. If Pen was suggesting it, I must not be
acting up to par.

I'd never admit to needing a break. That felt like
conceding to a weakness I couldn't afford. The show
must go on, and so must I.

"Let's do this." I said the words more as a pep talk
for myself.

Stepping back onto the stage, the roar of the crowd
washed over me, a temporary balm to my fraying edges. I
launched into my next song, the first hit and crowd
favorite "Book Boyfriend". It always got the crowd going
again after the break, and the lyrics flowed automatically.

I barely even had to sing, because the fans singing
the whole thing right back at me was almost as loud as
the sound system. Their presence, their voices that
were always so strong and steady, was a reminder of
why I was doing all this. For the fans, for the music, for
moments like these.

At the bridge, I gave a signal to the band to go quiet,
and I held the microphone out and let the crowd take
over.

The melody swirled into the mountain air, and the
words flowed around us all, telling the story of the
nerdy girl who wishes the heroes in her books would
come to life because they would be better to her than
the dumb boys in real life. I stood there on the stage,

swaying to the beat, and letting the fans completely take over.

They knew every word, every note, and the song pushed against my skin, into my heart, making it pound in my chest so hard I was sure the whole world could see it. The music seeped into me and I blinked, my eyelashes fluttering a million and two times in the course of the minute the audience carried the tune. Tears pricked at the edges of my eyes, and I sucked in a shuddering, deep breath as the final note hung in the night air.

It was magic.

For a tenth of a second, there was silence. I smiled, brought the microphone back to my mouth, and gave a long, happy, "Whoo hoo. You are absolutely the best fans a girl could have. I think you all had better come up here on stage and let me sit in the audience. That was fantastic."

I pushed through, song after song, the applause a distant echo in my ears. I was Kelsey Best, America's pop sweetheart, and I wouldn't let them see anything less than perfection.

The applause was still ringing in my ears as I moved into the next part of my set. Each song was a step closer to the end of the night, a step closer to rest. I glanced out at the audience, my gaze moving to where I knew Declan and his sister were in the VIP section. It was hard to see the actual faces with the glare of the lights on me, but I still sensed him over there watching me.

I hope he liked what he was seeing.

"Alright, everyone, we've got a couple more songs to go. Let's bring it down a notch and get cozy, shall we?"

Even though I'd indicated the next song was going to be a quieter song, they all erupted into squeals and screams. They knew what was coming.

The next song was another fan favorite. A ballad called "Cozy Nights". It was a love song that didn't exactly have a happy ending. I'd left the lyrics ambiguous, and there was plenty of speculation as to which of my former boyfriends the song was about.

Once the opening notes of the piano rang out, the crowd quieted, and the lights from people's phones went up over their heads. It was one of my favorite sights in any concert. I loved seeing those pinpricks of light glowing and swaying with the music like a million sparkles, joining the stars up above.

My voice carried the poignant lyrics into the night, and I stole a glance in Declan's direction. I shouldn't be able to see him, but with the dimmed lights, and the glow of the phones in the audience, I spotted him. His eyes were locked on me, and for a fleeting moment, it felt like we were the only two people in the world.

The song ended, and the crowd erupted into applause. I took a deep breath, prepping for the finale.

My feet and lungs were aching, but I pushed it aside, rallying for the end of the show.

This was the big climax of the night, and I gave it everything I had, the notes soaring, my heart pounding, and that last little bit of adrenaline pushing me to really take us out with a bang. The crowd was a sea of movement and cheers, and I let their energy carry me.

There was nothing like the exhilaration of a good crowd and their enthusiasm. It was an addictive feeling. Kind of like a really great orgasm.

I could use more of both.

That sounded like a much better idea than adding in another workout.

SIMPLY THE BEST

DECLAN

I was in so much damn trouble. I'd thought Kelsey was cute and adorable the day I'd met her and Wiener the Pooh. She had this sweet and engaging, girl next door thing going on that had starred in several of my fantasies since then.

But I'm sure that's how most people felt about her. The princess of pop, America's sweetheart. A talent to be cherished and savored for all generations. Her voice, more powerful and emotive than I'd ever realized, filled the air, her songs a mixture of energy and soul that the entire audience couldn't help but get swept up in. I watched, captivated, as she moved across the stage with a grace and confidence that was utterly mesmerizing.

Not to mention that ass had me on fucking fire. Every time she shook it in one of her dance moves, I just about came in my goddamned pants. I had to think of stats from boring-ass baseball and count the beads of the Bestie bracelet Jules had put on me just to keep my penis from poking right the hell out of the front of my jeans.

Each note she hit, each word she sang, resonated in a way I hadn't expected. It was more than just a performance. This whole experience was a display of raw talent and passion. The crowd was completely in her thrall, and so was I.

Kelsey Best, the pop sensation most people knew only from headlines and her music, was in her element and it was sexy as fuck.

The stage lights dimmed, casting a magical glow over the amphitheater. The crowd quieted, and for the first time in hours, we sat down on the long stone steps that acted as seats at Rust Rocks. She opened her mouth and pure fucking magic came out. It was a slow song, one I'm sure I'd heard before, but most of what I had on my playlists were the upbeat, poppy stuff. Good stuff to work out to. This... this was something else entirely, and it wound its way from my ears, down my spine, and settled deep in my stomach.

I leaned back, trying to appear nonchalant, as I pulled out my phone to lend another light in the audience, but the truth was, I was anything but. Or rather, I could be so much more to her.

She was a force of nature on stage. No wonder people went feral over her. I got it. I wanted to rush up onto the stage right now, pick her up, and carry her away to savor. I wanted her for myself.

Jules elbowed me, her grin teasing. "I think you're drooling, big bro."

I shot her a mock glare, but she just laughed, her eyes sparkling with mischief. "Can't blame you though. She's amazing."

"She's... yeah, she is." It felt ridiculous, this sudden, intense rush of feelings. I knew the difference between the crush of a fan and something real. But this, watching her pour her heart into her music, it felt like something more than either of those things. There was an undeniable pull, something that went beyond her celebrity.

And I was the fucking fool who'd told my agent today that I wouldn't do the fake dating thing.

I.

Said.

No.

Alexis growled at me. Like actually growled and told me she wasn't making any moves until the weekend. She had to have known I'd change my mind after seeing Kelsey in concert.

Kelsey sang this love song about being cozy with the one you love, and I swear to god she was looking right at me. Why would she do that to my heart? I was dead now. Deceased. Dust.

Jules nudged me again. "You're totally smitten, aren't you?"

I didn't answer right away. Smitten wasn't the right word. That was too shallow a feeling, too fleeting. This swirl of need in my chest was completely different, deeper.

"You gonna be okay there, big guy?" Jules' tone was a mix of excitement and a hint of concern. "Don't you dare embarrass me when we get to meet her after the show."

I meant to tease Jules right back, just like we always did when we gave each other shit. But I had nothing. I took a deep breath, trying to steady the whirlwind of emotions whizzing through me. "I'll be fine. It's just... she's not what I expected."

She was so much more.

Jules gave me a weird look, and out of all my family, she was the one who'd figure everything out. Shit. She was like a relationship Nancy Drew when it came to the lot of us.

Even though I'd told my agent I wouldn't do the whole fake relationship thing, there was still an NDA involved. Not that I was some big blabbermouth. I preferred to keep my personal life personal.

When the concert ended, the applause thundered through the amphitheater, and I thanked the residents of Morrison for putting up a stink and voting for an ordinance that ensured concerts here didn't go late into the night with encore after encore. The crowd began to disperse, and that meant I needed to get my shit together for the upcoming meet and greet. What would I say to her? How do you talk to someone who's just unwittingly turned your world upside down?

Jules linked her arm with mine, leading me toward the backstage area. "This is going to be epic. I can't believe we get to talk to her after the show."

Epic. That was one word for it. And all I could do was hope I didn't make a complete fool of myself. Jules already thought I was acting weird, and she wasn't wrong.

The security staff opened up the metal guard rails between the VIP section and the steps that led up to the stage. A whole gaggle of squealing teens and who I had to guess was their cool aunt made their way up to the backstage area.

I grabbed Jules and pulled her to the back of the line waiting to go to the meet and greet, and let the others get far enough ahead of us that they wouldn't overhear what I was about to reveal.

"What?" Jules narrowed her eyes at me, but then she smiled. "Oh, you're putting us last so we get more time with her. Smart."

"No. Listen." I took a deep breath and blew it out in a rush. "You have to swear on the collection of dolls I know you have hidden under your bed that if I tell you something, you can keep a secret."

"First of all," she held up a finger "those are going to

be collector's items because I got every plus-size Barbie ever offered. And duh. I am a vault of so many Kingman secrets I should be the head of the sports division of the CIA."

It was a perfect job for her. "I don't think that's a thing."

She made an I-know-something-you-don't face at me and shrugged. "As far as you know."

"Fine, lock this in your secret vault of secrets, and I'm only telling you because you'd figure it out anyway, and it needs to stay quiet. Like, legally. You got me?" I gave her the big brother stare down, which of course didn't intimidate her in the least, but she knew I was serious.

She pretended to zip her lips, then locked them with a key, and put the imaginary key down the front of her shirt. Yeah, no man would ever try to get that key, or I'd have to kill them.

I couldn't believe I was about to say this out loud. "Kelsey's people want to set the two of us up on a—"

"Are you freaking kidding me?" She smacked me on the chest. "Yes. You said yes, right? I knew it, I knew you were going to marry her. It's destiny."

"Whoa, whoa." Who said anything about marriage? "No. They want us to," I lowered my voice and looked around to make sure no one was paying attention to us, "fake date."

Her face went from open, wide-eyed excitement to

flat out denial. She shook her head, gave a thumbs down, and blew out a raspberry. "No. Absolutely not."

Huh. That's kind of what I thought. "I said no."

"Good, because the two of you are going to fall in love for real." She said it as an absolute matter of fact.

Why did I feel like I was negotiating my next contract with the Mustangs instead of admitting a secret to my baby sister? "I don't think that's how this works."

"As far as you know." She gave me the exact same shrug and look as before. "I have complete faith in you to make Kelsey Best my next sister-in-law."

"Jules." This was not how I thought this conversation would go.

She gave me a look that reminded me so much of Mom when she gave us something to do and expected it to be done. Deep instinct clenched at my chest, and I had to rub the spot over my heart.

This was the craziest conversation I'd ever had. The craziest idea.

But what if I didn't fake date Kelsey? What if I wooed her and got her to fall in love with me for real?

No. Ridiculous.

Maybe?

No.

Yes?

I had about two minutes to get my head out of my ass and decide. The backstage area was a flurry of activity, with VIP fans lining up for their chance to meet Kelsey. Jules and I waited our turn, and my heart rate went from just above normal to pounding like I was chasing some running back down the field.

I watched Kelsey interact with the fans just ahead of us. She was all smiles and warmth, but she had to be exhausted after all the effort she'd put into performing. At least when I played a game, I got breaks in between. She went full out for hours. But if she was tired, she masked it for her fans with professional grace.

But I saw the weariness in her eyes, the slight slouch of her shoulders.

Each time she leaned slightly against the table she was using to sign swag on for support, my hands clenched involuntarily, building an ache in my muscles. I gauged her energy like I would my own teammates', ready to act if she showed any sign of needing someone to step in and shield her. Like a fucking linebacker.

The sight of her, so vibrant yet clearly pushing her limits, sparked an instinct in me I hadn't known existed. It wasn't just admiration or the thrill of being near a celebrity. No, this was different, a deep-seated urge to protect, as if her well-being had somehow become important to my own.

It was irrational, this newfound concern for someone I hardly knew, but it gripped me with an intensity that was hard to ignore.

When it was my turn, Jules stepped slightly behind

me and fucking pinched me on the back of the arm. I jolted forward and turned and gave her a stare with an unspoken promise of retribution.

"Oh, Declan, hi." Kelsey stepped forward to greet us, but her foot snagged the tablecloth and she stumbled, lurching fast and headed for a crash.

My finely honed reflexes rose up, and I instinctively reached out to grab her, wrapping my arms around her to steady her. She barreled right into me, and I hugged her against my body to keep her upright.

"I got you," I murmured, holding her a little too long before I realized I was keeping her from getting back on her feet.

Cameras flashed around us, capturing the unexpected embrace, including that of my little sister. Kelsey laughed it off, thanking me with a grateful look in her eyes. "I'm gonna have to put you on staff, if you keep coming to my rescue."

The smile she gave me completely fritzed out my brain. I forgot how to talk. I forgot my own goddamned name. What did I do? I gave her a little salute.

What the fuck was that? Get it together, man.

"Kelsey, meet my baby sister. This is Jules, she's a huge fan."

Jules stepped up, gave me look that said not to be the dumbass she thought I was, and then held out her hand to shake Kelsey's like a normal person. She was bubbly with excitement though. "Kelsey, you were amazing, and I want to say thanks for representing us bigger girls so positively. Especially in an industry so focused on appearance. I appreciate the impact you've made on fatphobia in the media."

Kelsey blinked. That was Jules for you. Always defying expectations.

Kelsey's assistant slid a photo and a t-shirt onto the table, and Kelsey signed them both, then handed them to Jules. "You're exactly the kind of girl I do all of this for, so I'm really happy to hear you enjoyed the show. I'd love to chat sometime about your thoughts on teenage women and the body positivity movement."

Her smile was genuine as she chatted with Jules. My little sister was just a baby when our mom died, and our dad worked really hard to be sure she had positive female role models in her life. Kelsey was exactly that and I felt both grateful for it, and a weird sense of pride that I had no right to.

She looked over at me, and her eyes met mine, holding my gaze for a beat longer than with everyone else around us. There was a flicker of a question in her eyes I didn't know how to answer. But then I recognized the moment she put the mask of celebrity back on.

She didn't want Jules to know there was anything between us.

There wasn't.

Yet.

I was going to make sure there was.

"It was so nice to see you again, Declan. And genuinely nice to meet you, Jules. Thanks so much for coming to the show."

Oh. Shit. We'd just been dismissed. Perhaps my agent had actually told her people I'd said no to the dating proposal. I'd really fucked myself with that one.

Kelsey's assistant, the one who'd given me the tickets, held out a tablet and asked her to sign something. Yep. She was done with us. Just another set of fans that she was kind to, but in the end, we weren't in her life for more than the special moment we'd just gotten with her.

Dammit.

Jules grabbed my arm and yanked on it so hard, I was lucky it didn't fall off, and only because I bent down to save my ligaments and tendons.

She angry whispered in my ear. "Declan Dumbass Kingman, if you don't shoot your shot with Kelsey right this instant, I will take to social media and tell everyone in the world that you are a bigger wiener than Kelsey's dog, Pooh. And I promise you, the Besties will be relentless in a shared quest to get you to ask her out. So you might as well do it now and save the universe a lot of time and effort."

Jesus.

Jules ripped a bracelet off her arm and slapped it into my hand.

My cell phone number was on it. My fucking cell phone number.

"Give it to her and ask her if she wants to have dinner with you tomorrow night at Manniway's." Her tone brooked absolutely no argument. I either did what she said or faced dire consequences. And I didn't just mean about the social media campaign she threatened to lobby against me.

"Fine, brat, but if this backfires, I'm blaming you." What if she was already pissed I'd said no?

She gave me the patented Jules Kingman teenage eyeroll. "I promise to forfeit every game night from here to eternity if she turns you down."

Whoa. As competitive as Kingman family game night was, that was a huge boon, and Jules knew it. I'd hold her to it too. Just because she was the baby of the family, didn't mean we let her win.

I took a step closer to Kelsey and called upon the spirits of my suave ancestors to help me pull this off. I was going to win Kelsey Best's heart. But I was going to do it my way. With a little help from my sister.

"Say hello to Wiener the Pooh for me, will you?" I leaned in and brushed my lips across her cheek and slipped the bracelet into her hand.

Kelsey gave the sweetest little gasp, and I accidentally on purpose rubbed the scruff of my beard across her cheek as I pulled away. Then I grabbed Jules and guided her toward the steps and security. Just before we exited the backstage area, I looked back and gave her a wink and smile.

She looked down at the bracelet, then back at me. Her lips pressed together in a kind of shy grin that she was trying to hide, but she gave me a quick little nod, followed by a soft lick of her lips.

Fuck, yeah. I was in.

FLIPFLOP POSTS

VIDEO POST #1

Shaky, grainy video of Kelsey Best tripping and being caught by huge, hottie mystery man after her show at Rust Rocks, CO on Friday night.

Video voiceover and captions:

Hey Besties,

I cannot even.

Like... I'm swooning right now. This knight in shining armor legit saved our girl from falling flat on her face. Jake the jackass could learn a thing or two from this guy, am I right?

And LOOK at how she blushed and stared up at

him like he was chocolate... or cheese. I'm saying she wanted to eat him up.

And I think he's definitely thinking about how he wants to eat her too.

Who knows who this guy is, and does he have a brother for me?

#KelseyBest #Besties #BestieFlop #Denver #Rust-Rocks #GettingCozy #IHaveACrush #IfIFallWillYou-CatchMe #JakeCanSuckIt

---

VIDEO POST #2

Shaky, grainy video of Kelsey Best getting a kiss on the cheek from huge, hottie mystery man. He hands her something, walks away, and winks at her after her show at Rust Rocks, CO on Friday night.

Video Voiceover and captions:

Besties!

Oh. Muh. Gawd.

I've just gotten more footage of our mystery man. Apparently, this is also from the backstage meet and greet for VIPs after the show.

Did you see that? DID YOU SEE?

He kissed her on the cheek. And I think that looked

pretty damn familiar. Like, there's no way this was the first time they've ever met. Is it? IS IT?

And watch! He slips something into her hand. WHAT DID HE SLIP HER?

It's not paper, so it's not his number. I want it to be his number. WHAT IS IT?

Does that look like a Bestie bracelet to anyone else?

And that wink!;)

Get to sleuthing, Besties, because I have to know who this huge hottie is! He's actually taller than our girl, and I am living for it. He's got to be some kind of an athlete with a build like that. Or a lumberjack. Or a superhero.

#dead #dying #swooning #KelseyBest #Besties #BestieFlop #DoesHeHaveABrother #WhoIsThisGuy #Lumberjack #BeMySuperhero #Denver #RustRocks #MeetCute #JakeCanSuckIt

HOPEFUL ROMANTIC

KELSEY

I was so confused right now. I stared down at the bracelet that I'd been playing with for the last hour when I was supposed to be sleeping. But I couldn't. I was exhausted, but not tired. I hadn't felt this energized after a show this whole tour. I was keyed up and didn't know what to do with myself. Thank goodness I had the morning off after shows. I needed the sleep, but I was going to be dragging tomorrow.

Was I supposed to call him? Like for real?

This wasn't what I expected when we were set to do this fake dating thing. He flirted. With me.

Penelope said that his agent hadn't given any sort of official notification that he was in, but after that little show, he had to be. Besides, Skeeter had said that he'd at least signed the NDA.

Maybe he wanted it to look more natural than us just being seen together all of a sudden. That was smart. It would make it seem more authentic.

I glanced over at the clock. Two-twenty-two in the morning. I couldn't call him now. Besides, who actually called people anyway? I should just text him like a normal person. In the morning. He wouldn't see it until then anyway, I was sure.

> Hi.

Okay, I sent it. Excellent job, me. I don't know why I was so nervous. This was a set up.

But shoot. While I had his number, he didn't know mine. I could be any rando or a scammer texting him.

> This is Kelsey.

I meant to just set the phone down and try to get some sleep. I didn't. I stared at the message and considered figuring out how or if there was a way to unsend. But the three little dots indicating that he was typing popped up and I threw my phone across the bed.

Pooh made a snuffling snore and rolled over. "Sorry, Pooh."

I carefully folded the blankets back and crawled

across the big California king size bed to retrieve my
phone.

> Hi, Kelsey. I guessed it was you. I can
> count on one hand the people who
> have this number.

Ooh. So he didn't just give his number out to
every woman he met. It's not like I thought he carried
a bunch of beaded bracelets around with his name
and number on them or something equally as
ridiculous.

> Um, but don't you have a whole bunch
> of siblings?

> Yeah. But most of them can't be
> trusted with that kind of knowledge.
> Jules especially. As demonstrated by
> the fact that she had that bracelet all
> ready to go for me to give to you
> tonight.

Oh. Okay. That made more sense. Jules seemed like
a smart and savvy girl and the way he'd given it to me
had romance written all over it. But wait. He'd signed
the NDA, so he wouldn't have told her. So, she just
made it in hopes he'd give it to me at the meet and
greet? I did love a hopeful romantic.

That gave me an idea for a lyric.

I popped open the notes app on my phone, made a
quick note about being a hopeful romantic versus a

hopeless one. My heart skittered across several beats when another message popped up.

> I know it's late, but mind if I call? I'd rather talk than text.

Before I could overthink it, I typed back a quick thumbs-up and waited, the phone feeling like a live wire in my hand. The screen lit up with his incoming call. I took a deep breath and I answered.

"Hi."

"Hey. Hope I'm not keeping you up." His voice was a husky but smooth rumble over the line, and it sent a shiver and goosebumps across my arms. "No, you're fine. I was up... thinking."

"About your concert? You blew my mind with your performance."

"I did?" I was a sucker for a compliment about my show. It was hard not to be.

"Absolutely. You really capture people with your songs. It's not just your voice either. It was like you were singing just for me. Which is silly, I know. I'm sure everyone feels that way."

It was surreal, hearing him describe my performance, the admiration clear in his tone. But it wasn't in that flattery way that most people used when they talked about seeing me sing. His words were so genuine, and that was a bit of a surprise. Not that I didn't think he was capable, but a genuine compliment was rare in my experience.

"Thanks. I..." I almost told him I was singing to him. I had been for that one moment. "I work hard to be everything I can for my fans."

"It shows. You clearly work your ass off." He let out a soft sound that made me think he was smiling. "Although, I'll admit to being a bit of a fan of that too."

I had to keep back a little laugh of my own. "Of what? My ass?"

He gave a full on chuckle this time, and the deep resonating sound of it had my tummy feeling all tingly again. "Yeah, Kels. I am definitely an ass man. But I like every single one of your curves. A lot."

There he went, flirting with me again. Should I tell him he didn't have to do that?

Nah.

"Since you admitted that to me, I guess it's okay if I tell you I like a good, firm butt on a man too. I may or may not have watched some of your game highlights. Those pants you all wear are..." Masturbation fodder. Oh, geez. Good thing I didn't say that out loud. "Let's just say I'm a fan of whoever decided football players should wear super tight pants and bend over a lot."

"I'll bend over for you, if you bend over for me."

We were getting racy now, were we? Two could play at that game. "Mr. Kingman. I'm surprised. Are you offering to let me peg you?"

Yep. That came out of my mouth.

"I've never actually tried it, but if that's what turns you on, my sweet songbird," his voice was dripping with sensuality, and I found myself squirming, waiting to see what he'd say next, "I'd be game to check it out."

Oh god. He was serious. And now I was picturing him spread out on my bed, on his stomach, naked, waiting for me to... Or was he just calling my bluff? Crap. "I haven't done anything like that either. I've only read about it in smutty romance novels."

"Are you a big reader?" He changed the subject so easily, when I was still having naughty thoughts about what we could do to each other. "Who's your favorite author? Favorite series? What are you reading now?"

On one hand I was a little disappointed we weren't going into dirtier territory. But on the other, it was nice that he didn't have a one-track mind. If I was going to be spending time with him, and probably not in bed because this was fake dating after all, it was nice that he could actually carry a real conversation that didn't have anything to do with his career. "I don't get as much time to read as I wish I did, but I do love to when I have the chance. I've been working my way through this one author's dragon shifter series. It's got some good spice."

"Do they ride their dragons?" He emphasized the word ride, and I didn't miss his innuendo.

"Uh-huh." I paused for a little emphasis. "A lot."

"I'll have to read that one. Send me the author and title later, and I'll see if they have it at the library."

Declan was too good to be real. Super good-looking, taller than me, nice to kids and animals, he liked to read, and even used his local library? No. Where were his red flags?

That meanest player thing popped into my head. Maybe he was actually a giant douchecanoe but was hiding it from me. He wouldn't be the first.

I'd have to pay close attention. Although did I really have to? It wasn't like we were going to date for real.

We moved onto favorite TV shows and movies, and I tested him by mentioning one of Jake's action adventure blockbusters.

"It was just meh, honestly. To me, to be a good movie it's got to have some action, it's gonna have some comedy, and it needs a little romance. I'm not saying it has to be a romcom. But come on, we know it's always about a girl."

"What's always about a girl?"

"Everything. Fat bottomed girls make the rocking world go round."

I laughed. "Yep, we sure do."

I wasn't even sure how we flowed from topic to topic, but we seemed to cover it all. He told me an embarrassing childhood story about how his older brother had convinced him that the loud sound a toilet made was because there was a lion in it.

I found out we shared a love of dogs, and that growing up, they always had great big dogs that they named Bear.

My stomach rumbled, and Pooh woke up and growled at it.

"Was that your stomach?"

"Yes, and Wiener the Pooh. I think we'd better get a snack for both of us." I crawled out of bed and padded my way to the small kitchenette in the suite.

"I could eat." I heard the rustle of bed linens on his end and found myself wondering if he was wearing anything.

I was not going to do the cliché late-night phone call thing and ask him to tell me what he was wearing. I was not. I was not.

"What's on for late-night snacks? I've got, uh, a leftover smoothie, which looks like someone threw up or… I think this used to be a hamburger."

"Used to be?"

"It might have been a cheeseburger." He made a retching sound. Gross.

"I am generally a fan of cheeseburgers, but you're scaring me."

"Jules did mention you're a bit of a cheese connoisseur."

Oh no. "That comment about having a love affair with cheese is going to haunt me the rest of my life. But I wasn't lying. Cheese is the way to my heart, and Pooh's too."

"Good to know. I'll remember that for our first official date."

The mention of a date, even in jest, made my stomach flutter. This was all supposed to be fake, but it felt anything but.

We both found something edible and talked about everything and nothing, our conversation meandering like a lazy river. Eventually, I made my way back to bed and curled up under the blankets, phone cradled to my ear.

As the night deepened, so did our conversation. We touched on deeper topics—our dreams, fears, what drove us. It was intimate, real, and utterly terrifying in its sincerity.

The sky outside began to lighten, a soft, blue hue creeping in. We had been talking all night and continued to as the dawn broke. Our conversation was a soft murmur, a comforting presence. It was crazy, this connection I felt with him, but it was there, undeniable and growing stronger with each passing minute.

"I should let you get some sleep, Kels." His voice was reluctant, mirroring my own feelings.

"I think that should be the other way around." I didn't know his schedule, but an athlete must need a good night's sleep, and we'd been up all night. "Maybe just a few more minutes. I'm not quite ready to go to sleep."

I didn't want to let go of what we'd had together tonight. I wanted more. I hadn't realized how much I'd needed this, someone to talk to, to connect with on a level beyond the surface.

Declan chuckled, a warm, comforting sound. "Okay, Kelsey. A few more minutes. But get under the covers and get yourself tucked in. You need your rest."

Me? Why did I find it incredibly sweet that he was thinking about me needing rest, when I was thinking of him? To be honest, it was a first for me. "What if I'm not sleepy?"

He made low humming sound. "You need some help relaxing?"

"Always. I'm kind of a type-A person. I'm not great with doing nothing." I'd been go, go, go since I was a kid, but when I won *The Choicest Voice*, my career kicked that into an even higher gear.

Declan's voice softened, a hint of mischief in his tone. "Okay, Kelsey, close your eyes and imagine this..."

I did as he asked, sinking deeper into my pillows, the phone pressed to my ear, my eyes fluttering shut. But then he made this soft sound that was somewhere between a moan and a growl.

Holy shit, were we about to have phone sex?

"Imagine you're with me up in the mountains," Declan continued, his voice a soothing cadence in the quiet of the room. "The colors on the trees are a mix of reds and golds, and the sun is setting, painting the sky in shades of orange and pink."

Okay. So it was just me who was mad horny. Fine. I let out a contented sigh, the imagery vivid in my mind. "That sounds nice."

"There's a gentle, but warm breeze," he added, "and the only sound is the soft whirring of the old ski lift floating by overhead and the rustle of the aspens."

The scene unfolded in my mind, and I wondered if he was describing a real place. "I can almost hear it."

Declan made that same humming sound. "Now, imagine I'm there with you. I've set up a picnic in the trees, just for us."

I smiled at the thought. "What did you bring?"

"Your favorite," he said playfully. "Cheese, of course. All kinds of cheese."

I laughed, the sound light and carefree. "Perfect."

"And there's music," he continued. "But not from a speaker. I brought my guitar. I'm playing your favorite songs."

The thought of Declan playing guitar for me was unexpectedly intimate, sending a warm flutter through my heart. "I didn't know you played."

"I don't, but this is my fantasy, so let's pretend I do. I learned just for you."

Oh my god. Why was he so sweet? He continued in this vein for a while, painting a picture of our perfect imaginary date. His voice was a steady, comforting presence, lulling me into a place where I wasn't thinking about my next show or how I would get the songs for the album done on time.

As the minutes ticked by, his words became a soft murmur in the background, my mind drifting on the edge of sleep. I was vaguely aware of him talking, his words now a gentle, rhythmic sound that blended with the quiet of the night.

Eventually, his voice faded into the background, a

warm, comforting hum that filled the space around me. I felt myself slipping further into relaxation, the tension of the day melting away.

"Kelsey," Declan's voice was barely above a whisper now. "Are you ready to rest now?"

"Mmm," I managed, half-asleep.

"Sleep well, babe," he said softly. "Sweet dreams."

I drifted off, the last thought in my mind being Declan strumming my guitar and singing to me, music filling the air, and a sense of contentment I hadn't felt in a long time.

Then he was kissing me. And, man, was he a sloppy kisser.

I opened my eyes to find Wiener the Pooh licking my face, waking me up, wagging her tail so hard her little butt was going ballistic. I glanced over at the clock on the bedside table. I'd slept for five hours. Which, honestly, was rather good for me.

"Pooh, you didn't pee on the floor somewhere because I didn't take you out, did you?"

A soft knock came on the door and Penelope popped her head into the room. "I took her out. You were dead to the world. I pushed everything on your schedule because I don't think I've ever seen you sleep so soundly before."

I sat up and stretched and yawned. "Thanks, Pen. Hey, do you happen to know if the colors are on the trees where we're going for the festival this week? Or if they have places you can have a picnic?"

Maybe under a ski lift?

"I'll find out for you." She tapped on her tablet. "Also, you should check the FlipFlops I sent you. Our mission to get the world to forget you ever dated Jake is a go."

I normally didn't allow myself to scroll that addicting app, but when Pen sent me something, I watched it. Usually it was funny dog videos. She avoided sending me anything about me. Which was for the best.

I opened the messages and clicked on the first video. A superfan whose username I recognized because he, she, or they had been following me since my *Choicest Voice* days had posted. I watched it, and then I sunk back down into the covers to hide the blush I felt rising up my cheeks watching Declan give me a kiss on the cheek.

Maybe I let out one tiny giggle. Just one.

This wasn't real after all.

THE FAMILY THAT PLAYS TOGETHER

DECLAN

Waking up had never felt like such a shock to the system. My eyes flickered open, the numbers on the clock barely registering in my sleep-deprived brain. It was only a few hours since I'd finally hung up the phone with Kelsey. But even tired as hell, I felt more awake than I had in years.

I lay in bed, the ceiling a familiar friend, as I replayed pieces of our conversation in my mind. The laughter, the deeper confessions, the easy banter, it all swirled together, painting a picture of Kelsey that was so different from the pop star the world saw. She was real, funny, vulnerable, and incredibly easy to talk to.

We weren't playing again until Thursday night, and that gave me a rare day off during the season. Which was the perfect time to plan a real date with Kelsey. But how the hell did someone date a celebrity as big as her? My brothers and I had a hard enough time going out in public as it was. Especially in the Denver metro area. The fans were great, and usually very respectful, but there was no privacy, ever.

I also had no idea what her schedule was like. Did she even have time to herself? Didn't seem like it.

I headed down to my kitchen, and while I was throwing the ingredients into my blender to make a protein smoothie, something, or rather someone, caught my attention in my back yard.

I slid the glass door open and threw a frozen strawberry at Everett. Hayes snatched it right out of the air an inch before it should have hit Ev in the chest, who hardly noticed since he had his nose buried in Jules's phone.

"What are you dickheads doing in my backyard?" They were lounging on my outdoor furniture like they owned the place.

"Point of clarification." Jules, not looking up from her phone either, raised her hand, one finger in the air. Not the correct one for pointing either. "I'm not a dickhead. I'm a princess, and don't you forget it. Did she call?"

I gave her a death glare and wished, not for the first time in my life, that I had a Darth Vader level command over the force to use on any and all of my siblings.

Jules glanced up at me and shrugged. "What? I didn't tell them anything they didn't already know. You and Kelsey are trending on pretty much every social media platform right now."

Fuck. "I don't even look at that shit, much less care about it."

Everett finally pulled his face away from whatever he was watching on the phone. "That's why you have us. Between the six of us, we got you covered."

Six? Shit. That meant everyone except Chris. He didn't do socials either, and I'd followed his lead. But the rest of my siblings were all over it. Ev had huge followings on FlipFlop and InstaSnap. And Hayes and the twins did some sort of online streaming while they played video games and talked sports.

Dad insisted that Jules keep her socials private and anonymous as much as humanely possible. At least until she was eighteen.

I sat on the bench across from them. "What exactly do you think I need you for?"

Jules turned her phone around with a huge shit-eating grin on her face. A grainy as fuck, shaky video played, sound off. It was me catching Kelsey when she tripped backstage. Kind of. It was more like a blurry blob of me catching a blurry ghost of Kelsey. That had to have been taken from the top of the steps. Jeez.

I glanced quickly at the little heart on the side of the video that showed how many people had liked it. The number was so big, I wasn't even sure I knew how to say it out loud. There were also tens of thousands of comments.

My own phone buzzed in my pocket, and I pulled it out.

"Is that her?" Jules asked with wide eyes, more excited than on Christmas morning.

It was my agent. Just one line of text.

> Told you.

Clearly, she'd seen the videos of last night too. I wasn't dignifying that with a response. "No. It's Alexis."

"But Kelsey did call, didn't she?" Jules's voice went up an octave.

My response to her question was simply a raised eyebrow.

But since I had my phone in my hand, I sent a quick text to Kelsey.

> Good morning, sweet queen of hearts

I waited a moment to see if she was online, but those three little dots didn't appear, so I shoved my phone back in my pocket.

Jules joined me in on the bench and batted her eyes up at me, pulling the cute little sister card on me. "Declan. You're killing me. Did she call you or not? I have a vested interest in this relationship."

"Dude, did you actually slip her your number on a

Bestie bracelet?" Hayes held his phone out, showing another clip from last night.

Before I could tell him to fuck off, Flynn and Gryffen literally hopped over my gate and sauntered their way into my backyard too.

I was plagued with nosy brothers. "What are you two dickwads doing here? Don't you have a game today?"

"Yeah," Gryff said. "But it's at home, and it's not until this afternoon. So we thought we'd stop by and harass our celebrity older brother."

They both played for the Denver State University Dragons. Just like the rest of us had. And Dad made sure each and every one of us earned our spot on that team. No favoritism for us. Just reduced tuition since he had been their championship winning coach for years.

"And we're here to see if Hayes asked you to be our fourth tonight." The two of them plopped down on either side of Hayes and each gave him noogies.

Hayes took it in stride and shrugged at me. He never let shit like this faze him. Probably because he was the best athlete in the family and about ten times smarter than all the rest of us. We all knew it. "Isak's out until he gets his grades up."

Isak was a straight A student as far as I knew. "He is, huh? And this has nothing to do with what's trending on social media right now?"

"Dude. Of course it does." Flynn looked at me like I

was stupid or something. "The Besties have already found us. I got seven thousand new followers overnight. You have to game with us or we'll have a riot on our hands."

Gryff nodded. "Not to mention I'd have to cancel all eleventy-hundred dates I have lined up."

Like either of them needed help with the ladies. Ev might be our love guru, but the twins were sleeping their way through the entire student body at DSU. I wasn't helping them with shit. "No."

"You don't even have to say anything. Just play Schmadden with us. We'll even let you win. Make you look good for your new fans," Flynn said giving me a wink.

What the fuck was up with everyone offering to forfeit or let me win? That was some bullshit.

"You will not let me win, and you motherfuckers are going down." I pointed to them both and gave them my game day face.

"Yes." The twins high-fived over Hayes's head. "See you tonight after we pound Minnesota State into the ground."

The two of them gave Jules a quick kiss on the top of the head, which she swatted away, and then they were gone as fast as they had come.

That was enough family fun times for me today. "The rest of you all make like a twin and get out. I've got shit to do and none of it involves you chuckleheads."

Ev gave me an all too knowing look that I didn't like and did the whole fingers to eyes move. "You come to me when you need advice on how to woo your girl, Deck. Don't fuck this up by being a grump. You got me?"

"What he said," Jules chimed in. "We still need more women in this family. I expect you to do right by me."

The two of them walked out, but Hayes hung back. "Someday you gotta teach me how to get a girl like that, kay?"

"I'm sure you can get any woman you want. Why don't you go out right now and see." I gave him a shove out the gate and went back inside to figure out how the fuck I was going to woo my girl.

Oh shit. Yeah.

She was mine.

She just didn't know it yet.

My phone buzzed again with another text. This time it was from Kelsey, and I got a little zing. She sent a string of emoji. Yawning face, smiley face, music note. Then a brief message.

> Good morning, Mr. Kingman. Thanks for helping me get to sleep last night.

I hoped that Mr. Kingman bit was because I called her queen of hearts. I sent a quick text back.

> Let's do that again soon.

She replied with a winky face.

I wasn't sure what that was supposed to mean. But I wasn't going to reply until I figured out my next move. The day rolled out in a blur of halfhearted routines and distracted thoughts as I ran scenario after scenario in my mind for how to take Kelsey out on a date. I managed a light workout, but my mind wasn't in it, and I was afraid I was going to have to call Everett for advice. He would give me his love guru routine. It had worked for Chris.

I got several more texts from Alexis and I continued to ignore her. She was like everyone else who wanted to know if I was going to pursue Kelsey. The last time my phone buzzed with a text from her, it was accompanied by a link to a gossip site. There it was, the photo of me catching Kelsey at the concert, already making rounds on the internet.

I sighed, knowing this was just the beginning. My agent's text was full of questions and warnings about public perception. But for the first time, I found myself caring less about the media circus and more about what Kelsey thought of all this.

I texted Kelsey, really wanting to talk to her again, but my fingers hesitated. The magic we had last night wasn't going to happen during the day when she was surrounded by people. And it wouldn't happen on a public date either.

> How about dinner? No cameras, no media, just us.

I could bring her here to my house. Chris had beefed up the security in the neighborhood since the press went ballistic when he and Trixie had incited the media with a sex scandal. I'd just warn him she was coming and to close the figurative gates around the community. Or I could come to her. Stop by my favorite burger bar and bring cheeseburgers.

I waited, the seconds stretching into eternity. Then her reply came.

> I'd like that.

A smile spread across my face, a mix of relief and excitement. This was it. I was stepping into uncharted territory, but for the first time, the unknown seemed more exhilarating than frightening.

More dots.

> But I'm not in town tonight. We're getting ready to head up to Aspen to prep for the festival.

Shit. Of course. She was an international pop star and had a busy schedule.

Aspen was a good three and a half hour drive. I could do it. But not and be back in time to do the video game thing for Hayes and the twins. They'd understand me canceling for Kelsey fucking Best.

Before I could text back to tell her my plan, her dots appeared again.

> This might sound weird, and I understand if it's a no. But... we could do tomorrow. If you'd be willing to let me send my jet for you.

Shit. I should have thought of that. I shared a jet with Chris, Everett, and Hayes during the season. We didn't usually use it for anything but away games, but there was no reason I couldn't. It wasn't like I didn't have enough to cover the cost.

But there was something about the way she'd phrased that question. If I was willing to let her.

I sent a quick text to Jules.

> Hey. What were the other guys Kelsey's dated like?

I absolutely did not keep up with celebrity gossip, but I did vaguely remember hearing something about some jackass movie star.

Jules's message popped up a second later.

> Real D-bags. Why? We gonna rumble? I'll kick Jake Jay's ass under the highway.

Who talks like that? And the league thought I was

the meanest Kingman? They'd better never double cross the Kingman Princess.

> Cool your jets. Just doing some homework

Exactly like I thought. She was testing me out to see what kind of ego I had. I wanted to punch every dude who'd ever made her feel like she had to be smaller to feed their fucking sense of self-importance. If they couldn't be with a woman that was a bigger deal than they were, they had no business being anywhere near Kelsey Best. Fuckers. I typed back a quick text to Kelsey.

> Sounds perfect. Wanna watch the game with me? I promise there will be plenty of football players in tight-fitting pants for you to ogle.

She sent back the thumbs-up, the peach, the football, and the heart face emoji. I'd take that as a yes.

I headed upstairs to pack an overnight bag, hoping the invite was for more than a day, and seriously considered whether I should pack my uniform pants.

After dinner, I checked the scores of the college games and saw that the DSU Dragons did indeed beat Minnesota State. Good job. The boys would be in a good mood for this video game thing.

I played plenty of Schmadden in my day, and still liked to every once in a while. But Hayes was the real gamer. He'd even offered up a game night with him at a charity auction earlier this year that went for some big bucks.

I trotted down the street to his house, and he greeted me at the door. I hadn't been here since Chris gave him the house and we'd done a little house-warming and welcome-to-the-pros family party for him. This was big time for a twenty-year-old kid.

He had his living room set up like a mini arena, with four gaming rigs with cameras set up for stream-ing, headsets, and all, ready to dive into the virtual game. I had no idea how serious their streaming gig actually was. Hayes clapped me on the back, then rubbed hands together and put on his game face. "Get in losers, we're going to the gridiron."

He started up his live stream, did his intro, and cued each of us up. I had to school my face at how surprised I was at the production value these guys were giving. This was no joke.

I gave the screen a polite salute when he introduced me as their guest tonight. But then we started the game, and two minutes in, Hayes was already trash-talking, his focus locked on the screen, while Gryffen and Flynn, the twins, were laughing and giving it right back.

I'd forgotten how much fun it was playing games with my younger brothers. Especially when I got to smash their players into the ground.

We started off discussing the upcoming pro game,

analyzing plays and strategies. The twins, despite being in college, had insights sharp as any seasoned player. But Hayes was particularly keen, pointing out weaknesses in the opposing team's offense that I hadn't considered.

As we played, the chat on our livestream was a constant flow of football talk... until it wasn't.

"So, big bro," Flynn said, his tone so sneaky and sly, I knew what was coming. "Everyone's talking about that catch at the Kelsey Best concert. You planning to romance her or what?"

I tried to brush it off, focusing on the game. "That's nacho, bro."

Hayes, ever starving, perked up. "Nachos? Whose got snacks?"

Gryffen grinned and it wasn't because his player on the screen just scored. "Kelsey Best is a snack."

Dumbasses. "It's nacho business."

The chat on the side of the screen where their fans interacted exploded. It was like someone had opened the floodgates and every Kelsey Best fan in the universe found the livestream and decided to join in. Questions, comments, and speculations flooded the stream.

Hayes laughed. "Looks like you've got a whole new fanbase, Declan. Kelsey's Besties are all over this."

Flynn, ever the joker, chimed in. "Should we start calling you Mr. Best now?"

The site they streamed to struggled under the

sudden influx. Comments scrolled faster than we could read, a blur of excitement and emoji. Then, with a stutter and a freeze, the stream crashed, and the screen went blank.

We sat there for a moment, stunned.

"Guess we broke the internet," Hayes said, a hint of awe in his voice.

Flynn leaned back in his chair, whistling. "Man, Kelsey's fans don't play."

I shook my head, trying to hide my own shock. I'd caught a few of the comments in that chat. This thing with Kelsey, it was no longer just about a showmance or fixing public perceptions. It was about her. About us. Whatever this was turning into, it felt bigger than the both of us.

I shook my head, trying to dismiss the whirlwind of attention around Kelsey and me. It was overwhelming, this sudden thrust into the spotlight for something so personal. But amidst the chaos, there was an undeniable thrill, a sense of something beginning, something real.

*H*ey Besties!

Okay, here's the recon.

Our handsome hottie from the concert is the delicious six-foot-five Declan Kingman, who is a football player here in Denver. His team is... the blue horses?

Now, I know absolutely nothing about the sports ball, but as far as I can tell, his job is smash.

In fact, I may have spent a little too much time watching highlights of him cosplaying the Hulk during his sports ball games. He's really good at smashing.

Just saying.

And... did I mention he does have a brother (for me). In fact, he appears to have several brothers. Too many to count.

[Oprah meme]

You get a brother, and you get a brother, and everybody gets a brother. Let me tell you, Besties, they are all lookers too.

I know it might just be a dream on my part, but is anyone else hoping we might see an appearance of Mr. Smash at the music festival this week?

I'm headed up to Aspen, and if you're there, be sure to keep those phones at the ready, because as huge and hot as this guy is, he shouldn't be hard to spot. Tag me in your posts!

Mz. Besties' Bestie

THE WAY TO A WOMAN'S HEART

KELSEY

*T*he moment Declan stepped into the hustle and bustle of the backstage area for the stage I'd be using at the festival, the room shifted on its frenetic axis. His presence was like a calm amidst the storm of my usual pre-show preparations.

"Hey, Kels. Where's Wiener the Pooh?" His greeting resonated with a confidence that didn't overpower but somehow reassured. Everyone in the room paused, their tasks momentarily forgotten as they turned to look at the unexpected visitor. Maybe I had forgotten to mention to anyone that he was coming, or maybe he was just that hot and they were all as awestruck as I was.

This was supposed to be for show, but I sort of wanted to keep him to myself.

"Hi. I'm so glad you could come up. You're here earlier than I thought." Pooh, who I'd tucked firmly by my side because I didn't want another snake incident, gave a whole volley of little yips, and wiggled hard to get out of my arms.

I almost dropped her, and would have, but she went flying straight into Declan's arms. Then proceeded to slobber all over his face. Lucky girl.

"Hey there, little beast. I like you too, but let's keep that tongue to yourself, huh?" He gave her a couple of scritches behind the ears and then tucked her under his arm like a football. Her little butt stuck out behind his elbow and her tail was still going ballistic, but she didn't try to get away. She liked it right where she was.

I was not jealous of my dog right now.

"I think she likes you. Want a little tour of what we're doing to prep for next weekend?" I waved my hands at the craziness, staff, and crew floating around like busy bees setting up different elements of the show. "Or, no, you don't care about lighting timings and stuff. I can just—"

He grabbed one of my hands and gave the inside of my wrist a soft kiss. "I'd love to see a day in the life behind the scenes. You put a lot of effort into this, so, yes. I'm interested."

Huh. "Cool."

Penelope came over with her ever-present tablet

and had me approve a few things. "I'm also sending you the head of the dance team. She wants to hire some new backups."

"Oh good." We'd been continuing our search for more plus-size dancers. Hopefully we'd found some. "I want to go over a changeup I'm thinking of for the second set."

Declan stood by my side as I went through the motions of my day, only relinquishing Pooh when my dog walker came to get her for some potty breaks. He watched me talking to the sound guy and got a funny look on his face. "Do you have to approve every single detail of your show?"

There was no judgment in his tone, although it did sort of make me wonder if he thought I was crazy. "I'm a bit of a control freak when it comes to my shows. I just want them to be great."

"They are great, babe." He looked at me like the words he'd just said were more like, "Duh, babe."

And also, why did I like it so much when he called me babe?

While the girls and I rehearsed some new moves in the afternoon, Declan disappeared with Pooh. But I trusted him with her implicitly. Probably bored and just taking her for a walk. He might say he was interested, but really, who would be? The minutia of everything we did to get ready for a show even felt tedious to me these days.

"Citrus with a vitamin C boost or peanut butter

banana with a B-complex boost?" Declan popped up behind me and I jumped a good foot. He held two big plastic cups out toward me from some kind of smoothie place. Pooh was at his feet, literally licking his shoe. "Both have added protein powder."

I stared at him like he'd grown a third eyeball. "What's this?"

Obviously, it was a smoothie, but had he gone out and bought me a snack? Who did that?

"I figured if I was getting hungry, you must be starving." He shoved one of the cups into my hand and took a sip off the straw from the one he kept. "Or at least needed an energy boost. You've been going for hours. I'm tired just thinking about how much you've accomplished already today."

"Thanks. But you didn't have to do that." I took a long swig. Mmm. I loved peanut butter and banana. I was starving actually.

He gave me a lopsided smile that reached up to his eyes and had them sparkling. "And when you've finished that, I'm kidnapping you and Wiener here for the rest of the day."

My team exchanged glances, unsure of how to react. Skeeter stepped forward, shaking her head. "Kelsey has a strict schedule today, we can't just—"

Declan raised a hand, his movement gentle but firm. "I know, and I respect that. But she deserves a break. She works harder than anyone I've ever met."

His words weren't just flattery. They were spoken

with a sincerity that made my stomach flutter. Must be the smoothie.

Declan looked at me, his gaze soft but unwavering. "Only if you want to, Kelsey. I don't want to overstep. But you need a little time off, so you don't crash and burn later."

I took another sip, waited for the brain freeze to pass, and then gave him my best faux quizzical look. "What is this time off you speak of?"

Penelope gave me a small nod and a smile. "Maybe a short break wouldn't hurt? The show isn't until Friday, and we can easily handle the rest of today's checklist."

I knew that checklist up one way and down the other, and so did the rest of the crew. We always power loaded the front of the week in case there were any problems along the way. But we were ahead of schedule. It looked like Skeeter was going to protest again, but Penelope made a face at her, and mouthed "Pee Arr."

Skeeter rolled her eyes but looked own at her phone and started typing something, which I decided was her approval. Not that I needed it, but I liked having everyone on the same page.

"Okay, let's do it." I said but wagged my finger at him. "But just for today."

Declan's smile widened, and he took my free hand to lead me away. Pooh trotted along right at his heels as if she'd been trained to do exactly that. She absolutely never did that for me unless I had a treat in my hand, and even then, she was usually jumping and barking.

"How did you get her to do that?"

He looked down at Pooh and then gave me a wink. "That's between me and my girl, Pooh."

I looked down to where Pooh was licking his shoe again and noticed a blob of light brown goo. So he'd won over both our hearts with peanut butter. Smart man.

Wait. I didn't mean my actual heart like I was in love with him.

He obviously had plans. I hoped he understood I couldn't just go hang out in a coffee shop or a restaurant. Not without security and advanced notice to the staff that I was coming. Otherwise we'd completely disrupt their day and their business. He should get that, he was a bit of a celebrity himself. I'm sure his sports fans were crazy about him too.

Or was that just me?

"Wait, one sec." I stopped and turned to address my team. "Thank you, everyone. And why don't you all take a break too? I'm sure you could use it."

There were murmurs of surprise and gratitude as my staff realized what I'd just said. We never did this. But they worked just as hard as I did. I gave them all a little wave, and Penelope gave me a thumbs-up. If this was what fake dating Declan Kingman was like, I was going to enjoy it way more than real dating anyone else.

He led me to a big black SUV, where some of my security people were waiting. One of them opened the back seat for us to get in. Declan gave him a light slap on the back, in a sort of "I got this" way, and shut it, then opened the front passenger door for me. His demeanor protective but not overbearing. It was clear he was looking out for me.

"We're good, ladies and gents. Take the rest of the day off."

No security? Well, if anyone could pull that off, it was Declan. Just that air of confidence he had about him would keep most people at bay. His six-foot-something wall of muscles didn't hurt either.

Looked like he'd thought of everything, because there was even a fluffy sheepskin lined box in the backseat, strapped in with the seatbelt for Pooh. I showed it to her, and she immediately claimed it for her own with a little bark, three turns around and around, and then she sat looking forward expectantly like she was just waiting for us to get on the road.

"Where are we going?" I kind of hoped it was that picnic he'd described, but unless he'd hidden the blanket, basket, and a guitar in the back, probably not.

"Somewhere a little less flashy, and where the papps and fans aren't going to look for us." He steered us out the main part of town and I was surprised to see we were getting on the highway.

Did a place like that even exist? "So not in Aspen?"

"Aspen's fine, but a little too posh for my tastes.

We're going to head over to Bear Claw Valley. They've got a nice ski resort with all the amenities, but the actual town is full of regular joes who refuse to let the place get all gentrified."

Sounded too good to be true. "How did they do that?"

He shrugged and looked over at me a little sheepishly. "The Kingmans own most of the land up here. My dad didn't want to see his hometown get turned into some kind of place only richy rich people could afford to live in like some of the other mountain towns. So he... invested."

I should do that. My dad handled most of my money and a lot of it was just invested. I did pay off my parents' house in San Diego and bought the strip mall my mom's shop was in with my first big advance. But other than my apartment in New York, that I hardly spent any time in, I didn't actually own very much.

The drive to Bear Claw Valley was tranquil. But I kept catching Declan sneaking peeks at me. There was something in those looks that made me wonder more than once what he was thinking about. Like his glances were hungry. We had skipped lunch.

I had to stare out the window so I didn't look back at him with something else I was hungry for. Yes. That was better. Look at that tree, and that one. And those big rocks. Maybe I could spot a deer or a mountain sheep. That was a thing in the mountains, right? Anything to distract myself from the way I wanted to... Nope. No. Not going there. This was business. Even if it didn't feel like it right at this exact moment.

Declan's ease behind the wheel mirrored the comfort I found in his presence. I needed to tamp thoughts like that down. But I hoped that when this was all over and we fake broke up, we could still be friends. I liked him. A lot.

This mountain area was so beautiful, and he wasn't lying about colors. The leaves on the trees were like jewels. He slowed as we drove past the sign that identified the town of Bear Claw, and it was like something out of a movie or a book. Little shops on a main street, lots of pickup trucks, and we pulled into the parking lot of quaint bar nestled at the edge of town.

He parked the car, and I grabbed Pooh, clipping on the leash in the pocket of the car seat. "It's okay to bring her in here?"

I hesitated next to the car. We weren't the only ones in the parking lot and that meant there were people I didn't know inside. I hadn't gone to a place that wasn't either filled with other celebs or people who worked for me in ages.

Declan took my hand with a smile and a chuckle, reading my apprehensive expression. "You're not going to cause a riot by walking in here, Kels. We arranged for it to be a private event. Just a few old friends of the family, here to watch the game with us."

He had asked if I wanted to watch a game with him.

People did that at sports bars, I guess. Wait. Who was we?

Inside, the bar was cozy and inviting, a stark contrast to the glitzy venues I was used to. The few people present greeted us with warm smiles and nods, clearly accustomed to the Kingman family's presence. Only a few eyes lingered on me, but no one took out their phones and started filming or hopped up to ask for an autograph or anything.

Weird.

Declan led me to a group sitting in a corner booth. "Kelsey, meet my brothers Chris and Everett, and this is Chris's fiancée, Trixie, and our youngest brother, Hayes."

Their welcoming smiles instantly put me at ease. Introducing me to his family was a gesture that meant more than he probably realized. I'd never brought anyone home to meet my parents, especially not someone from the dazzling world of celebrity. But here I was, meeting Declan's family in a setting so normal it made me wonder what it would be like to bring him home to my mom and dad.

Not like that was ever going to happen.

LET'S TALK ABOUT SACKS, BABY

DECLAN

*K*elsey greeted my brothers and Trixie with a warm, genuine smile, her laughter mingling with the low hum of conversations. People couldn't help but be drawn to her. It was like watching a natural magnet in action.

We grew up with enough celebrities in our lives, not just sports stars, but models and Hollywood types from the De le Rein side of the family, that it took quite a bit for a Kingman to get starstruck. But even Chris and Everett, who were arguably the most famous among us, were a little bit in awe of the star power of my girl.

I was definitely teasing Hayes later about the way he blushed and forgot how to talk when Kelsey shook his hand. Not that I didn't feel the same way. They all behaved in a pro manner, but I got looks from both of them that said exactly how badass it was to be here with her, just hanging out.

I needed them to keep their shit together, because if anything went down, they were my first line of defense. Nobody was going to touch Kelsey, or even look at her funny. Not on my watch.

The bar was alive with laughter and conversation, but my focus was entirely on her. She was effortlessly charming, lighting up the room, and I was determined to make a lasting impression by letting her have a real night off. This was no celebrity hotspot. Simply good people, decent food, and a football game.

My world. Fuck, I hope she liked it.

After we ordered and our mountains of wings and beers came, she and Trixie talked about books. I was going to make sure I got a list of the ones Kelsey wanted from Trix later so I could get a couple. The game started, and the bar got pretty rowdy. L.A. was a big Denver rival.

Kelsey's eyes went wide, and she grinned at the shift in the mood. She tucked Wiener the Pooh between us on the bench to shield her from some of the noise. "You're going to have to explain what's happening. I got nothing until the halftime show."

Trixie leaned over and fake whispered, "I'm mostly in it for the football player's butts."

Kelsey looked at her and said, "Right? That's what I'm saying."

Chris gave Trixie a tickle for that comment and pulled her in under his arm, giving her a kiss on the top of the head. Kelsey got a cute little thinking face, pulled out her phone and typed something in.

"Just an idea for a lyric." She shoved it back into her pocket and smiled. This one was new to me. I'd seen a lot of her smiles, but that one had some excitement mixed with relief. Interesting. "Okay, now, who are we rooting for, and how do we know when to cheer?"

I wrapped my arm around her and pulled her close to my side, just like a real first date. "The boys here are all about the throwing, and running, and catching, which is fine. But I play defense."

"So your job is to stop the guys on the other team who are trying to throw and run and catch. Got it."

Hayes leaned in close. "He's the best one at doing it too."

Everett nodded and said, "Yeah. Glad he's on our team. I've been smashed into the ground enough times by him. Wouldn't want it on game day."

"Try being a quarterback when he's on defense." Chris stretched his neck from side to side as if he was actually sore from having recently been sacked. "Who do you think he practiced on to earn that most sacks in the league title?"

Kelsey got all wide-eyed and looked at me like I was a lesser-known god she hadn't heard of. Then she tipped her head to the side and got a sly look. "Do sacks have anything to do with balls?"

Hayes snorted the sip of beer he'd just taken out his nose.

I gave a little suck on my teeth and waggled my eyebrows at her. "Yes. Big balls need big sacks."

"I like her," Everett said.

I'd punch him in the face right now, because I knew he was thinking impure thoughts about my girl, but I was too busy staring into her twinkling eyes. "I like her too."

Pooh gave a little bark and wriggled around panting. She crawled right up my leg and tried to crawl her way up my shirt too. Her tongue was already trying to lick me.

Kelsey gasped and grabbed Pooh off me. "Don't you be a Gretchen Weiner and try to horn in, naughty little poop."

Pooh looked contrite and tucked her head into Kelsey's chest, but I swear to god, she peeked an eye out, looked at me, and licked her lips. "I think she might be hungry. The bar has a doggie meal with rice, carrots, and chicken."

"She's hungry for something alright." Kelsey scooted off to the end of the bench and set the dog on the floor next to her. "Let's see if she'll eat some food."

We went up to the end of bar and I ordered the doggie meal. It only took a minute for the bartender to grab it and a bowl of water. Pooh dug right in and forgot about the rest of the world.

Kelsey tilted her head, her eyes twinkling. "Is this where you teach me your secret tactics?"

"I don't keep secrets, Kels."

Something flashed through her eyes, but I wasn't sure what. In a second, she gave me a small slap on the arm. "I meant your football tactics. How you play the game."

Were we playing a game right now?

"Ah, I see. Then, yes." I stood up straighter, towering over her and the room. I swept my arm across the space. "Picture this, the field is a chessboard, and I'm the knight, ready to make my move."

Kelsey laughed, playing along. "A knight in shining armor?"

"Yep." I always wanted to be her knight in shining armor. "And my mission is to protect our realm from invaders."

She mimed holding a football and danced from foot to foot like she was going to run around me. "And I'm the invader, right? Trying to break through your defenses."

I had no defense against her. But I was going to catch her. "That's right. But here's the thing about a good defender, we anticipate every move. It's not just about brute strength, it's about outsmarting the offense, getting in their heads, and knowing what they're gonna do."

Stepping into her space, I backed her up against the wall at the end of the bar. "So if you, as the runner, decide to go left," I moved slightly to my right, "I'm already there."

Kelsey moved to the right, her eyes locking with mine. "And if I switch directions?"

Without missing a beat, I matched her movement. "Then I adapt, always one step ahead."

The air between us was charged with a playful tension. I put one arm up against the wall and leaned in closer. Her lips parted and her tongue peeked out before she pulled her lower lip between her teeth. My eyes locked on that lip, then flicked up to her eyes.

"What if I'm unpredictable?" she asked, her voice laced with a challenge.

I closed the gap between us, my voice low. "Then I have to use all my skills to keep up. But I'm always up for a challenge."

For a moment, everything else faded away. There was a spark there and I wanted nothing more than to let it set me on fire.

Kelsey whispered up to me, "I think I'm starting to like this game."

"I play to win, Kelsey."

She raised an eyebrow, a playful smirk on her lips. "Is that so? Well, I might just let you catch me to see if you're as good as you say."

Fuck yeah.

She slipped out from under my arm, picked up her

dog, who was definitely not done eating, and headed back to the table.

Mmm. I did enjoy the chase.

I was more determined than ever to win her over. This was no game to me either. It was the beginning of something I couldn't, and didn't want to, ignore. I was head over heels in love with Kelsey Best.

By the time the football game was over, Kelsey was cheering and booing the players on the screen along with the rest of us. I'd have to get her a Mustangs jersey of her own. With my name and number on the back.

We got up, ready to leave. I'd love to hang out longer, but I wanted to get back to her hotel safe and sound to prove to both her and her people that I could take care of her for a night off.

"That was kind of fun. I still don't understand a thing about football, except that some of those guys need to work on their dance moves when they score." Kelsey pointed to Everett and Hayes. "I expect to see better from you two."

Everett did a little spin, worthy of a popstar, and pointed his finger guns at her. "I've got moves you ain't even seen yet."

"Oh boy." Kelsey looked up at me. "Where did you find this one?"

"The backyard, I think. We had a very productive cabbage patch." I put my hand on her back and guided her through the bar toward the front door. She gave some sweet waves to the people still gathered, and I'm quite sure she made the day for Tex, the old guy who owned the hardware store in town.

Just before we reached the door, the bartender swooped inside. "Bad news, Kingman. I've been holding off a camera happy crowd out there for the last hour. Told them this was my place, and we were closed for a private party, and they couldn't come in. But they wouldn't go away."

Damn.

Kelsey took a long breath that I didn't like one bit. "Guess our time pretending to be regular people is over."

I jerked my chin toward the back. "Plan B?"

The bartender shook his head. "Naw, I saw a group of them head back that way too. They've got you figured out."

"It's okay. I'm used to it. Even this couple of hours out of the spotlight was nice."

"I've got plans you ain't even seen yet, sweetheart." I whistled to the boys and waved them over. "Plan C. The papps are outside waiting for us."

Trixie groaned. "Where's a rooster when you need one?"

"What?" Kelsey stared at us all like we were insane.

"A story for another night." Trixie patted Kelsey's shoulder. "Let's just say we've got experience with the press and the paparazzi, as does Luke Skycocker."

Kelsey leaned over and stage whispered to me. "I know she's saying words I understand on their own, but not when you put them in that order. I can't wait to hear this story."

"I promise to tell you after we make it through this gauntlet and get you home safe and unphotographed." I turned to Chris, Everett, and Hayes, and nodded. They knew what to do.

The flash of cameras was like a sudden storm, blinding and disorienting. Paparazzi swarmed around us, shouting questions and snapping photos. The manager, who'd been a solid shield inside, looked apologetic as he held the door, powerless against the crowd outside.

Chris, Everett, and Hayes immediately sprang into action. The three of them pushed out into the parking lot, forming a wall of Kingman with me between Kelsey, Trixie, and the relentless cameras. Their imposing figures were a clear message, but the photographers were undeterred, and we were surrounded and couldn't move without someone getting hurt.

Kelsey grabbed the back of my shirt and pressed her mouth to my ear from behind. "We need to be seen together, remember? Let's just give them their shot."

I clenched my jaw, the protective instinct roaring inside me.

"One picture," I growled loud enough for the paparazzi near us to hear. "Then everybody back off, or I swear I'll smash every camera here."

Kelsey stepped forward, her hand finding mine, and struck a pose for the cameras. Her grip was firm, reassuring, as if she was the one grounding me instead of the other way around. She gave the cameras a smile, but it didn't reach her eyes. The shutter clicks went wild, the flashes intensifying.

"Alright, you got your damn picture." I held my hands up and glared at the people taking pictures. I didn't yell. I just used my best linebacker growl. "Back off. Now."

To my surprise, they actually started to disperse. It might have been because Wiener the Pooh peed on the closest guy's shoe and looked like she was gearing up to shit on them too. Good dog. She was getting more cheese and peanut butter treats from me later.

I picked Pooh up and wrapped my arm around Kelsey, shielding them both as we made our way to the car. The tension in Kelsey's body was palpable, a stark contrast to the relaxed atmosphere we'd just left.

"You good?" I asked, once we were safely inside the vehicle. Chris and Trixie got into another SUV, and Everett and Hayes were going to follow. I'd prepped them that we might need an escort back to Aspen. I'd left nothing to chance with this date.

I needed Kelsey to see that I could take care of her. No one else ever fucking seemed to. No wonder she was exhausted.

She let out a long breath, her smile returning, but this time it was genuine. "Yes, of course, thanks to you. That kind of stuff is just part of the deal. I hope you don't mind too much. I should have warned you before you signed up for this."

It stung, hearing her accept continual harassment as part of her everyday life. I wanted to protect her from that, from everything that made her feel less than the amazing person she was. "I knew what I was getting into, babe. I'm here for it."

I was already thinking of ways to keep her from that kind of frenzy again. She deserved better, and I was going to make sure she got it.

The drive back wasn't exactly quiet. I didn't say anything, but Kelsey hummed a tune I didn't recognize. I wasn't even sure she knew she was doing it either. Her fingers did this little dance as she stared out the window, and if I had to guess, she was picking out the tune on an imaginary piano.

The hotel's valet was deserted when we got there, but we parked in front anyway. This was the kind of hotel that was host to presidents and popstars and they knew how to both be discreet and take care of their guests.

The boys were blocking us in on the driveway, so it wasn't like anyone would try to steal my rental. Everett and Hayes got out when we did and flanked us like my own personal offensive line until we got to the elevator. A few people in the lobby murmured, and I'm sure a few more pictures were taken too.

"Wow. I think they're more intimidating than my

own security team. Maybe I should hire professional football players in the offseason."

She wouldn't need to. Not if I was there with her.

The boys gave us a little salute as we got in the elevator, and Kelsey blew them a little kiss. Hayes caught it. The little shit.

A tension zipped between us as we stood listening to the horrible elevator music. I had the incredible urge to grab Kelsey, push her up against the wall, and kiss the bejeesus out of her. I had to bite the inside of my cheek and wrap my fist into a tight ball at my side not to.

When we reached her floor, Kelsey's room was the only one. Of course she had the suite all to herself. We stood together in the small foyer area between the elevator and the doors to her room. She turned to face me, her eyes searching mine. There was a vulnerability there that made my heart kick against my ribs.

"Tonight was... it was something else," she said, her voice a soft murmur.

"It was." My gaze dropped to her lips, then back to her eyes. I wanted to kiss her, to feel that connection that had been growing between us all night. But I held back, respecting the boundary we hadn't yet crossed.

Kelsey bit her lip, a small gesture that sent my thoughts spinning. "Declan, I..."

"Whatever you need, Kelsey, I'm here," I said, my voice low. I reached out, gently tucking a strand of hair behind her ear. Her skin was warm under my fingers, and she leaned ever so slightly into my touch.

For a long moment, we just stood there, the space between us charged with unspoken words and unacted desires. The urge to close that gap was overwhelming, but I knew this moment was hers to lead.

She exhaled slowly, her breath mingling with mine. "Goodnight, Declan."

"Goodnight, Kelsey." I stepped back reluctantly, my hand lingering near hers before I finally let go.

INSTASNAP POST

[Screenshot of the photo of Kelsey Best and Declan Kingman on the front page of the CelebsSightings.com website]

esties!

Best TEAs!

Kelsey has been spotted coming out of a sports bar in a town near Aspen, CO with none other than Mr. Football Smashie McHotsalot Declan Kingman.

AND THEY ARE HOLDING HANDS.

I'm dead.

I'm alive.

I am living for this.

And look at the way he's protecting her from the

paparazzi! He's holding them back, keeping our girl safe.

Your Bestie here heard he growleed at them and basically told them all to eff off, (but in more polite terms), and that his brothers acted as bodyguards so he and Kelsey could slip away.

WHERE DID THEY GO NEXT?

Are they dating? Are they just hanging out? Are they friends? Are they more? I neeeeeeeeds to know!

Your BFF,

Mz. Besties' Bestie

#Swooning #WhereCanIGetAKingman #Aspen #MusicFest #KelseySighting #Besties #KelseyBest #Friendstolovers? #SuckOnThisJake

THE FIRST KISS IS THE DEEPEST

KELSEY

I blew out a long breath and leaned against the door. I'd thought he was going to kiss me.

I don't know why I thought that. There were no cameras here to catch us. This wasn't real. This was not real. It was all a set up and I apparently needed constant reminding of it.

I watched him take one step away, two, and then he spun around, stared at me, probably thinking I was a total weirdo for just standing there propped up against the door like this.

"Fuck it." In less than a second, he crossed back to me, cupped my chin in his hand and wrapped his other arm around my waist. "Tell me right now if you don't want this, Kelsey. Because if you don't stop me, I'm going to kiss you, and I'm not going to regret it one little bit."

I forgot how to speak. I forgot how to breathe.

"Tell me you don't want me to kiss you." His eyes went from mine to my lips, where they stayed. He was already so close I could feel his breath on my lips.

My mouth kicked in before my brain. "Kiss me."

Before I even finished saying that final vowel, his lips were on mine. He both pulled me tight against him and pressed me back against the door. He was every-where, surrounding me, taking up all the air, all my thoughts, stealing my heartbeats and taking them for his own.

His tongue slid across mine, and I was lost in his taste. I finally remembered how to move my own muscles and pushed my hands into his hair. We fit so perfectly together. Not just our mouths, but our bodies. I didn't have to stoop to be level with him, and I reveled in the primalness of him being taller than me, bigger than me.

And of course, my mind went straight to how we would fit together in bed. I wouldn't have to be afraid I would squish him.

Declan swept his tongue over my lips, breaking the kiss far before I was ready to.

"Don't stop." My voice was so soft and breathy that I hardly knew what I was saying. How could he? I grabbed the collar of his shirt and pulled him back down to me.

But the kiss he gave me this time was light and teasing, not like the all-consuming kiss from before. "If we don't stop now, I'm going to have a hard time saying goodnight."

Then don't. I didn't let those words slip out of my mouth though. "We already said goodnight."

He pressed his cheek to mine, and god how I enjoyed the scratch of his beard on my skin. He whispered in my ear, "I know, and I should have walked away then, but you're so fucking tempting, Kels."

He was trying to tell me we shouldn't be doing this. Of course we shouldn't. This wasn't a real relationship. We'd just gotten caught up in the night. This shouldn't have happened.

Pooh whined at my feet. I blinked down at her, surprised she was even there. How the hell had I forgotten my poor, sweet poochie poo? She was probably dying to get to the patch of grass out on the porch and curl up in her bed. She was not used to late nights.

I wasn't used to getting the daylights kissed out of me.

"I'm going to go." He said the words but didn't move.

"Where?" I had a bed that was plenty big enough for the both of us.

"I need to head back down the mountain. Can't miss practice tomorrow."

Oh yeah. He had a whole life that didn't revolve around me. "Oh. Right. Of course."

"Come to my game this week." He ran a thumb across my bottom lip. "Thursday night."

"Okay." Everyone on my staff was going to murder me for taking a second evening off. Especially the night before the first show of the festival. But I couldn't resist. I needed to see him again.

Because, umm, the press would go wild seeing me at his game. That's why I needed to see him again. Not because I wanted to rip his clothes off and see exactly how big every single part of his body was.

He took a step back and shoved his hands into his pockets. I wanted to believe it was because he had to restrain himself from reaching for me again. "I'll message you when I get home."

"Call. I'll be up."

He dragged his eyes from where they were glued to my lips up to my eyes, and he shook his head like I was being a brat. "You need your rest, sweetheart."

Like I was going to be able to sleep anytime soon. "Maybe you can tell me another story to help me get to sleep."

Pooh whined again and Deck knelt down to pat her head. "Be a good girl, I'll see you in a few days."

When he stood back up, he stepped close and brushed a light kiss across my lips again. "I'll talk to you in a few hours."

And then he was gone, and I was a pile of goo.

I waved the key over the fancy lock and spent another good three or more minutes leaning against the back of the door hoping he changed his mind and would knock. He didn't.

He wouldn't. That was just dreaming on my part.

"Come on, Pooh. Let's go drown our sorrows for having a crush on a hottie football player in some cheese."

After I got her out for a potty and then settled in for the night in my bed, I grabbed my guitar. There were at least a dozen messages waiting for me to respond to from Skeeter and Penelope, but these days, if the muse was going to show up, I was going to ignore the world.

My creative inspiration had been a source of stress for a while. Where the ideas used to flow so easily, it seemed those days were over. I used to be able to just reach out into the universe like there was any number of tunes, lyrics, and ideas for songs, and all I had to do was just pluck one down.

Now I had to work for it, and while I always wanted to make the best art I could for my fans, I worried that I wasn't giving them my all.

Or maybe I'd given them too much.

I grabbed my phone and scrolled through the recent notes I'd written. They were sappy and happy and different from anything else I'd come up with in months. I strummed a few chords and started playing with the song I'd tried out at the Rust Rocks concert the other night.

I'd meant it to be something a bit slower and ballad like, but with these new lyrics, maybe it was supposed to be lighter and poppier.

When my phone rang a few hours later, I hadn't even realized how much time had passed. I set the guitar down, pleased that I had a good half a song on paper. But there was also a buzz of anxiety right behind my breastbone that that was all I had to show for songs on the next album. That studio date was approaching much faster than I liked, and I just wished I had made a whole hell of a lot more progress.

"Hey, you." I tucked the phone next to my ear and curled my feet up under me on the couch. I was trying really hard to sound nonchalant. This was just a new friend letting me know he'd made it home after a long late-night drive. "Made it home all right?"

"Yep. You kept me awake the whole way."

"I did?"

"You and 'Book Boyfriend', 'Strength', and 'Cozy Kind of Love', and a couple dozen or so more songs."

He'd listened to my music on his drive? That made me smile in a silly, stupid, happy way. "I like that I kept you company on the way home. Sleep tight. I'll see you on Thursday."

I wanted to spend the whole night on the phone with him again, but I didn't want to be the reason he didn't do a respectable job of doing his footballing in the morning. I'd hate if he got smashed instead of doing the smashing because he was tired. "Goodnight."

He hesitated for a moment before he said goodnight back and we hung up. I set the phone down on the couch next to me, stared at for a long time, picked it back up, ready to dial his number again, and then rubbed my eyes and checked the clock. Ooph. It was almost four o'clock in the morning.

Sleep was the last thing on my mind. A pang of guilt nudged me about the time I'd taken off today and the impending game on Thursday. I had to make sure no one could say my work at the festival this weekend was slipping because I'd starting seeing someone new.

Especially not the record company. I needed them on my side.

I reached for my phone, hesitating for a moment. Was I really about to wake up my team at this ungodly hour? But this was crunch time, and they'd understand. They always did.

Penelope's familiar groggy voice came across the line. "Kelsey? Everything okay?"

She sounded more alert than I'd expected. I should have messaged her when I got back to the hotel. It was a rare event that she didn't know exactly where I was and what I was doing. She'd probably been worried. Or wanted the tea on how my faux date night went.

I don't know why I wanted to keep the events of the evening a little bit private. Something just for myself.

"Hey, Pen. Sorry to wake you, but I had an idea. Can we get some work done now? I'll give everyone Thursday evening off."

There was a pause and then a soft chuckle. "Only you would call at four in the morning with a work proposition, Kels. Let me round up the troops, and no one expects to have another night off, especially right before a show. Don't worry about that."

"Thanks, Pen. And everyone is going to get Thursday off anyway. I'm headed back down to Denver for Declan's game."

Pen switched over to Facetime and waited until she could see my face before she spoke again. "I just wanted to make sure I was talking to the real Kelsey Best and that you hadn't been taken by aliens or some other such body snatchers."

Okay, yes. It had been... never since I'd taken two evenings off in a week, during a tour. Or maybe ever. I'd even continued to work through two bouts of COVID. I had big plans, big dreams, and a lot to get done to accomplish them.

"I just think it's good for the whole cover story, being seen at Declan's game. And, you know, Jake hasn't drunk dialed once since those first photos leaked. This fake dating thing is doing its job and I want it to continue to."

Penelope's voice took on a knowing tone. "Of course... that's good. It's what you wanted."

I shuffled uncomfortably. "Yep. It's everything I wanted. Nothing more."

She frowned at me, and I almost gave in and told her about the kiss. But it wasn't a big deal. Just a little mistake. Wouldn't happen again, so there wasn't anything to tell.

"Alrighty then. If you say so. Give me twenty minutes to gather the team leads and we'll be up to your suite, coffees in hand. Then later, you can tell me about where Declan kidnapped you to tonight and every single detail of what you did."

Penelope was onto me, thinking there was more to my sudden schedule change. But I couldn't let on, not even to myself, that Declan was more than just a strategic move.

True to her word, Pen and the rest of the team shuffled into the living room of my suite, coffees in hand, in various states of dress, within half an hour. We dove into the logistics for the Aspen festival, discussing stage design, setlists, wardrobe, and choreography.

Skeeter joined us a couple of hours into the morning work session. "Glad to see you're back on track. I just got off the phone with the PR team at the label. They've gotten you into Saddle Rock on Thursday night for an intimate acoustic show where you can test out some of your new songs for the upcoming album. It's a perfect promo to hype up your new stuff."

Well, damn.

Skeeter was right. This was the perfect opportunity, and I rarely got to play intimate venues like Saddle Rock. But I hadn't revealed to anyone that I didn't have any new songs ready. Pen probably had a clue, but as far as the rest of the team knew, I had time worked into my schedule to song write.

Not to mention that prioritizing my personal life over the business was not something I did.

Skeeter and Big Marine Records would shit bricks.

I glanced over at Pen, and she nodded, reading my mind. "Let me see what I can do."

KELSEY WAS HERE

DECLAN

I'd fucked up.

Took things too far, too fast, and now Kels was avoiding my calls. She responded to my texts. Mostly with selfies that showed her with her crew, working. God, she was a machine. Even during late-night texts, she was still at work, usually working on a new song.

I shouldn't have fucking kissed her.

But she'd kissed me back, disintegrating every one of my brain cells. I could still taste her on my lips.

And then she hadn't talked to me for three days.

But she was here. I knew because Jules had sent a pic of her, Trixie, and Kelsey in the Kingman box.

I also had a whole host of messages from my agent.

Half were about how Swoosh had contacted her about opening talks about the shoe deal again, and the other half were asking what the hell she was supposed to tell Kelsey's people.

I'd told her to stall, which she didn't like one bit. I'd gotten an entire lecture in text form, complete with GIFs about how irritated she was with me. As far as I was concerned, if she hadn't communicated my decision, that was her problem. What was going on between me and Kelsey was all I cared about.

I loved football, but today, I wanted nothing more than to get this game going so I could pound some Bandit ass into the grass. Because the sooner we won, the sooner I could see her.

Every single thing I had to do before then was either my job or something standing in my way. I didn't have space to think about anything but football and Kelsey.

The camera team was set up in the media room with their green screen and their cameras getting to record our player intros. Fuck, I'd forgotten it was media day. It was a routine thing, we said our names and alma maters. And it was the last thing I wanted to do.

If it wasn't in my contract, I'd have told them all to fuck off. Instead I got dragged into the media room, gear, and all.

Chris was up first. He stepped in front of the camera, his trademark quarterback confidence on full display. "Chris Kingman, Denver State University," he said, flashing a charismatic smile that had no doubt won over fans and reporters alike. They took a bunch more pictures of him posing and I rolled my eyes at least a hundred and twenty-seven times.

Everett followed, his tight end stature imposing even on camera. "Everett Kingman, Denver State University," he announced, winking at the camera as if sharing a private joke with every viewer.

Then came our rookie, who was already killing it in stats. "Hayes Kingman, Denver State University Dragons, baby," he said, giving a nod to say he was ready for whatever the game threw at him. They made him record it again without the "baby."

The film team seemed pleased, each of my brothers having given them exactly what they wanted.

I stepped in front of the camera, feeling its unblinking eye on me. The media team waited, and at one point gave me a signal that they were rolling. I remained silent, just glaring into the lens. I let my playing do the talking.

The PR folks exchanged glances with the film team. This wasn't the first time I'd recorded the exact same intro. They knew better than to expect a charming one-liner or a flashy smile from me. I don't know why they even bothered. They should just use the same old one.

But I thought about how Kelsey had given those papps what they wanted with the picture, and then we'd been left alone. I guess I could give just a little too.

"Declan Kingman, Denver State."

After a few tense seconds, the PR team member behind the camera gave a surprised nod. "That's... that's good, Declan. Thanks."

I stepped away, feeling the eyes of my brothers on me. Chris and Everett were ever amused by my refusal to talk to the camera so this had surprised them too. Hayes looked a bit puzzled and I kind of liked that I'd confused our resident genius. But none of them said anything. Smart men, all of them.

With the PR task checked off, albeit to no one's satisfaction but my own, I grabbed my gear and headed out.

"You're pacing like a caged grizzly." Chris joined me on the sidelines.

I crossed my arms and took up a wide stance, trying to play it cool. "Just ready to tear it up."

He clapped me on the shoulder, his knowing look telling me he saw right through me.

"Kelsey's in the suite," he said, almost conspiratorially. Of course Trixie had told Chris that Kelsey was up there with them.

"Right." I had to clear my throat or risk him hearing the edge of excitement in my voice. "Just makes today's game a bit more interesting."

"Then show her what the biggest, baddest player in the league looks like."

I nodded, my focus narrowing as I glanced up toward the suite.

Mile High Stadium was a cauldron of noise and expectation like always. There was nothing like a home game. The weight of my gear felt familiar, comforting, but there was an added charge in the air today. Kelsey was here, and I wasn't the only one who knew it.

The big screens in the stadium, normally lit up with pre-game stats or games to keep the crowd entertained, all had Kelsey, in a Mustangs baseball cap and a blue and orange t-shirt, splashed across them. She gave the crowd a little wave and they freaked out.

"Wait, did we just score a touchdown and I didn't notice?" Everett teased. "I didn't know we could do that before the game even started."

"Shut up."

Hayes jogged over, a big grin on his face. "We gotta make you look good in front of your girl. You want Ev and I to do the Kelsey shuffle when we score?"

When, not if. That was the kind of confidence that kept our family supplied with national championships and bowl rings.

I couldn't keep the smile off my face this time. Damn. I scowled at him and narrowed my eyes, putting that game face back on. "You do that, kid. But when the defense gets on the field, watch and learn how to really impress the ladies."

The whistle blew, and like a switch, the world narrowed down to just the field, the play, the rush of the game. As a defensive lineman, my job was to be an unmovable force. When the special teams filed off and Washington had the ball, I dug my cleats into the turf, crouched low, my muscles coiled and ready to destroy.

Across the line, the slow-ass quarterback eyed me warily. He knew I was coming for him, and every nerve in my body sang with anticipation. The ball snapped, and I exploded forward, the world shrinking to the space between me and my target.

The quarterback dropped back, eyes scanning for an open receiver. I bulldozed past their left guard, a surge of adrenaline pumping through me. The quarterback's eyes widened in panic as I closed in. I launched myself, my body a perfect blend of power and speed, tackling him to the ground with a satisfying thud. The crowd erupted, a tidal wave of noise and energy that washed over me.

Two minutes in, and I had my first sack. That was the way to start a game. My teammates swarmed around, patting my helmet, their voices a chaotic blend of congratulations and excitement.

Still on the ground, I chuckled, breathing hard. "Just warming up, boys."

In the heartbeat of stillness as I rose to my feet, my gaze drifted involuntarily to the suite above. Was Kelsey watching? My heart hammered, not from the exertion but from the thought of her eyes on me. What did she think of this side of me, so different from the man who'd pinned her against her door and kissed her like our lives depended on it?

I shook my head slightly, forcing my focus back to the game. I couldn't afford to be distracted, not when I needed to be at my best. But the question lingered, an unspoken echo in each play.

Each subsequent play blurred together, a relentless rhythm of aggression and strategy. But in those fleeting moments of pause, my eyes would betray me, seeking her out repeatedly. I channeled every conflicting emotion into my performance.

Today was more than just a game. It was a statement, a message sent across the field and up to the woman who had unwittingly upended my world. Every tackle, every defensive move, was sharper, as if I were carving my message into the very field with my bare hands.

In between plays, I caught glimpses of my brothers on the sidelines, their grins wide, their teasing remarks lost in the roar of the crowd. We were a unit, a family on and off the field, and today that bond felt even stronger. Especially knowing Kelsey was hanging out with the rest of the Kingmans.

God, I hoped my dad wasn't too much for her. Or the twins. It would be just like Isak to make a pass at her with his teenage hormones raging and filling him with confidence.

After a particularly hard tackle that turned the ball over to our offense, Chris gave me a good couple of smacks on the helmet, all hyped up. "Damn, Deck, you're earning that meanest player nomination today. We're gonna win this game for your girl."

The final whistle blew, marking our victory. The stadium erupted in cheers, the sound echoing off the stands. I was buzzed with the adrenaline of the win, my body still thrumming with the energy of the game.

As I made my way off the field, I caught sight of the press area, a flurry of activity as reporters jockeyed for position, cameras, and microphones at the ready. I hesitated. The last thing I wanted was to face them, but I knew it was part of the deal, especially after a game like today.

A PR rep from the team nudged me toward the cluster of reporters. "They're going to want to talk to you, especially after today's performance. You tied your game sacks record from last year today."

I nodded, steeling myself. I could handle this.

The reporters descended the moment I stepped into the designated interview area, their questions overlapping in a cacophony of curiosity and expectation.

"Declan, was your performance today inspired by Kelsey Best's presence?" one of the reporters shouted over the din.

I paused, my initial instinct to tell them it was none of their damn business. But then I thought of Kelsey, of how this all reflected on her. I couldn't afford to be the asshole they expected.

I fixed the reporter with a look, my voice rough but

controlled. "Let's just say it's always good to have support in the stands."

His eyes went wide, and I recognized the look of surprise that I'd even responded. After that, all their hands went up, and they basically started shouting random questions at me. The PR guy started calling on them for me.

"Are you two officially dating?" The next reporter went there, pushing my boundaries, and he knew it.

I clenched my jaw, the urge to snap my mouth shut and not say another word rising. But I kept my cool. For Kels. "That's personal," I said bluntly. "Today, we're talking football."

The questions kept coming, a relentless stream about the game, about Kelsey, about my aggressive play today, and the meanest player nomination. I answered them with the same no-nonsense responses, giving them just enough to satisfy their curiosity but keeping the details of my personal life close to my chest.

After what felt like an eternity, I finally broke away from the press, the PR rep giving me a nod of approval. "Handled that well, Kingman."

I didn't care about their approval. All I cared about was seeing Kelsey.

I made my way through the stadium's inner corridors, my mind a whirlwind of anticipation and nerves. What would she say? How would she react after what had happened?

As I approached the family and PALs meet up

spot, my heart raced. I could already imagine her there, her eyes meeting mine, that connection reigniting between us. This was it. The moment I'd been waiting for since I first stepped onto the field today.

But she wasn't there. I'd told Jules and Trixie to bring her here. Maybe they were still up in the suite?

The suites were exclusive access, but there were still other people up there, so it wasn't exactly a safe haven, The longer she stayed up there, the more it would be a glass fishbowl in the sea of the stadium.

My phone buzzed with a message from Jules.

> Operation Best Sneak is a go. Be in the family area in 10.

I couldn't suppress a grin. Trust Jules to come up with something like this.

Ten minutes later, the family area was still buzzing, and I suspected most people were still hanging around hoping to catch a glimpse of Kelsey's star power. I couldn't blame them. I pretended not to notice a thing and just swiped through my phone. But all I was doing was looking at my messages over and over, waiting for a tip off.

Then I saw them. A group of 'maintenance staff' comprised of three football-player-sized men, and two shorter, softer... men pushing a large utility cart, the kind used for moving heavy equipment. They were followed by my dad, who looked like he was slightly humored that his path was being blocked by this bizarre maintenance crew.

The utility cart was covered with a tarp, but the slight, irregular bulge at one end was a dead giveaway. How they'd gotten away with this was anyone's guess. As they neared, one of the 'staff' who was unmistakably Jules under a baseball cap, shot me a covert wink.

They rolled the cart into the far corner of the room, and the 'staff' formed a barrier around it, holding brooms, and I think Trixie was pretending to dust. Until Chris walked over and threw her over his shoulder.

She squealed, and that created the distraction I needed. I moved over toward the cart as inconspicuously as I possibly could and lifted the tarp. Underneath, Kelsey sat curled up, a mischievous smile on her face. "Hi there. Fancy meeting you here."

A short snort-laugh popped out before I could hold it in. I reached down, helping her out of the cart.

"I didn't want to miss the chance to see you after the game," she said, her voice soft.

"I'm glad you're here," I replied, my heart racing. "I've been thinking about you. A lot."

Her smile widened, and for a moment, it felt like we were the only two people in the world, but I felt a whole host of eyes on us. I turned and pointed my finger around the room like a sword. "Everybody's going to be cool, right?"

There were lots of murmurs agreeing, but one little

girl raised her hand like we were at school or something. I pointed to her and said, "What?"

"My brother said I'm not cool."

I looked over at said brother and scowled. "Sweetheart, if there's one thing I know, it's that older brothers who think their little sisters aren't cool, are dumb."

Kelsey gave her a wink and a nod, and the little girl looked up at her dad, who was another of our linesmen, and said, "Told you he was dumb."

The rest of the room still gave us some looks, but they understood the pressures of celebrity better than most and grabbed their families and got on their way.

Kelsey stayed quiet but smiled at everyone and returned waves to the kids. When it was just the Kingmans left, she relaxed. We stood there for a moment, just smiling at each other, the noise and chaos of the day gone. "I've had my fair share of sneak and peeks, but having a whole fake maintenance crew straight out of an episode of Scooby Doo was a first."

"Anytime you need some Kingman ninjas to sneak you out, or in, or whatever, we got your back," Isak said, and then he and the twins moved into a legit Charlie's Angels pose.

"All right, I think that's enough K-Team for one day." My dad made a round 'em up circle with his hand. "Ms. Best, it was nice to meet you, and I hope we'll see you again soon. Don't let this one talk football all night."

"Dad." I was going to have to interrogate both Kelsey and Jules later to find out just how much damage control I'd have to do after leaving Kelsey in the clutches of the men in my family for the last several hours. Like... did he bring out the baby pictures?

"I'm sure you can think of something much more fun to do with your girl tonight." Dad gave Kelsey a wink and then made my entire family file out like we were all still kids in school.

"Did... your dad just..." Kelsey's mouth hung open as she stared at the backs of my family walking away. "Did he imply that we should..."

I can't believe she had to spend an entire game in the suite with them without me. I had a feeling I'd be hearing how much they'd embarrassed me for years. Years. "Do me a favor and forget you ever met any of them."

"Uh, no." She laughed and I loved the sound of it so much, I'd forgive anyone for embarrassing me just to hear it over and over. "The Kingmans are unforgettable."

FLIPFLOP

THE LEAGUE OF AMERICAN FOOTBALL FLIPFLOP ACCOUNT PROFILE

@TheLeagueAF

WE'RE BESTIES NOW

MILE HIGH STADIUM FLIPFLOP ACCOUNT PROFILE

@ItHappensAtMileHigh

KELSEY'S HOUSE

THE DENVER MUSTANGS FLIPFLOP ACCOUNT PROFILE

@DenverMustangs

WE'RE A KELSEY-KINGMAN STAN
ACCOUNT NOW

SAVE A HORSE, RIDE A COWPAL

KELSEY

*a*fter the last person left the family room, we stood together for a second, not saying a word. My world was never quiet. It was all hustle and bustle and cameras and needing to be heard. Not with Deck. He found these kinds of spaces for me, and I didn't know whether the quiet was a good thing or not.

"Hey," he said in a way that was a new greeting, starting our meeting all over again but with just the two of us here. His voice carried that same deep, resonant tone that had sent shivers down my spine during our phone calls.

"Hi," I managed, my voice a little breathless. I was suddenly acutely aware of how close he was standing, how I could feel the heat emanating from his body. "You were incredible out there."

I honestly only sort of understood when to cheer, but every time he'd taken a player on the other team out like a freaking zombie hunter, I'd shouted and screamed.

The way he moved, the way he carried himself—it wasn't just confidence. It was a deep, unspoken understanding of his own strength and ability. It drew me in, igniting a flame that I was trying really hard to pretend wasn't a roaring inferno in my libido.

Which wasn't good. This couldn't happen. We both might have some attraction, but in reality, this couldn't actually happen.

I thought I was attracted to Declan Kingman before. I'd pissed off my agent and my record label rearranging my schedule just to see him again.

He was a gentleman, he was great with my dog who clearly had as big of a crush on him as I did, and his protectiveness made me a little bit swoony. But I'd convinced myself that he was just being a pro and fulfilling our fake-dating agreement.

That was for the best. We both needed to be pros about this. I did not have space in my life for another relationship disaster.

I hadn't quite compartmentalized that kiss though.

A hint of a smile played on his lips. "Glad you enjoyed the show."

"It was more than that," I confessed, my words

tumbling out before I could censor them. "Seeing you out there, the way you... took control of the game. It was... it was hot."

Declan's eyes darkened, a spark of something more flickering in their depths. He stepped a little closer, taking up all the air in the room. He placed a knuckle under my chin, lifting my face so I had to look up at him. "Is that right?"

Nothing prepared me for watching him play live. Not the hours of highlight reels I'd obsessed over, not watching a game on TV with him and his brothers. Not even reliving that kiss on the quick flight down. His performance on the field added a raw, primal edge to the feelings that were already complicating my life.

Seeing him turn into a feral bear on the field had me wishing I'd brought extra panties. I understood now why they called him the meanest player in the league. At first, I'd been worried that meant he wasn't a nice guy. Which was patently wrong.

His aggression, his dominating presence, probably scared the poop out of the opposing team. As it should. He'd really taken some of those other players down hard, and every time he did, I got one hell of a thrill.

I nodded, my usual poise faltering under his intense gaze. "I mean, I never thought I'd say this about football, but watching you play... it's kind of a turn-on."

What was I doing? This couldn't happen. Stop it. Stop flirting. Stop telling him how hot you are for him.

There was a charged moment of silence as we stood there, the air thick with unspoken words.

"Let's get out of here."

I knew what he was asking, and I became a giant wiener. "Where do you and the boys usually go to celebrate?"

"You want to go out?" He shook his head, and his eyes went up, looking at nothing except maybe something in his mind, thinking. "Kels, I'm not sure it's a smart idea. It could get crazy with fans and paparazzi."

I was immediately struck by just how much he'd made it his job to keep me safe. But if I'd come down for his game and pissed off my agent and label, they expected me to have something to show for it. And just because I was famous, didn't mean I couldn't have a life and be seen out on the town. With some careful planning.

I smiled and gave him a wink. "Don't worry, I've got moves you haven't even seen yet. Let me handle it."

I quickly messaged Penelope. She'd flown down with me and was ready for this.

> Secure that venue for post-game celebration. Make it exclusive. Can we send out a message to the Mustangs and their partners?

Penelope was a miracle worker. I didn't even know how she made half the stuff happen that she did. A fairy godmother wand or something. Within minutes, she texted back.

> All set. Private rooftop at Manniway's. Security in place. Cowgirl network already spreading the word to players and PALs.

I showed the message to Declan who lost his forehead with how impressed he was. "Wow, that was fast."

I winked at him. "Welcome to my world. Let's show them how to celebrate a win, shall we? Wait, what's the Cowgirl network and PALs?"

"The partners and lovers of Mustangs players. They call themselves the Cowgirls."

I snort-laughed. "Because cowgirls ride mustangs?"

He grinned and waggled his eyebrows at me. "They sure do."

Penelope had a black SUV waiting outside the players' entrance to the stadium. We'd waited around inside long enough that there were only a few paparazzi and fans still holding out for us. I waved to them as he escorted me to the car, and when a couple of the photographers got a little too close before I was in and the doors were shut, Declan growled at them. Like a bear.

God that was hot.

Stop it, lady libido. Enough with the thinking every single thing he did was hot.

When we arrived at the place, Declan told the

driver to go around back and then pointed out where my security could discreetly usher us in. "You've been here? I thought you weren't a partier."

"This is a steakhouse owned by Denver's former quarterback Johnston Manniway and his wife, Marie. He just opened it at the end of the summer. It's not a club, but it is a hot spot for local celebrities." He placed his hand right at the spot on my lower back that had my body going into high alert at that single touch. "Your assistant chose perfectly. They know how to keep raving fans at bay, while also not making them feel like they don't matter."

The private rooftop buzzed with excitement and was already filled with Mustangs players and their partners. These people knew how to respond to a party invitation. I saw Trixie and waved to her. She motioned me over to the circle of women she was with. "Oh, you must be the Cowgirls."

A man wearing a Mustangs t-shirt as if it was a fashion-statement and not sports paraphernalia, standing on the edge of the circle, raised his hand. "I'm a cowboy and also a big fan."

A woman who was just a smidge older than the rest of the group and was so freaking classy looking in a flowy shirt, belt, and pressed trousers, I was incredibly jealous, pulled the young man into the group and kept her arm wrapped around his shoulders. "Yes, you are, and we're all a little bit jealous you've taken our handsome safety out of the running for most the eligible

Mustang."

He shrugged and smiled. "Yes, but he's still in the running for best butt. Just saying."

There were a lot of head nods and murmurs of agreement, and it was clear on at least half the faces that they were thinking about said butt in a fond but lustful manner.

Trixie cleared her throat and brought everyone's attention back from football buttsville.

"Everyone, while she probably needs no introduction, this is Kelsey Best. Kelsey this is everyone." Trixie introduced the women in the circle one by one. I repeated them all in my head to try and remember as many of them as I could. "And this is Marie Manniway, our de facto head cowgirl."

The classy woman extended her hand to me. "Nice to meet you, Kelsey. Now tell us about this little showmance you're having with our boy Declan."

Uh. "Showmance?"

"Yes, sweetheart." She didn't smile and tapped her well-manicured nails along her silky shirt sleeve. "I'm asking if this is for show, or if the lovey dovey eyes you were making at him during the game are real."

Gulp.

"Girl," another woman in the group, whose name was maybe Kierra, pointed at me, grinning. "No way this is fake. She's got it bad, he's got it bad, and we've all got it bad for how bad they've got it."

"Wait," the woman standing next to her said, "is that bad?"

Cowboy lifted his phone and showed a video posted by the League of American Football on FlipFlop that showed me in the Kingman suite, cheering and indeed making eyes directed toward the field. Although I wouldn't have said I was thinking lovey dovey thoughts at that moment. More like I was eye-fucking Declan from all the way at the top of the stands.

"We all saw it, clear as day. As did, let's see," he glanced at his phone and snorted, "so have one-point-eight million other people so far today."

Well. That had better satisfy my agent and the label that the jaunt down to Denver was worth it for the free publicity I'd just gotten. That was a hell of a lot more than the four-hundred-ish people who'd be at the Saddle Creek show. The one where I was supposed to sing new songs that I still hadn't written.

Trixie gave me a little squeeze. "Don't worry. Marie does this to every newbie. She's a bit protective of the Mustangs players. And... you know, none of us want Declan to get anymore grumpy than he is, which he would be if he got his heart broken."

I did not understand why everyone kept saying he was mean or grumpy. How had that moniker been foisted onto such a sweet cinnamon roll of a guy?

Marie crossed her arms and gave me a slight glare. "You're not going to break Declan's heart, are you?"

"I can honestly say ladies, that if anyone is going to

get their heart broken here, it would be me." Which was exactly what I was afraid of and why we could not get into a real relationship. "I think Declan is in love with the game."

I glanced up from the circle and Declan was staring directly at me from over by the bar where he stood with his brothers. God they were—

"Formidable, aren't they?" Marie cut into my thoughts.

"I was going to say hot, but yeah, let's go with formidable."

"See," Cowboy said. "Come on, Marie, come to the Bestie side. We have cookies. Christmas tree sugar cookies."

Declan said something to the men around him, pushed off the bar, and moved his way through the crowd to my side. "I've been chosen to sacrifice myself to find out what you all are talking about over here. The looks you've been shooting our way are making our cute and adorable Hayes nervous."

Marie looked at him, then at me, and I knew she was going to expose us both right then and there. She knew this was a fake relationship. I could see it in her eyes. "We've been debating whether to rename our group of Mustangs partners and lovers."

I clearly needed more faith in the world and the women around me.

Declan frowned but looked to me for confirmation.

"I suggested cowpokes." I shrugged and pretended

this blatant little lie was all I'd been thinking about for the past ten minutes.

Everyone giggled, but most also shook their heads. Trixie vetoed the idea. "That's a good one, but I think Wyoming would get mad at us."

Like... the whole state? The wild, wild West was weird. I liked it.

"Partners and lovers pretty much covers it," another woman said. "So how about CowPaLs?"

Marie nodded sagely. "Doesn't quite have the same ring to it, does it? We'll keep workshopping that."

"We need something like Kelsey's Besties," Cowboy, whose name I needed to learn and then recruit him to be on my PR team, declared. "Anyone can be, and honestly pretty much everyone is, a Bestie."

"Which is why we were consulting your girlfriend, Declan." The way Marie said girlfriend, it was so clear she was asking him to confirm the relationship. This was such a test, and I held my breath waiting to see if he'd pass it.

Although, I wasn't sure exactly whose test it was.

"One I intend to now steal from you all." A lively song started up and Declan took my hand, pulling me toward an area cleared of chairs where a few people were dancing. The minute we hit the floor, everyone else crowded in too and we all started shaking our little boo thangs.

And Declan could dance.

Like, *dance* dance. He had rhythm and moves. Who

could ask for anything more? A man who could play a violent game of football and dance like the music flowed through him was more than I could ever resist. Ever, ever, forever, ever.

Okay. Fine. We were not going to be in a real relationship, so there was no harm in my having a little crush on him, right?

Right.

Bad.

Too bad.

And too late.

I had more than a little crush. And it would never be anything more. I'd see to that.

I laughed and danced right along with him, matching his moves, and getting nice and close. I prayed for a dirty dancing song to come on next. Instead the beat shifted into a slow, tender melody. Declan extended his hand with a playful glint in his eyes. "Shall we show them how it's really done, sweetheart?"

I took his hand, my heart skipping a beat. "Only if you promise not to step on my toes."

Declan's hand slid down and rested gently on my lower back, guiding me with confident ease. We moved in sync, lost in the music's embrace. His gaze, intense yet soft, locked with mine, speaking a language only our bodies and the music understood.

"When were you going to tell me you could dance?" I was surprised by his smooth moves. Was there anything sexier than a dude who could really dance? He wasn't just moving his hips around, he could keep up with my backup dancers.

He leaned in, his breath warm against my ear. "I'd rather show you."

The world around us faded, leaving us alone in our own little sphere. His grip tightened slightly, pulling me closer, as if we were alone in the room.

"Is this all part of the show?" I murmured, my voice barely above the music.

Declan's lips curved into a mischievous smile. "Do you want it to be?"

The song dwindled to a close and I didn't want to let go. This electricity between us had me in a chokehold. It was more real than any showmance or any other romance I'd ever had. What did that say about my past relationships?

Trixie pushed through the other people around us with her phone out. "Kelsey, Declan, you guys are blowing up the internet. Look at these hashtags, #KelsandKing and #Delsey."

She flipped her phone around, showing us a feed of photos and videos from tonight, each one with us in the center. There we were, dancing, laughing, looking like a couple straight out of a fairy tale. My heart skipped a beat at how perfect we looked together.

Declan took the phone from her, scrolling through the images with a frown.

I leaned in to look, my stomach doing somersaults.

Each picture, each comment, it was all so public, yet so intimate. A part of me thrilled at the attention, but another part worried about how real it all seemed.

One picture caught my eye, a candid shot of us during our dance, where I was looking up at him with what could only be described as adoration. It was a look I couldn't fake, a moment of genuine emotion caught on camera for all the world to see.

Wow. I really needed to rein this in. If anyone else saw that, they'd think I was in love with Declan Kingman.

And from the look on his face in these pics and videos, unless I was crazy, he was in love with me too. We would definitely have the world fooled. I was almost fooled myself that this was real. But it wasn't. It wasn't, couldn't be. Ever.

LEAVING ON A JET PLANE

DECLAN

*S*omething was different about Kelsey tonight.

I'd been prepared to rush her out of the party when we saw how social media was blowing up. Those posts were far too up close and personal to me, and some of those clips had definitely come from people here on the rooftop with us. But she wasn't bothered by it at all. She'd smiled and said she wanted to dance some more because she was having fun.

My girl might appear like she was having fun on a daily basis to the world around her, but I saw how her life was taking a toll on her. There were dark circles under her eyes that she hid with makeup and those smiles that made me go weak in the knees. But she was also more relaxed tonight, hanging with my teammates and our friends and family, than I think I'd ever seen her.

She needed this. Needed downtime in her life. I had the whole damn offseason to refresh and re-coop. When was her offseason? Never. And I was worried as fuck she was going to crash and burn.

So we stayed. Although, I gave a lot of my team-mates and their partners the side eye for posting about us on social media. They knew how much I avoided that kind of shit, and I expected better from most of them. But could I really expect anyone not to get starstruck in Kelsey's presence? Probably not. Her star was so much brighter than everyone else in the whole damn world. And not because she was an ultra-famous musician.

Everett slapped a bottle of beer into my hand. "If you're not careful, brother, that woman is going to rock your world and then break your heart."

"Shut up." I took a swig of the beer and didn't even bother looking at him, not that I could tear my eyes away from her anyway. The Kingman family resident love guru was going to tell me what he thought regardless.

"I'm serious." He leaned against the bar and watched her with Trixie, Marie, and the others along with me. "You're so fucking in love with her the whole damn world can see it. On national television I might add."

"I don't care what's on TV or FlipFlop or wherever."
I only cared what she thought.

"She's got a long line of broken hearts in her path.
Have you seen what a wreck her last guy is? You're
already a sullen asshole. None of us want to see what
you'll turn into when she moves on. Although it will
make for a killer album, I'm sure."

I had to grip my bottle real fucking tight so I didn't
slam it down and sock Ev in his stupid mouth. "The
other fuckers she dated were boys who cared more
about their hair than her. She's not going to break my
heart."

"They always do, my man. They always do."

Shit. This wasn't about me. Although, I did recognize the Kingman family trait of trying to look out for
one another. My happy-go-always-getting-fucking-
lucky-with-a different-woman-in-his-bed-every-night
lothario of a little brother wasn't as love 'em and leave
'em as the world thought he was.

I set my beer down and clapped him on the shoulder. "The right one won't. Kelsey is my one, Ev. And
I'm going to make sure she knows that. You'll know
when you find the one too."

Her face was illuminated by the soft rooftop lights,
and she was talking and laughing with a group of the
Mustangs' partners. The party was winding down, the
pulsing beat of music replaced by a softer, more intimate vibe. Her eyes met mine, holding them in a
moment that charged the whole night with electricity.

If ever I was going to make my move, let her know how I actually felt about her, it was tonight. I'd never lied to her, but I hadn't told her the truth either. I'd instructed my agent to continue to stall about that stupid fake relationship thing so I had the time to woo her. It was time to find out if my plan had worked.

I crossed the rooftop, the sea of people parting for me. Not like they had much of a choice. It was either move or be mowed down by someone twice their size. Because I was on a mission. I gave a small jerk of my chin, asking her if she wanted to get out of here. With me.

She gave me a nod, and I swear there was a twinkle in her eye that promised something more once we were alone.

We made our way through the rest of the crowd and met in the middle. Her hand slipped into mine, sending a current of heat straight through me. Her touch was light, but the way she held onto me was another whisper in that promise of more.

We waited at the back entrance for the car, and I was ready to crawl the walls. How did one go about telling the girl he loved that he wanted to spend the rest of his life with her? Maybe that was a little too dramatic. Better to just start with what I could give her in the here and now.

I was either about to completely fuck this all up irrevocably and blow this whole relationship up or take it to the next level. I was almost sure she wanted this thing between us to be more, but I could be kidding myself.

But if I was wrong, I'd rather know now. "I have next week off. It's our bye week."

She looked up at me, surprise flickering in her eyes. "That means no game? A week off?"

"Yep, and I want to spend it with you." I held my breath as I said it, laying bare the truth of what I wanted, what I needed.

For a moment, she was silent, and I could almost hear the rapid beat of her heart.

"I'd like that," she said softly, and it was all the confirmation I needed. "But I have to get back to Aspen tonight. The jet's waiting for me at the airport, and then I have three shows back to back for the festival. Plus a small gig at Saddle Creek that, umm, I had to reschedule so I could come tonight."

She'd rearranged a show. That revelation sent a rush of warmth through me. "You did that... for me?"

I knew what a big deal that was. Her career came first. She worked hard to get where she was and wouldn't have changed her schedule just for the sake of showing off our relationship for the media. Her fans meant everything to her.

Her eyes flickered with vulnerability, and I was going to make sure she knew she could trust in me one hundred thousand percent.

"I did," she admitted, a faint blush coloring her cheeks. "I wanted to see you play."

There was something more she didn't say, and I'd give her time if that's what she needed. I reached out, tucking that strand of hair that was always falling in her eyes. Her skin was soft under my touch, and I could feel the heat radiating from her.

"Then let me make it up to you," I said, my voice low and sincere. "Let me be there for you during your shows. I'll be your number one fan, cheering you on from the sidelines."

Her smile grew, lighting up her face. "You'd do that? Be my groupie?"

"Kelsey Best's personal groupie?" I chuckled, the idea both amusing and incredibly appealing. "I can't think of a better way to spend my week. Let's do it."

"Like, right now? You don't want to meet me up there? Don't you need to pack or something? Trust me, Aspen does not have any place to buy clothes if you're not buying ski bunny straight sizes."

So I wasn't the only one who'd been there, done that, and not gotten the t-shirt. Regular stores didn't make clothes in my size and hadn't since I was in high school. I couldn't even imagine the wardrobe Kelsey must have to tote around the country.

I sent a quick text to Hayes, making him my designated errand boy. He was my little brother after all, and wasn't that what they were for?

> Hey, do me a solid and grab my go bag and bring it over to Rocky Mountain FBO.

You fleeing the country after all the media mess?

> Headed back up to Aspen with Kels.

Ooh. Fancy. I'll be there.

Get me tickets to the festival?

Pretty please? With whipped cream and a cherry on top?

I'll do your chores for a week.

I'll do your taxes.

He was a math genius. He'd probably save me like a gazillion dollars.

> I'll see what I can do.

Less than an hour later, we were in the air along with Penelope and Pooh. The cute AF little dog took one look at me, about wagged her tail off sniffing my shoes, and then decided my lap was the best place on the plane to sit.

I'd rather have Kelsey on my lap, but I'd take the little love noodle since PDA probably wasn't going to happen on a flight less than an hour and in front of her assistant. That wasn't my kink.

Kelsey was my kink.

But I had to figure out how to show her that without scaring her away like I had with that kiss.

The jet's engines hummed softly as we landed in Aspen, and Penelope, ever the attentive and hard-working assistant, was already on her iPad and phone, coordinating our arrival. But she didn't look like she was happy with her results.

"So, it turns out every hotel room, AirBnB, VRBO, and any other accommodation I can book online is completely sold out. Even the camp sites can't accommodate anyone else."

"Thanks for trying, Penelope, but my family has a little cabin over in Bear Claw. I can stay there."

Kelsey put her hand on my arm and the zing I got from her touch was not from static electricity. "I think it would look good if you stayed with me."

Holy shit. Was she inviting me to her room? Maybe I'd misjudged how she felt about that kiss. My brain cells all went straight to my dick, and I leaned in close and brushed my lips over her ear. "I think I can do better than make it look good, sweetheart."

Kelsey shot me a mischievous glance. "You'll get the luxury of my couch tonight. But don't worry, it's designer."

Fuck a duck. I'd been right to trust my gut. But okay, I could play along. Being that close would still give me a chance to romance her. "Ooh, designer? Well, in that case, I'm honored."

Her security picked us up in a big SUV and took us back to her hotel. Even this late at night, there was a crowd around the entrance. The hotel had the entry cordoned off so people couldn't get too close, but that didn't stop them from taking pictures and shouting questions at us.

I wrapped my arm around her to shield her from most of the cameras and prying eyes, and it felt like neither of us even breathed until we were well inside. I got that the attention was unavoidable, but I didn't have to like it. Where Kelsey hadn't seemed bothered by it at the party, she leaned into me now.

Once we were in the elevator, she relaxed again. "Someday I'd love to go somewhere that a thousand people weren't always trying to take my picture."

Fuck if I wasn't immediately trying to think of ways to make that happen for her. It probably wasn't going to happen this weekend, but I would find a way to give her that tiny bit of peace that she craved.

"It's not that I don't love my fans. I do." Her shoulders slumped just a little, and she seemed more tired today. "It's hard to be on all the time."

"I get it, babe. Why do you think I ignore the cameras most of the time? They don't need every piece of me. And I promise your fans would live if you kept just a tiny bit of yourself for your own too."

Penelope looked up at me wide-eyed like I'd just declared the zombie apocalypse was about to start and she wasn't up to date on her katana skills. "Kels? I... I didn't know you felt like that."

"It's okay, Pen, I don't most of the time. I promise, it's all fine, and I'll be all smiles again by tomorrow morning."

Hmm. I recognized someone trying to people please when I saw it. "You're allowed downtime, Kelsey."

"Ha." That not-a-laugh slipped out and she covered her mouth with both hands as if she could force it back in. "You're hilarious. Have you met me?"

As we entered Kelsey's lavish suite, Pooh bolted ahead, claiming the couch with a triumphant leap. Kelsey chuckled. "Looks like Pooh's got dibs on the best spot."

"I guess I'll have to negotiate with her then," I replied, eyeing the couch. It wouldn't even be comfortable for someone half my size. And I'd happily stay there all night. Because it made her comfortable and that was my number one priority right now. That was the first step to getting her to trust that my interest in her was more than for show.

Penelope clicked on her tablet again and gave a quick rundown of tomorrow's schedule, her professionalism unfazed for even a moment. But listening to Kelsey's schedule had me exhausted and all I had to do was watch her do it.

"Alright, I'll leave you two to... settle in. Kelsey, I'll knock when it's time for your early rehearsal tomorrow." She gave me the tiniest of eyebrow lifts and some eyeball pointing to Kelsey. I swear she was encouraging me to make a move.

"Thanks, Pen," Kelsey said as Penelope slipped out, leaving us in the privacy of the suite. Just us. And Wiener the Pooh.

"I really am glad you're here, Declan. Even if it's just the couch for now." Her voice was soft, a subtle mix of teasing and sincerity.

I sat down, testing the couch's limits, and patted the cushion next to me. I'd intended that to bring Kelsey to me, but Pooh and her tail went ballistic as she jumped into the spot and spun in circles. I gave her little ears a rub and then patted her butt, letting her know she was welcome, but also to get her to sit and calm down.

Kelsey came over and sat next to me, testing the couch out with a little bounce and a frown. "I know this isn't extremely comfortable. It's for... well, someone a bit smaller than you. I'll bequeath you at least ten of the four hundred-ish pillows on the bed."

"I think I'll probably need to strategically place them on the floor for when I inevitably fall off."

I leaned back, stretching my arms along the back of the couch, and wrapped one arm around Kelsey's shoulder, feeling a bit like a teenager making a reach during a movie. "I wouldn't be anywhere else. But just so you know, I'm holding out for an upgrade to a real bed someday."

Kelsey laughed, the sound light and genuine. "I've got a guard dog to protect me."

She patted her dog on the head and gave her a little scratch behind the ears. Pooh looked at me, to her, and back to me again, and then curled up, pushing Kelsey further away from me with her little butt. When Kels tried to pick Pooh up, the dog growled at her and scurried into my lap.

"Oh. Gretchen Wiener the Pooh, don't you be a mean girl and try to steal my man." Kelsey wagged her finger at her dog who just gave a little whimper and then licked my arm.

Kelsey huffed out a quick laugh. "I think she just said, 'I licked it so it's mine' to me."

"Is that how it works?" I leaned over and ran my tongue along Kelsey's bottom lip. Her eyes fluttered shut and she sucked in a soft gasp. I mentally crossed my fingers that I hadn't just fucked up again.

With her eyes still closed, she whispered, "Yeah, that's how it works."

Kelsey's eyes slid open, and her gaze met mine, a hint of something deeper flickering there. The moment lingered, the beat of our hearts the only sound in the silence.

"And that's my cue to go to bed." She stood up to head to her bedroom, gathering Pooh, who gave a disconcerted sigh and made sad puppy dog eyes at me, into her arms. Kelsey paused at the door, looking back at me. "Goodnight, Declan. And thanks... for being here."

"Goodnight, Kelsey," I replied, watching her disappear into the bedroom. I wanted so fucking badly to follow her in there, spread her out on the bed, and feast on the passion I saw in her. But if I played the game exactly right, she'd want me there as much as I wanted to be.

*H*ey Besties,
Whoever is out there saying this budding relationship between our girl Kelsey and Mr. Hottie Football player a.k.a Declan Kingman is a publicity stunt... I have just one word for you.

DeLULU.

There's no way. Did you SEE how he looked up at that box during the game? Did you see how he had his arm around her, trying to protect her from people taking pics of them I might add, at the rooftop party at Manniway's?

(side note: Who ever heard of a steakhouse with a whole-ass vegan menu? My intel says Marie Manniway, classy AF wife of former quarterback Johnston Manniway. Their stuffed mushrooms were to die for BTW. If you're ever in Denver and want a fancy meal but don't eat cutie patootie cows, you gotta go to Manniway's.)

AND...

Guess who's been spotted in ASPEN???

Yeah. You guessed it. A certain football player we all now have a crush on.

AND... AND

He's staying at the same hotel as Kelsey and crew. I cannot confirm nor deny that they're sharing a room, but I will say that I happen to know that there are NO rooms for sale or rent in the entire area right now. The music festival has the entire freaking mountain sold out. There aren't even campsites!

AND... AND... AND

IF none of that is proof enough that the big bad football player is truly in love with America's sweetheart and that she loves him back, just check out this (possibly sketchily obtained) really long lens photo of him taking Wiener the Pooh for a walk this morning AND scooping poop!

SCOOP

-ING

POOH'S

POOPS.

Nobody does that if they don't love said dog's owner a lot (or are a professional dog walker).

We know Kelsey would NEVER let anyone she didn't a THOUSAND percent trust and love with Pooh.

THIS RELATIONSHIP IS LEGIT.
I REST MY CASE, your honors.
Your BFF,
Mz. Besties' Bestie

[pic of Declan bent over pooper scooping, Wiener the Pooh trying to lick his face]

DEDICATED TO THE ONE I LOVE

KELSEY

The stage lights blazed above me, transforming the music festival into a whirlwind of colors and sounds. I was backstage, my heart thumping in rhythm with the bass, a heady mix of excitement and nerves churning within me. The sea of faces I could see from the side of the stage mirrored my anticipation, awaiting my arrival on stage.

With the intro of my first song playing, adrenaline surged through me, and I bounced from foot to foot, raring to go. This was the feeling I lived for, the energy I sought out that I could only find on stage. It hadn't failed me yet. The crowd's cheers erupted into the crisp, fall afternoon air as I took the stage. The familiar rush of performing engulfed me, a tidal wave of pure euphoria. My voice soared over the adoring fans as I belted out the opening lines of my very first hit song, still a fan favorite after all these years.

Halfway through the first set, at the transition, my gaze swept across the audience, looking for Declan. I found him, and he wasn't alone. There were Kingmans everywhere. I thought I'd met them all, but there was no mistaking at least three fresh faces that were definitely all related. How many siblings did he have? Maybe they were cousins?

I was an only child, and my parents, shy of the limelight, rarely attended my shows, though they were incredibly supportive. My dad managed my money for me, but they loved their life minding their shop, going to fish-fry Fridays. The Kingmans represented a different kind of family, something I didn't know I longed for – a lively, loving family.

During the instrumental intro to the next song, I leaned closer to the microphone. "This next song goes out to some amazing people in the audience this afternoon. To the Kingman family, who've shown me the warmth of being part of something bigger, something beautiful."

The crowd's roar of approval acknowledged either the personal nature of my dedication or the fact that most of my fans were female, and the Kingman men were fine AF.

I put my all into the show, and my final set ended on a power song. I'd put everything into this performance, and while the adrenaline had kept me going, it had barely been enough to get me through. I could already feel that ever-present, after-show exhaustion ready to hit me hard.

I really needed to prioritize getting better sleep. Maybe then I wouldn't be so tired. I was really starting to struggle to get through the days. I just didn't have the same energy I did when I was sixteen, eighteen, or even twenty-two. I felt like a freaking old lady at twenty-six.

But that was the life I'd chosen. Nobody said this go-go-go life was easy. A lot of musicians turned to drugs to keep them going. Jake had even suggested I get a 'prescription' or two and that he could hook me up. That was the beginning of the end for us.

There was no time for a real break, just some dinner, a shower, and a costume change before my second show tonight. Another performance awaited me at the Saddle Creek Bar, and I could feel the fatigue gnawing at me.

I gave lots of waves to the audience and even blew some kisses toward the Kingmans, but in my dressing room, I collapsed into a chair at the makeup vanity. The stage makeup did little to mask the tiredness in my eyes, and I couldn't have that. There was absolutely no time to be tired.

Penelope would be here any minute and she didn't need to see me like this.

My phone buzzed on the vanity and seeing a

message from Declan pop up helped more than anything else.

> Incredible performance. My brothers are freaking that you dedicated a song to us. Pooh and I can't wait for the next one.

Declan's constant support basically since the day we'd met was a boon that I was getting addicted to. Part of me yearned to fall into his arms, to reveal all the vulnerabilities behind my superstar facade. I couldn't. That would be exposing too much, too close to getting emotionally entangled.

I forced myself to smile even though no one could see it but me. Then I replied with more cheer than I felt.

> Thanks. See you soon.

Okay, so that wasn't exactly cheery. Close as I could get right now. Hopefully he didn't notice.

I needed to pull myself together before anyone saw me like this. I stood up, ready to change out of my costume and wash my face. A wave of dizziness hit me. Shit. That wasn't good. I was probably just dehydrated. I steadied myself, inhaling deeply, and promised myself a power nap. "Just one more show. You've got this."

I was splashing water on my face when a soft knock on the door warned me that it was a different kind of showtime. I called out, hoping my voice didn't betray my exhaustion. "Come in."

Penelope walked in, Declan and Pooh trailing behind her. The sight of them was like a balm, but it also reminded me how much I had to keep up appearances.

"You were phenomenal, Kelsey," Penelope said, her eyes scanning my face with concern. "But you look a bit... off."

I dabbed my face dry with a towel, forcing a smile. "Just the usual post-show adrenaline crash. I'll be fine."

Declan stepped forward, Pooh wagging her tail beside him. "You sure? You look like you could use some rest."

I hated that they could both see through me, but I wasn't about to admit it. "I'm good, really. Just need to eat something. Maybe a power nap before the next gig."

Penelope eyed me, not quite convinced. "I can postpone the Saddle Creek show again if you're not up to it."

"No, no, absolutely not." No way I was letting those fans wait on me a second time, not to mention, I did not have the mental energy to deal with the fallout from the record label or the haranguing I'd get from Skeeter. "The show must go on, right? I've never let a little tiredness stop me before."

Declan came closer, his gaze soft but filled with a silent question. Pooh, sensing the mood, sat down at my feet, her head tilted as if she, too, was worried.

"I appreciate the concern, guys, but I've got this." I moved to the vanity, grabbing a wipe to finish removing the stage makeup. "I can't disappoint all those fans waiting at Saddle Creek. Or your whole-ass family. How many Kingmans are here? Every single one in the whole wide world?"

Declan chuckled, but his eyes remained on me, full of unspoken care. He accepted my change of topic, but I hadn't fooled him. "Sometimes I lose track of how many brothers I have. But they're all here. Hayes took my request to bring me clothes as an invitation to come up to Aspen. And once Princess Kingman found out, that meant everyone else knew. It's not like any of us can say no to her."

A giggle popped out, and it felt good. "No, I don't suppose you can. It was fun to see people in the audience I know in real life. So, I guess, thanks for bringing them along to the show."

Penelope clapped her hands together. "Okay, let's get going if we're feeding you and sneaking in that power nap."

Declan picked up Pooh and used her to point at Penelope. "She's definitely getting that nap, even if we have to guard her door."

Back at the hotel, I went straight to focusing on my songwriting notebook. Tonight's acoustic show was supposed to be my new stuff and I didn't have any new stuff. Declan watched me from across the room, a knowing smile on his lips.

"You should take that nap, Kels." His voice was gentle yet firm, and it did something funny to my lower belly. Something flippity-floppy.

I shook my head, stubbornly clinging to my notebook. "We're waiting for food, and I need every spare minute to work on this song. I want to try it out tonight."

Declan walked over and gently but decisively closed the notebook. "The song can wait. You need to rest, even if it's just for a few minutes. The food will be here when you wake up."

"I don't need a babysitter." I knew full well he was just being nice, trying to take care of me. And that's what made me snap at him. Because I was scared I was going to fall for him.

Nobody took care of me but me. Well, and people I paid to take care of me. Declan was neither of those things. He cared because he was... good. Yeah, not because he was in love with me. Nope.

He didn't even flinch at my petulance. Probably from years of actual babysitting a little sister. In fact, he chuckled like he was about to enjoy what was going to happen.

"Think of me as your personal relaxation coach." He crossed to me in three steps and wrapped his hands around my waist. Then he picked me up.

He.

Picked.

Me.

Up.

I gasped and squealed and threw my arms around his neck. "What are you doing? Put me down. You can't just carry me around."

The last time I'd been picked up by anyone, I was probably five or six. I was taller than my dad by the time I was twelve, so it wasn't like I was the kind of girl anyone just randomly picked up and threw around. I'd been way too big for anyone to do that in a very long time.

"Sweetheart, I'm making it my job to carry you around." To prove his point, he took me from a princess carry to throwing me over his shoulder like a rag doll. And then he slapped me on the ass. "I was built for carrying you to bed."

Eep. To bed?

"Fine, fine. Carry me to the couch and I promise to, like, meditate for a few minutes or something." I could definitely do some deep breathing just to let my lungs catch up to my heart beating out of my chest.

He settled me onto the couch, his presence enveloping me in a cocoon of safety and warmth.

I tried to muster a glare, but it melted away under his attentive gaze. I conceded, my body already sinking into the cushions.

Declan pulled me gently against him, and I had to admit, my head did fit very nicely in that spot on his chest just under his shoulder. "I'm not stopping you from working if you want to, so tell me about this song."

I nestled against him, the comfort of his embrace lulling me. Friends could snuggle, right? "It's about finding something real in a world of make-believe. About recognizing what's genuine in a sea of facades."

His hand stroked my hair, a tender gesture that undid the last of my defenses. "Mmm. I think we both know something about that."

My thoughts floated around the idea of the song, of Declan, of us. His heartbeat was a steady rhythm beneath my ear, a promise of something steadfast and true.

In that moment, nestled in Declan's arms, the world faded away, and I surrendered to the quiet embrace of sleep, safe and content in a way I hadn't felt in a long time.

When I woke up, it felt like a thousand years later, but by the smell of the food that had been delivered, it was probably only a few minutes. The song I'd been working on was still ringing around in my head, and the whole melody was there just waiting for me to pluck it down.

"Did you know you hum when you sleep?" His voice was soft and like that warm blanket you don't want to crawl out from under.

"I do? I mean, I did when I was a kid. But I didn't know I still did." No one who'd been in my bed in the past few years had mentioned it.

"It's cute." He shifted a little so that we could look at each other but didn't actually make me get up. I didn't want to. "Do you remember the song you were dreaming about?"

"I do." Oh. Ohh. I had a song. Like the whole damn song. I'd been grabbing at scraps of tunes, and fragments of lyrics for months, and now I had a whole-ass song running through my head as if it was on the radio and I'd heard it a hundred and twenty-seven times in a row. I popped up and scrambled for my notebook. What if I lost it? It was right there now, but it wouldn't be the first time the music had slipped away from me before I could get it on paper. "Would you grab the food? I'm going to write a bit of it out really quick."

After the food, a shower, and a quick change into a new, much more casual outfit than I would normally wear, I was ready for show number two of the day.

Saddle Creek only held a few hundred people, and it was mostly just me and my music to entertain them tonight. I hadn't done a show like this in years. Not since that first year on the road after I'd won *The Choicest Voice*.

That year had been brutal. I wasn't always sure I'd make it in this business back then. But I hadn't quit. I sure wasn't going to now, even if this tour didn't have that same spark as before.

As I stepped onto the stage, the warmth of the old wooden and warn platform felt like a physical touch. The crowd was buzzing with a vastly different energy, a mix of mostly locals and a few lucky festival goers, all eager for a more personal performance.

I'd give them all that I had.

I spotted Declan right away, seated at a front table with, of all the Kingmans he could have invited, his dad. Declan's eyes locked with mine, and for just that brief moment, it felt like we were the only two people in the room.

But once the lights went up, the faces faded away, and there was just me and my guitar. And the music.

I opened with a slower, more sensual song, one that allowed me to pour all the emotion I was feeling into the lyrics. It was something I'd written years ago, but that hadn't ever made it onto an album. I'd considered it kind of locked away in a vault of songs that would never get to be heard. But it was good, and with each verse, I remembered why I'd written it in the first place.

It was about those giddy feelings when you've got a crush and realize you're falling in love with someone for the first time.

The audience loved it, and that gave me the push to throw myself into the performance, feeding off their energy. I launched into the new song that had come to me today, and even though I'd never performed it even once before this, it poured out of me like sugar and starlight. At the bridge, a wave of dizziness hit me, and I closed my eyes, singing through it, letting the music carry me.

The song was good. It was going to be a hit, I could feel it in my bones.

I didn't open my eyes again until the last long note faded. Why wasn't the audience clapping? Or, wait, were they? I couldn't hear over the whoosh, whoosh, whooshing in my ears. I reached for the earbud but lost my balance on the little stool I was propped on.

The guitar fell, and I should have been able to hear the awful crunch of the wood on wood and the discordant notes of the strings reverberating, but I couldn't. My senses were failing me. I tried to push through, I swear I did. I needed to finish the set, but my body had other ideas.

In the haze, I saw Declan rising from his seat, his eyes the only thing I could see at the end of the tunnel, and they were... pissed. He was saying something, moving toward the stage, but his voice sounded so far away.

FIRST AND DOWN

DECLAN

J'd spent plenty of time in bars, but Saddle Creek was something else. This wasn't a bar, it was the facade of one but for rich, entitled pricks. If it meant I got to watch Kelsey sing the song she'd been humming against my chest and see it bloom into something so fucking deep and meaningful that I wanted to goddamned cry, well then, I was going to be a rich, entitled prick. Who got to sit in the front row.

She was a vision, her voice captivating the audience with every note. But while she had us all dazzled, something wasn't right. It was that same something I'd seen in her after her performance earlier today.

Kelsey was on the verge of burnout, and it pissed me off that she had to do these two shows back to back. I understood hustle. But her manager should be fired for letting her work herself to the bone like this. Who the fuck took care of Kelsey when she wouldn't take care of herself?

Her sweet, young assistant, Penelope, tried. I could see how much she cared, but she was also obligated to do what Kelsey, and probably her record label and manager, told her to do. After this show, I was going to conspire with Penelope to get Kelsey some time off, or at least some fucking sleep.

As her song continued, I noticed her gripping the microphone stand more for support than performance. Then she closed her eyes. To anyone else, I imagined they thought she was just really getting into the music. But my spidey senses were screaming that something was wrong.

"Son." My dad grabbed my shoulder. "I know that look. She's going down. Get up there. I'll call nine-one-one."

My muscles reacted faster than my brain. Her voice faltered, a note cut short. She swayed, her hand reaching out to grasp something for balance. I lunged forward, shouldering past club staff and security with the best of my defensive line skills. Time went into slo-mo, but my focus was pinpoint on my way to her.

I reached Kelsey just as she collapsed, catching her before she hit the ground. The world around us faded into a blur. All that mattered was her in my arms. I gently laid her down on the stage, my hands shaking but efficient as I checked her pulse and breathing.

Her pulse was there, steady but faint. Her breathing was shallow. I should be relieved she was alive, but I wanted to murder someone for letting this happen to her in the first place. Her record label, agent, manager, assistant, me, and even her were my current hit list. But that needed to wait. Once I knew she was going to be okay, I was protecting her the way I should have already. To get her out of here, to somewhere quiet and safe where she could rest, recover.

With careful urgency, I scooped Kelsey into my arms, her head resting against my chest. I could feel the heat of her skin through her stage clothes, a stark reminder of her vulnerability.

"Make way," I barked, my voice cutting through the stunned silence of the crowd. The sea of people parted, their faces a mixture of shock and concern.

Every step was fueled by a fierce protectiveness. I was not just carrying a superstar off stage. I was carrying the woman who had unknowingly claimed my heart, the one I'd do anything to keep safe.

The paramedics must have been close by because they were coming in the back door and met me back-stage. I gently laid her down on their stretcher, brushing her hair from her face. Her breathing seemed to have steadied, but she was still out cold.

Penelope dashed toward us, clearly freaked the fuck

out. I knew exactly how she felt. "Kelsey? Oh my god, oh my god."

"Did she hit her head?" one of the EMTs asked.

I wanted nothing more than to keep holding her against me, to feel her breath on my neck so I knew she was alive. But I stepped back so the medics could do their jobs. "No. I caught her before she hit the ground."

"Drugs?"

Penelope pointed her phone like a weapon. "No. Kelsey isn't that kind of rock star. She does not do drugs."

The paramedic didn't even look at her and kept on with his tasks like a pro. "We're not here to accuse or arrest anyone, lady, we're just trying to help her."

"Is she going to be okay?"

"The doctors will know more once we get her to the hospital." The EMT looked at those of us surrounding her. "But her pulse is steady and she's breathing fine."

Now I was the one who was ready to pass out. She was going to be okay. Fuck, I hoped there wasn't something seriously wrong with her.

"Who's coming with us in the ambulance?"

Penelope looked right at me. "Go, Declan. I'll be right behind you with her security detail."

I nodded and followed the EMTs out to their bus. There was barely room for me in the back, but I squished myself in and tried my best to keep out of their way. Luckily Aspen isn't a big community, and we were at the hospital before I even had time to worry that she still hadn't woken up yet.

One of the EMTs put her hand on my arm. "Don't worry, kid. AVH is a level-three trauma center, and Flight for Life is just a dispatch away."

None of what she'd just said actually made me feel any better.

They whizzed her into the emergency entrance and all I could do was trot behind them, listening for any scrap of info to know that she was okay. "Twenty-six-year-old female. Lost consciousness. No head injury, no indication of drug use. BP one-twenty over eighty, heart rate seventy-two, pulse ox ninety-five."

The doctor took one look at Kelsey, blinked a few times like she recognized who she was about to help, and then got that I'm-in-charge-now look. "Take her to exam one. Let's get some fluids pushed and see if we can wake up sleeping beauty."

Then the ER staff whisked her away, and I was left standing in reception, staring at the wide-eyed receptionist. "Was that Kelsey Best?"

I nodded and put my finger up to my lips. "Yes, and let's keep that between you and me and the doctor for the moment. I'm sure Kelsey would appreciate that."

"Oh, yes. Of course. We treat all kinds of celebrities here so, uh, I'm totally used to it." She glanced back toward the double doors they'd rolled the love of my life through.

"Can you fill out her paperwork, Mr. Kingman?"

The receptionist held out a clipboard to me. I hadn't told her my name. So either she was a Mustangs fan, or a Bestie. I'd bet on the latter.

"I've got this." Penelope stepped up beside me and took the clipboard from the woman. "Do we have news on her condition yet? I'm trying really hard not to freak out."

I shook my head. "Not yet."

My thoughts whirled between worrying that there was something seriously wrong, like a tumor or worse, and being sure she'd just worked herself to exhaustion. The chaos this would cause in the media was the last thing she needed either way. Whatever I did next, it would have to be as secret as possible, to protect Kelsey. Not just her health, but her privacy and peace of mind as well.

The doctors were still assessing Kelsey when my dad, my sister, every single one of my brothers, and Trixie came into the waiting room and surrounded me and Penelope. Trixie had a big bag on her shoulder, and Pooh popped her head up out of it, looking as forlorn as I felt.

Chris shook my hand and then pulled me in for a hug. "We've got you, brother."

"Declan, how is she?" my dad asked, glancing around the waiting room with suspicious eyes. "Do we need to set up a wall of Kingmans to keep the press out?"

He did love to scare the media away, and I was grateful for it.

"Not yet. When they took her back, her vitals all sounded more like she was taking a nap than hurt or sick, so..." I replied, my voice tight.

My dad placed a reassuring hand on my back. "Son, you need to get her away from all this. I recognize someone whose been pushing themselves too hard. If she were one of my players, I'd have already benched her."

"I know. But I can't tell her what to do." No matter how much I wanted to right now.

"No, you can't. Because you're a good man, and you were raised right." He gave a nod of his head toward the doors to the ER. "But you're not the only one who knows she needs quiet and to recover from this somewhere out of the spotlight."

I nodded, my mind racing for what I could do. "Assuming they release her, I don't want her to walk into a whole mess of media. What if I took her to the cabin?"

Dad shook his head. "It's overflowing with Kingmans. We can skedaddle, but that is the first place the press are going to look for you two, and without the rest of us there to keep nosy media and fans at bay, it won't be restful or private."

My old man was right. Since our relationship was public, they'd definitely find us there. That was low-hanging fruit. "What about Mom's old place? The little cabin near the lake?"

His eyebrows rose, considering it. "Nobody's been up there in years, and it's nothing fancy, Declan. Nothing like what Kelsey's probably used to."

Maybe she needed that. "Dad, right now, fancy is the least of our worries. She's going to need rest, and that place is perfect. Secluded, quiet, and away from prying eyes."

He nodded slowly. "It's a good spot. Peaceful. Not to mention... only one," he glanced around at the rest of the family, eyes stopping briefly on Jules and then Penelope. "Never mind, you'll figure it out."

Penelope, who'd been filling out the mountain of papers, had also clearly been paying attention to our conversation. She looked between us, her expression a mix of gratitude and the same determination to help Kelsey and keep her safe that I felt. "Is it safe? Is there food, a place for her to sleep, play her guitar, take Pooh for a walk? That's all she needs. She might be a gazillionaire music star, but she's really just a normal person like the rest of us. Aside from her enormous talent and the jet."

"It's safe and it's got the basics," I assured her. "I'll make sure she's comfortable. And I'll stay with her, look after her."

Skeeter, Kelsey's agent, burst into the waiting area, her face a mask of concern that didn't quite reach her eyes. She scootched her way into the circle and grabbed Penelope's arm. "Pen, oh my god, is she okay?"

Her gaze quickly searched the space as if she'd see Kelsey just saunter out. "Can she continue? We can't afford to cancel the rest of her shows. The record company is already on my back for rescheduling this one. Can they wake her up, give her some stimulants or something to get her back on her feet?"

I felt my jaw clench at her words. It was clear where her priorities lay, and it wasn't with Kelsey's well-being.

"No, they cannot. And you should be fired for even suggesting it." My patience snapped. I would never hit someone, but my fists were curled and ready. "Kelsey needs rest, not more pressure. If you or the record label can't see that, then—"

My threat was cut short as Kelsey's doctor came over. "Mr. Kingman? Oh, umm okay, lots of Kingmans, I see. Declan Kingman, you brought her in. Does she have any immediate family?"

Uh-oh. Didn't they ask for immediate family when something was really wrong? Penelope interjected before I could say anything more. "No. She's only got her parents, and they're in California. Do I need to call them?"

"No. Ms. Best is doing fine. She's awake, and we're moving her to a room for some more tests and observation. But it's past visiting hours so only immediate family members are allowed in to see her."

She was awake.

She was fine.

I was going to kill her.

"I'm her fiancé."

My family all froze, trying really hard not to react to my lie. Probably the first one I'd ever told in front of all of them. They all knew it and all they all understood.

"Then come this way please." She led me through the hallway toward the hospital room. "We'd like to keep her overnight for observation, but she's stable, and by all accounts healthy, save for some mild dehydration. We'll have some more results from blood tests, but my diagnosis right now is that she's overworked and exhausted. See if you can get her to take some time off, Mr. Kingman."

That's exactly what I was going to do. She left me standing in the doorway to Kelsey's room. I stood there for a full minute, clenching, and unclenching my fists. I'd watched my family almost fall apart when my mother died. She was my dad's entire world, and I honestly don't know how he carried on without her. For us kids, I guess.

I couldn't imagine how my life would be destroyed if I lost Kelsey. And she didn't even know how I really felt about her. I'd been afraid she'd get scared off if I let her see how deep my feelings already were for her. The logical side of my brain told me it was insane to fall in love with someone so fast. But I had.

And I'd be damned if I let her kill herself working. I wanted to spend the rest of my life with her, and I wanted that life to last a long, long time.

I quietly crossed the room and pulled the visitor's chair next to her bed. It was hardly big enough for my ass, but I would sit there as long as she needed me to.

I took her hand in mine and pressed my forehead to her knuckles. "I'm here, babe."

She stirred and her eyelids fluttered open. "Declan."

I stared deep into her eyes and kissed those knuckles I'd been praying over. "Jesus, Mary, and Joseph, you scared the shit out of me, Kels."

"I scared me quite a bit too." She swallowed hard and then clasped her other hand over mine. This one was connected to the IV pushing her fluids, and she stared at it like it was an alien growing out of her skin. "I've never been in the hospital before."

"As far as hospitals go, this one is nice." What an inane thing to come out of my mouth. I needed to tell her I had real feelings for her, that none of this was fake, no showmance. The words got stuck in my throat. Stuck behind a week's worth of lying to her.

"I don't like it. Can we leave now?" She sounded so small and scared. I'd never seen her like this before, and I wanted to wrap her up in my arms and tell her I would take care of everything.

"The doctor wants you to stay overnight for observation."

She frowned at that, and she blinked like she was

trying to hold back tears. I couldn't handle tears, not from her. I'd carry her out of here myself if she cried.

"Will you stay with me? I know you don't have to be here, this is your vacation and all, but—"

"I do have to be here. I have to be here with you." I wouldn't be anywhere else.

"Okay." She still looked so scared, fragile even.

Fuck it. I stood, picked her up, and then sat back down on the hospital bed with her in my arms. The metal creaked beneath us and I was sure I'd be paying later to replace this contraption, but it would be worth every penny to hold her in my arms.

I laid back and settled Kelsey between my legs and against my chest and stroked her hair. She didn't say a word, but after a few minutes, her muscles relaxed and her breathing turned heavy. She fell asleep in my arms, and it was exactly where we both needed to be.

"I've got you, Kelsey baby. I've got you."

ASPEN DAILY NEWS: KELSEY BEST HOSPITALIZED AFTER ONSTAGE COLLAPSE

By Emily Johnson, Entertainment Reporter

In a shocking turn of events at the much-anticipated Aspen Music Festival, superstar singer Kelsey Best was hospitalized last night after collapsing onstage during her performance at the Saddle Creek Bar. The incident, which left fans and fellow musicians concerned, occurred shortly after the beginning of her set. This was Best's second performance of the day, having headlined the Friday opening lineup.

Witnesses report that Best appeared increasingly fatigued during both performances, eventually leading to her collapse. In a heroic effort, Denver Mustangs' star defensive end, Declan Kingman, who was present at the event, quickly intervened. Kingman, who has been recently rumored to be in a relationship with the singer, rushed to her aid, carrying her offstage to safety.

Best was taken to Aspen Valley Hospital, where she is currently under observation. However, fans are warned that she will not be taking visitors. Hospital staff have reported that she is stable and recovering. The cause of the incident is believed to be exhaustion and dehydration, highlighting the intense pressures faced by artists in the entertainment industry.

Kelsey Best's team has yet to release an official statement regarding the incident or her current health status. However, it is understood that her upcoming performances at the festival will be canceled.

In an unexpected twist, it has been confirmed by sources close to Best that Kingman identified himself as Best's fiancé. This revelation will likely spark a frenzy among fans and media alike, as the nature of their relationship has been a topic of much speculation in recent weeks.

Declan Kingman remained at the hospital with Best, further fueling rumors about their relationship's seriousness. Fans have taken to social media to express their concern and support for the singer, with hashtags like #GetWellSoonKelsey and #KelsandKing trending.

This incident raises important questions about the

grueling schedules and demands placed on performers, calling for a re-evaluation of how the industry cares for its artists' health and well-being versus profits.

ASPEN DAILY NEWS reached out to Kelsey Best's management for further comments and wishes her a speedy recovery.

BESTIE4EVER: Sending all my love and prayers to Kelsey! Get well soon, our queen! #GetWellSoonKelsey

MusicLover1998: Shocked to hear about Kelsey collapsing. It's a wakeup call about the pressure these artists are under. Wishing her a speedy recovery.

KingmanFan: Declan Kingman is a real-life hero! Stepping up like that shows his true character. #KelsandKing

TheChadMan52: She should eat more slads and get some exersice

BestiesBestie: re: TheChadMan52: Eat a bag of dicks, Chad. And learned to spell.

SongbirdSoul: Rest up, Kelsey. Your health comes first! Looking forward to hearing your beautiful voice again soon.

SurprisedBestie: Wait, did I read that right? Fiancé??? When did this happen? #KelsandKing

AspenNative: It's always sad to see something like

this happen. Hope she gets the rest she deserves. Much love to Kelsey from Aspen!

HeartStruck: Declan Kingman as Kelsey's fiancé is the plot twist I didn't know I needed! Wishing Kelsey a quick recovery and lots of happiness!

BotGuy1984: Fake news. Wake up Sheeple!

Sheeple: re: BotGuy1984: Why everybody always trying to wake me up? I'm woke already.

RealityCheck: Fiancé or not, let's focus on what's important – Kelsey's health. Celebrity life isn't as glamorous as it seems. Get well soon, Kelsey!

TuneInFan: Just shows how much we don't know about celebrities' private lives. Hoping Kelsey makes a full recovery and takes the time she needs.

KingmanPrincess: WE LOVE YOU, KELSEY

MUSTANG, TAKE ME AWAY

KELSEY

I awoke to the soft beeps of hospital equipment and the murmur of voices. My eyelids felt heavy, my body drained, but a sense of urgency nudged me awake. As my vision cleared, the first thing I noticed was the heat of Declan's body holding mine. He had his arms wrapped around me, but with my own arms crossed underneath his so that he was holding my hands in his.

The absolute feeling of being protected, secure, and taken care of by this man stirred something deep inside of me. I'd been holding him at arm's length this whole time and had missed out on this for far too long. How could I have denied myself this?

Because I was scared to let any of my feelings be real. I'd been running on fear for a while and somehow hadn't noticed. All of these thoughts were quickly overshadowed by the memory of collapsing on stage. It was like a cold splash of reality. Fear and fumes were all that had kept me upright for... well, if I was just admitting it to myself, for this entire tour.

I was so damn tired, and I couldn't ignore it any longer. It wasn't just physical exhaustion either. I didn't want to believe it, but I knew full well that I couldn't write songs like I used to. Except for the one that had popped into my head fully formed yesterday. That had been a miracle. But also an anomaly.

The music used to just be there for me. Like I could reach up into the ether and pluck down the next song. But they weren't there. Little blips of lyrics or a note or two floated around, but I had to work to hear them, and even when I did, they crumbled in the light of day like a wilted, unwatered plant.

I didn't know what to do about it. So I just kept pushing. If I could just push through, I was sure I could get to the other side of this.

But pushing had landed me in the hospital. Pushing had let down all my fans. Pushing through was all I knew how to do, and now I was scared to even try again.

What was I going to do?

Declan's hands gently squeezed mine, and he

nuzzled my neck, rubbing his beard along the sensitive skin in a way that made me want to lean into him even more. He whispered in a hoarse, sleepy voice. "Hey, hey, hey, you're safe, you're okay. I'm here."

I swallowed hard, keeping a sob I didn't expect to pop up down where it belonged. "Okay."

That was all I could manage at the moment.

He squeezed me tighter but sat us up, and for the first time, I realized he'd wedged himself into this tiny hospital bed with me. The bars had to be digging into his legs and sides, and I was definitely squishing him. I should move, let him get up and probably take a full breath without the constraints of me and the metal, but I couldn't quite talk myself into moving from what felt like the only place I could recharge.

"How are you feeling?"

"Umm." I wasn't entirely sure how to answer that. I actually felt more rested than I had in a long time. But mentally? I was shaken. "I'm thirsty."

That was as much as I could commit to in this moment.

Declan's soft chuckle rumbled in his chest, and I felt it all up and down my back. "That, I can fix, sweetheart."

He grabbed me around the hips, and I realized I was wearing one of those flimsy hospital gowns and nothing else. Oh geez. My whole-ass backside was naked and had been pressed against him all night.

Declan moved me off his lap and he slid off the side

of the hospital bed. I watched all his muscles flex as he stretched. God, he was so strong, and I wanted him back in the bed with me, keeping me safe from the outside world for just a little bit longer. I shivered and pulled the flimsy blanket up to my chin.

"The nurse was here to check on you a couple times, and I think she wanted to kick my ass for being in that bed with you. But she left this jug of water for when you woke up." He poured me a cup and handed it over.

I was more grateful to have something to do that wasn't thinking or talking about what happened than I was for the water.

Before we could say more, the door burst open. Skeeter, my manager and agent, stormed in, her face a mask of concern that somehow didn't quite reach her eyes. "Kelsey. Thank god you're awake. Can you perform today? The label is freaking out."

Declan's body tensed, and I saw the anger flicker in his eyes. He stepped between us, ready to confront her, but I touched the back of his arm, stopping him. "She's not doing any more shows, Skeeter. She's exhausted, and she needs rest."

Skeeter's eyes widened, and she took a step back, clearly not used to being challenged. "Declan, I appreciate your concern, but this is between me and Kelsey. The record company—"

"Skeeter, I can't." Knowing I had someone on my side was what would give me the strength to fight this battle that I'd known was coming for a while. I'd been avoiding it, ignoring it, hoping it would go away. It wasn't just a battle against Skeeter or the record label. It was against my own instincts too. But I had to do it now while I had this fresh, new fear motivating me.

Her eyes widened. "But Kelsey, you have to. The festival—"

"No," I cut her off firmly. "Last night scared the shit out of me, Skeeter. I don't want to let down my fans, or the label, or you, or anyone. But I don't have anything left right now."

Declan stayed silent but stood beside me, like my own personal guard dog. No wonder Pooh had fallen for him so hard. I was right there with her, and that scared me almost as much as ending up in the hospital.

Skeeter's face turned a shade of red I don't think I'd ever seen on a human being before. "Do you know how much is at stake? The label—"

"Look. If I go out on that stage today, I'm afraid it will be my last show." I wanted my voice to come out stronger, but there was a waver in it that I hated. For the first time in a long time, I wasn't going to do what I thought would make everyone else happy, or believe in me, or love me. That was really scary too. "Ever. Go tell the label that, Skeeter. I need a fucking minute to myself, or I'm done."

My heart was racing, and we all knew it because the monitor next to me was going crazy. I imagined the nurses or doctors were going to be in here any minute thinking I was having a heart attack.

Skeeter opened her mouth to argue, but a look from Declan silenced her. She huffed and slid in one last warning. "You have a contract for another album, little girl. Don't forget that."

She stormed out, and it was a good thing too, because I think Declan was about to punch her in the face. Not that I think he actually would, but he was not a happy camper right now.

Once she was gone, I turned to Declan. "Thank you, for backing me up. I... I needed to do that myself."

He nodded, understanding. "I know, and I'm so fucking proud of you for telling her off, babe. I just hate seeing you pushed around. She's supposed to work for you, for your best interests, not the label."

"I've trusted her for a long time, but maybe I need to evaluate a lot of things about my career." I lowered my eyes and stared down at the pattern of the blanket, blinking back tears that just seemed to sprout up. "I hate that I feel so overwhelmed with everything and I can't really see through to the other side."

Declan cupped my chin and lifted my face so I had to look at him. He leaned down, kissing my forehead. "I'll always be here for you, Kels."

I'd scared him too. And I knew he wanted to be here for me, but I couldn't have him forever. I barely had him for a week. He had a real life to get back to, and I didn't want to interfere with that. But I was going to take him for the few more days I had him.

I just wished there was a way we could avoid the outside world for just a little while longer. But the press was definitely waiting, and I needed to make some kind of statement to my fans. I already wanted to hide under my blankets.

With Declan.

I closed my eyes, leaning into his touch. Despite the chaos going through my head, in that moment, his touch gave me a sense of peace.

The room was quiet now, save for the occasional beep of the hospital monitor. My feelings, my vulnerabilities, were laid bare to him, and he was still here. He looked down at me, his eyes filled with concern and something else.

"I want to take you away from all of this, Kels. The media, the shows, everything. You need time and space if you're going to... get your groove back." He changed that look of worry to a twinkling smile. "And if you trust me, I've got something already arranged."

Did I trust him? I wasn't sure there was anyone I trusted more. He'd worked his way into my life in a way I never expected and certainly hadn't let anyone else, except maybe Penelope.

"I trust you."

"Good girl." He grabbed his phone and tapped a text message while I mentally fanned myself. I already knew I was a people pleaser, but being called a good girl by a rough and tumble man like Declan did things to a lady.

I didn't get time to consider what that meant, because in two seconds, there was a knock on the door. Damn, our little bubble of solitude was already getting busted into. That didn't last long. I supposed it was a doctor or Pen needing to work on my statement for the press or... three carbon copies of me walking through the door?

I did a double, or rather, a triple take. Two of the impersonators were way too short to be me, but one was almost tall enough. They all had on my dark bob wig I used when I was trying to throw the press off, a Denver Mustangs puffy jacket, dark glasses, handbag with a dachshund sticking their head out the top, and a Kingman in the same Denver Mustangs jacket on their arm.

But only one of those dogs gave a yip and wiggled their butt so hard the whole bag shook. Penelope slid off her shades and gave me a wink. "Your escape plan has arrived."

I stared, slack-jawed, at the other two. They took off their glasses too and turned into Jules Kingman and Trixie. On second glance, the dogs in their bags were— I snort-laughed—stuffed toys. "What in the world is going on?"

Penelope crossed over to me and Pooh just about jumped out of the bag to get to me. I gave her a kiss and a snuggle. "Hello, my sweet stinker poop. I missed you too."

"Are you actually okay, Kelsey? I... I really hope you are. I'm so sorry if I didn't take care of you like I should." She shook her head and pressed her lips together like if she didn't, she might break down.

"Pen, you've been taking care of me all along. I'm the one who needs to do a better job at taking care of myself. I am going to need your help to stave off Skeeter and the label though. She's big mad freaking out." I had a feeling that was going to become a bigger problem that I could handle at the moment. It would have to wait. "Because I'm going to take some time off this week, and I want to find a way to make that up to the fans, especially the ones who came all the way up to Aspen for the music festival. You're my best Bestie and always have a line on how I can make them happy. So you put those talents to work, okay?"

She looked away but nodded. "I'll take care of everything. I promise."

"I know you will. Now what's this getaway plan you've cooked up?" I had a feeling it was a plan we'd executed before, but this time it was Kingman style.

Jules stepped up and grinned at me. "There are already a lot of people hanging outside the hospital. Mostly well-wishers, because there are a lot of people pulling for you, Kelsey. Just in case you didn't know. But there's press too."

Trixie interjected with a groan. "You already know how much I super-duper love the press. So any chance I have to pull one over on the paparazzi, I am so in."

"Right." Jules nodded with way more enthusiasm than I thought a ruse like this called for. "See, most people know about your wigs and having your dancers and stuff all dress like you to try and throw the press off. But we're going bigger. We've paired each of my brothers up with a look-a-like for you, and we've all got fake dogs. We've got a whole friggin' fleet of black SUVs. We'll all leave the hospital together, and even if they think they've figured out which Kelsey and Declan are the real ones, which, no they won't, there's no way anyone is going to be able to keep up with the game of which car are you in."

This girl was a mastermind. I loved it.

I crawled out of the bed and took just a couple of minutes in the bathroom to change into the matching outfit that Penelope had brought for me. I decided not to look in the mirror, because I knew I wasn't going to like the bags under my eyes that I could literally feel. But I caught a glimpse anyway.

This was the last time I wanted to look like I was death warmed over. I pointed to myself in the reflection. "Take better care of yourself."

Declan poked his head in. "And let me do some of that taking care of too. Ready?"

I was so ready to get out of here. Or maybe it was the anticipation swirling in my stomach wondering what kind of plans Declan had for us. "Yeah. Let's go."

The eight of us were joined by three of my dancers, already in costume for this ruse, and only slightly distracted by the three Kingman brothers that had been assigned to them, Flynn, Gryffen, and Isak. Lord help them, every man in this family was way too good-looking for anyone's good. The whole lot of us pushed through the doors that led out to the parking lot of the hospital, and it was like one of those slo-mo scenes in the movies where the dream team headed into the fray shoulder to shoulder. And there was one hell of a battle waiting for us.

Penelope and Everett were at the front of the pack and took the brunt of the camera flashes and barrage of questions from reporters. Jules and Hayes flanked me on one side and Trixie and Chris were on the other. The dancers and the other boys were behind us, and I don't think anyone even said a word to me until we got into the back of the third SUV.

What happened after that was like a dance of the fricking sugarplum fairies, but with big black SUVs. Even I wasn't sure which car I was in. And it fooled the press and paparazzi too. In a few minutes, four vehicles pulled off and headed into town, while another four were on the road I recognized as the way to Bear Claw Valley.

Declan had mentioned that his family owned a lot of the land around here. Soon enough, I got to see some of it. We pulled up to a big, gorgeous cabin. It looked right out of a magazine for mountain getaways.

But even as I imagined what staying in a place like this would be like, we only got out of the car long enough for the driver to be picked up by Chris and Trixie.

"Come hop up front with me." Declan opened the front seat passenger door for me. "You and I will be the only ones who get to see where we're going."

I watched wide-eyed as he pulled onto a dirt road that had been mostly hidden by bushes and trees. And that road kept getting steeper and steeper until I swore we were about to drive off the side of the mountain. When I was about to get a cramp in my hand from white knuckling the armrest, we pulled to a stop in front of a cabin that looked about the same size as the truck.

Declan turned to me and grinned like he had the best kept secret. "So, how do you feel about a getaway with a ruggedly handsome football player to a mysterious cabin in the woods? I'll be there for your protection, just in case you're worried about wild animals or ghosts."

"Hmm, sounds like the start of a horror movie." I licked my lips. I didn't mean to, but the thought of spending alone time with Declan in a cabin that would barely fit the two of us inside had my heart speeding up for another reason, and thank goodness I was no longer hooked up to all those monitors because he would know exactly what he did to me. Too late now. Might as well give in to the feelings I couldn't lie to myself and say were fake anymore. "Or a really cheesy romance. Which one are we starring in, Mr. Kingman?"

My question came out a whole lot breathier than I'd intended.

His grin widened and he pitched his voice like a movie announcer. "Imagine a world, a rustic paradise, where the Wi-Fi is weak, but the connection," he pointed to his heart and then mine, "is strong. Where there's only one comfy bed, but it's big enough for two."

One bed. Big enough for two.

He was being corny and cute, but there was no mistaking what he was asking.

Was I really going to do this? Was I ready to stop pretending, stop worrying that if I let myself fall in love again there would only be heartache? I was. "One bed for two? Declan, are you trying to seduce me with promises of ghost protection and wilderness survival?"

"Only if it's working." His tone turned a bit more serious. "This is my mom's old cabin, and no one outside the family even knows it exists. It's a place where you can breathe, Kelsey. No pressure, no cameras, just you, me, and nature. Plus, I make an excellent campfire hot chocolate."

I pretended to ponder, tapping a finger against my lips. "I'll agree, but only because I'm intrigued by this campfire cooking and the idea of you protecting me from ghosts."

Declan's smile turned warm and affectionate. "Good, then welcome to your cabin retreat."

His words sent a flutter through my heart, a mix of excitement and trepidation. The idea of spending time away from everything with Declan, in a secluded cabin, was both terrifying and exhilarating.

Until we got inside and I saw exactly how big... or rather, small that one bed was.

OFF SEASON

DECLAN

I swear to God when we were little, all eight of us kids used to sleep on that bed. When I was eleven, it had been nine feet high and six feet wide, and soft as a downy chick. But looking at it now, Kelsey and I would be sleeping on top of each other.

And I wasn't actually sad about that.

Holding her in my arms last night felt so fucking right that not having her there would be a personal tragedy. I wanted very little more than to lay in her that bed and make hot but sweet love to her. So why wasn't I doing that?

Because she needed rest. But didn't someone say an orgasm a day keeps the doctor away? I was definitely walking on eggshells around her right now because, while she might have scared herself into taking a real break from the super-stardom life for a hot minute, she'd also scared the shit out of me. My head went to all the worst case scenarios when she'd gone down.

I didn't know if I could live through losing her like my dad lost my mom. I wanted to wrap her up in cotton fluff and hide her away like Rapunzel. But Rapunzel was never happy living in her castle. Mine wouldn't be either.

She looked at the cabin, her expression unreadable. "It's... cozy and... secluded."

I almost laughed. What she meant was that the cabin was a shack in the middle of nowhere. "Exactly what you need. I think Pooh is going to have a blast."

I opened up Pooh's bag and she went sniffing all over the place. There were lots of interesting things for her to smell. She immediately found several bushes that needed to be peed on. City pooch was going to have a lot of fun on her vacation, I could tell.

Now to convince Kelsey that she would too. She had her arms wrapped around herself and was chewing on her bottom lip. "You're not going to like hanging out with me on vacation. I don't know how to do nothing. It's uncomfortable, like something underneath my skin is itchy."

She'd be okay once I got her things inside, started a fire, and convinced her to take a nap. With me. We wouldn't be doing nothing.

I knew very well that someone who was a high

achiever like her couldn't just sit still. That wouldn't actually be restful to her. But she did need to refill her reserves of energy, of creativity, of the things that made her who she was. Having a tight-knit family around me and refusing to interact with the media most of the time had insulated me from the worst of that. Who did Kelsey have to do that for her?

Penelope was great and all, but there was only so much she could do, and Kelsey's agent needed a good swift kick in the ass if you asked me. Later, when we were cozy by the fire and I had her soft and supple in my arms, I'd ask her about her family. Surely, she had a base of support there.

I popped the back of the SUV open. Penelope and my dad had made sure we had bags with a few days' worth of clothes, some food, and even Kelsey's guitar. She moved to help me bring the bags in, but I gently intercepted her and turned her back around, giving her a shove back into the cabin. "You're not lifting a finger while we're here. Remember, you need to rest."

"You're a regular mother hen, aren't you?"

She had no idea how to be taken care of. If I had my way, she'd want nothing more by the time I was done with her. "You are going to be a spicy patient, aren't you?"

She rolled her eyes and stuck out her tongue at me. Was she doing these things on purpose? Because the more I thought about her mouth, the harder it was going to be to... let her rest.

I unpacked the groceries in silence, running scenarios in my head on just how quickly I could get her into that bed. To nap. Maybe snuggle. Nothing more until I didn't see bags under eyes. She was quiet but also grabbed up the broom by the door to sweep the stray leaves out, despite my warnings to her already.

"Go on now, test out the bed, take a nap," I said, gently taking the broom from her hands. "You're supposed to be resting, remember?"

She sighed. "You're bossy, you know that?"

"You want to see bossy, baby?" I picked her up and quite literally tossed her onto the bed. I should have grabbed the blanket and covered her up, but I couldn't resist covering her with my body instead. She squealed and giggled and wiggled, and though I liked to see a little fight coming back into her, the more she squirmed, the more I wanted to keep her right where she was. "Because I can be bossy."

A soft blush rose up her cheeks and damn if it wasn't the prettiest thing I'd ever seen. "Don't you get up from this bed, my little songbird, until I tell you that you can. Understand?"

"And what happens if I do?" She was being bratty and prickly, and testing me to see if I was going to keep my promises. I always did.

I pulled one of her hands out from between us and pressed it over her head and into the soft pillow, then the other, to see how she reacted to giving up some of her control. The way her eyes dilated and her breathing went all ragged, she liked this. Even if she wasn't ready to admit it. "I promise you're going to be a lot happier if you do as you're told."

"I can't do nothing. I told you that. I don't think I even know how to relax. I don't want to just lay around in bed all day." With that last sentence her eyes flashed, going wide for a second as she realized what lying in bed all day implied.

"I promise you won't be bored." And to prove it, I lowered my mouth to hers and I kissed her. I kissed her like it was the only thing I'd ever wanted in my entire life. I kissed her to show her that there was nothing fake about the way I felt about her.

This kiss was nothing like the one in her hotel a few days ago. That had been a little promise of what could be. This was fire. She moaned into my mouth and opened for me almost instantly. There was no teasing, no testing, only taking and giving all the pent up tension that had been building between us from the very beginning.

I swept my tongue over hers, tasting her, wanting and needing so much more. I might have her pinned down to the bed, but she was no passive woman I could control. Kelsey sucked my bottom lip in between her teeth and then soothed the sting with a soft pass of her tongue. She dueled with my tongue to see who got to taste more and pushed against my grip on her arms until I finally relented and let her free.

She immediately pushed her hands into my hair and gripped the strands, holding me right where she wanted me. Fuck, I was going to lose myself in her, and I wanted that, wanted it so much it hurt.

But I didn't bring her up here to fuck her.

Did I?

No.

Fuck.

I tore my mouth from hers but couldn't quite talk myself into breaking the contact entirely yet. I buried my face in the crook of her neck and kissed and nibbled my way up her throat, to her ear. Then I whispered to her, "I told you we wouldn't be bored, sweetheart."

Before things could get completely out of hand, I rolled off the bed and stood at the foot, staring down at the way her hair was splayed across the pillows, how her mouth was swollen from my kisses, and the gorgeous flush across her cheeks and neck. There would be no resisting her like this, and she and I both knew it.

"I'm..., yeah, that wasn't boring." She touched her lips and looked up at me with bedroom eyes that were going to kill me. My dick was screaming at me to crawl back into that bed with her and make her forget the rest of the world existed outside of the two of us.

But my heart wanted more than that. Sure, I wanted to fuck her, but I wanted her love even more. And that's why I turned around and went back to putting away the groceries. She needed to know I was serious about taking care of her, not just trying to get laid.

I'd take care of her every want and need. Not just my own.

Pooh raced in through the door yapping and wagging her tail. She ran in and out of my legs and then jumped up on the bed, wiggling and waggling all over Kelsey. She laughed and let her dog run roughshod all over her. "You're not bored either, are you poo-poo? I think you like the fresh air and room to roam, don't you?"

"Since I'm not going to get you to take a nap, let's take her on a little walk. get some of that fresh air into you."

Kelsey raised an eyebrow, and I saw that look that said if I got back into bed with her, she'd stay there. "I thought you wanted me to rest."

Oh god, was that an invitation or what? Nope. Not taking the bait. Instead I was going to romance her. I grabbed the picnic basket that I'd requested Hayes grab from one of those posh places in Aspen, and a blanket.

"Trust me, you're going to love this." I handed her Pooh's leash and tipped my head toward the door. "Come on, girls. Nature awaits you."

The walk to the lake was a leisurely stroll. This little cabin of my mom's was originally built as a fishing cabin specifically. And we were the only people with access to this piece of land, so it remained as untouched as the day she bought it.

Kelsey's cheeks were pink again, but this time because of the sunshine, crisp autumn air, and the exercise. She already seemed to breathe easier, her steps lighter amidst the rustling leaves and birdsong.

I knew just the spot to take her to. The lake was surrounded by blue spruce and ponderosas, and we had a really nice grove of quaking aspens. But there was one old Douglas fir that was as big as the Christmas tree in Rockefeller center, and we'd had plenty of picnics under its shade for the first ten years of my life. There were a lot of fun memories up here and I wanted to share at least a few of them with Kelsey.

Because I wanted her to feel like family.

I wanted her to be family.

Mine.

I wanted Kelsey to be my family.

A soft breeze swirled the fallen leaves around our feet and a ray of sunlight shone down right along our path. I shivered, but not from the cold, more like awareness flittered over my skin, and my chest contracted. Someone up above was telling me that what I wanted was exactly the right thing.

I took Kelsey's free hand and led her through the last patch of trees on our path and into the open shores of the Kingman lake.

"Oh. Wow. Declan. This is... awe-inspiring. I didn't know places like this even existed in real life. It looks like something out of a fantasy movie."

"It's the perfect place for that picnic I promised you." I spread out the blanket, plopped down the basket, and then dragged Kelsey down with me, settling her on my lap. "This is where you can come when you just need to get away from it all."

She ran her hand down the side of my cheeks and stared into my eyes for so long that the scenery around us faded away. There was only me and her and the beating of my heart. She leaned in and pressed her lips to mine.

This kiss wasn't as frantic and needy as the one at the cabin, but it was just as delicious. I was trying my best to be good and romance her, but if she asked me to strip her bare and make love to her under this tree right here and right now, I would.

Instead, our moment of peace was shattered by our god damned phones. I'd meant to leave them behind but had forgotten them in my jacket pocket. I hated that we even got a signal up here and was going to murder whichever rich entrepreneur decided to put cell phone towers on Bear Claw mountain.

Both of our phones erupted into swarms of buzzes. Something must be going on and unless it was the zombie apocalypse, I didn't care.

"Dammit," I muttered, pulling them out. Mine was messages from my agent. Something about Swoosh loving the 'good press' from last night and wanting to seal a deal. Frankly, that was sus. I'd be rethinking that when we were back to real life. But today I was ignoring everything. There was also a whole string of messages from Jules too. But the only one I read was the final one that told us the fam was going to do game night on Sunday.

Depending on how Kelsey was feeling, I think she'd enjoy game night. Although, I'd have to be ready to show her exactly how competitive I really was.

Kelsey's phone was a frenzy of notifications, but I didn't want her to see any of them. The world was bound and determined to keep her under its thumb.

She peeked over. "What's happening?"

"You're getting bombarded," I said, scrolling through. "Messages from Skeeter, Penelope, and a bunch of others."

She snatched the phone from my hand and exactly what I didn't want to happen manifested right then and there. Her face fell, and I could see her muscles tensing up, her anxiety spiking as she read a message from Penelope. "There are rumors that you're bullying me into canceling shows and speculation that you're... mean off the field too."

"That's bullshit," I growled. They wanted me to be mean? Well fuck them all. Frustration took over, and in one swift motion, I hurled both our phones as far as I could into the lake. They disappeared with satisfying splashes.

"Declan," Kelsey exclaimed, half-shocked, half-amused. Pooh barked and waded into the water like she was chasing a stick.

"I'm tired of everyone needing something from us and speculating on who we are, how we feel about each other, and what we should or shouldn't be doing. Right now, we need this – peace." I looked at her, hoping she'd understand.

She bit her lip and laughed. And it was the first genuine laugh I'd seen from her maybe since the first day we'd met. So I did the only thing I could think of when something so perfect happened. I picked her up so she had to wrap her legs around my hips and her arms around my neck. I kissed her, and this time I wasn't stopping for anything.

INSTASNAP

MUSICGOSSIPMAG

@MusicGossipMag

Bio: Want to know what's going on with your favorite bands and singers? We've got the tea.

[Pic outside of the hospital of Declan and Kelsey in disguise as they hurry to the SUV]

Is Declan Kingman just a big bully? He's been nominated as the meanest player in the league. If you've seen him play and take out quarterbacks like rag dolls, you know he deserves the award. But is this rough and gruff linesman pushing pop star Kelsey Best around off the field? Just look how he's pushing her into the car. And does she look scared to anyone else?

@IncognitoMosquito: That man is a walking red flag. I'm glad someone else is finally seeing it. #walkingredflag

@KanYayKing: She's just playing the victim, like most women do #IsaidwhatIsaid

@JakeJayOfficial: Do I need to go to Colorado?

@BestiesBestie: You're delulu. She's scared because people like you send paparazzi to take pictures like this. He's protecting her. #TeamKingKel

@KingmanPrincess: Declan Kingman is the nicest guy you'll ever meet, unless you're a quarterback for the other team #TeamKingman

@OopsImBritneyAgain: Kelsey! Wear a yellow shirt if you need help #FreeKelsey

---

GOSSQUEEN101

@QueenofGoss

Bio: I keep track of celebs so you don't have to. Join my newsletter!

[Pic of Declan and Kelsey at the hospital, looking rushed]

Is Declan Kingman more than just a tough guy on the field? Spotted: #KelseyBest looking less than thrilled as Declan practically shoves her into an SUV. Is our pop princess under the thumb of this gridiron giant? #DeclanAndKelsey #TroubleInParadise?

@MusicLover1994: This looks so sketchy! Declan seems too intense. #WorriedForKelsey

@Trav88: Come on, guys, you're being so dramatic. He's just protective. Leave them alone! #TeamDeclan

@PopStarSleuth: Not liking this vibe. Is Kelsey okay? #RedFlag

@BestiesBestie: He's protecting her, not bullying! Look at the care in his eyes. People need to stop twisting things. #TeamDelKel

@MosquitoIncognito: She's the one controlling him if you ask me. She's always been controlling and bitchy.

@Boomer411: Media making a mountain out of a molehill, as usual. #DramaAlert

THECELEBSCOOP

@CelebScoopOfficial

Bio: We've got the scoop on celebrities. Find us at all the award shows.

[Blurry pic of Declan and Kelsey at a distance]

Mystery or Misery? Caught this pic of Kelsey and Declan. She looks exhausted, and he's all muscle and might. Sources say she's been MIA since. Is it a protective boyfriend or something more controlling? #WhereIsKelsey #KingmanControl

@BestiesBestie: "Declan's a sweetheart, not a monster. The media is so quick to judge without knowing the facts. #SupportKelseyAndDeclan"

@Mystery_Maven: Something's definitely off here. Kelsey never looks this down. #Concerned

@GridironGuy: Declan's a beast on the field, maybe off it too? #KingmanControl

@SashaFollower: I don't think she looks scared, more like tired? #MixedFeelings

@GossipHound24: Did he force her to take time off? That's not cool. #FreeKelsey"

STARBUZZDAILY

@SBDUSOfficial

Bio: Official account of @BuzzDaily's celebrity reports.

[Pic of Kelsey looking fatigued with Declan standing over her]

Pressure or Protection? Kelsey Best seen looking weary as Declan Kingman stands guard. Is it just us, or does it seem like she's not there by choice? Fans are worried – is Kelsey really okay? #KelseyUnderPressure #DeclanGuardianOrGoon?

@KELSEYFOREVERFAN: I just hope she's okay! She's been working non-stop. #LoveKelsey

@SkepticalViewer: "Why's everyone blaming Declan? He might be helping her. #GiveHimABreak

@NoSmokeWithoutFire: There's something we're not seeing here. Can't put my finger on it.

@KBestAddict: Why is no one talking about how she almost fainted on stage? #HealthFirst

@BestiesBestie: She's clearly exhausted and he's there for her. That's true love, not control! #DelKel-Forever

POPMUSICGOSSIPGURU

@MusicGossiper-Pop

Bio: We're the music gossipers. I'm Pop Gossip. Follow our other accounts for country, rock, rap, and EDM, and catch up with us all on our website.

[Pic of Declan leading Kelsey, who is partly obscured]

Whisked Away or Whisked Apart? Declan Kingman seen leading a barely visible Kelsey Best. Rumors swirl of her 'taking a break' – but is this a romantic getaway or something more sinister? #KelseyVanishingAct #DeclanDominance?

@BestiesBestie: A secret getaway sounds romantic to me! They deserve some peace and quiet. #LetThemBeHappy

@MosquitoIncognito: Taking a break or shirking her responsibilities? What about all those fans who paid for concerts she isn't doing?

@TruthSeeker101: Disappearance? That sounds serious. #WhereIsKelseyReally

@RomanceReader: "Maybe it's a secret getaway? Let them be. #RomanticEscape

@ConspiracyTheorist: Doesn't anyone else think this is all for publicity? #StagedDrama

@DailyDiva: I don't like this... Kelsey always seemed independent. #NotLikeHer

FAMECHASERZ

@FameChaserzzz

Bio: Like tornado chasers, but cooler

[Pic of Kelsey looking dazed beside Declan]

Shocking Sight! Latest snap of Kelsey Best looking dazed and confused next to Declan Kingman. She's known for her vibrant performances, but this? Fans are asking - is this a retreat or a retreat from freedom? #SaveKelsey #DeclanDilemma

@WorryWart: Kelsey doesn't look good, guys. Is she being controlled? #ConcernForKelsey

@DefenderOfTruth: "Media always exaggerates. They're probably just taking a break. #ChillOutPeople

@KelseyBestieFan99: I just hope she's getting the rest she needs. She deserves it. #RestUpKelsey

@SuspiciousMind: Something's up. Declan's look says it all. #EyesWideOpen

@BestiesBestie: People always assume the worst. Declan is her knight in shining armor, not the villain! #ProtectKelseyAndDeclan

THE BANGXIETY IS OVER

KELSEY

*I*n a world of boys, Declan was a man. God, was he ever a man.

Up until now, I wasn't sure I'd ever actually dated a real man. Because none of them had ever treated me like a real woman. I'd been a thing to the rest of them. A sex object, of which some of them were ashamed of but wanted anyway. I'd been a means to an end for so many. A way to get what they wanted and look good while doing it.

But none of them had ever made me feel like this. I felt taken care of, felt protected, felt adored, and never had anyone made me feel so damned loved.

And it scared me.

And I was tired of being scared.

Since the day I decided to try out for *The Choicest Voice* singing competition, fear had been my main motivator. What if they don't like my singing, what if they tell me I'm to chubby to be a pop star, what if I don't write songs the record label likes, what if I put out an album that flops? What if, what if, what if...

For months my fears had been about whether I could even write songs anymore. Without the music, what was I?

I'd left all those questions unanswered and did everything I possibly could to make sure I never found out. Because I was sure it would be the end of everything. My hopes and dreams, my career, my life, the world.

I knew I had anxiety about my career that bordered on unhealthy, but it had served me for a while. I hadn't seen how much I'd let that mindset bleed into everything else. Including my love life.

No wonder I was a wreck.

While Declan was so sweet and sexy and had set up everything to take care of me like no one else ever had, he couldn't fix me. Only I could do that.

I had to quash the fears that were no longer serving me. I would start with the one right in front of me. It was the scariest of all because it meant more than my career or fans or livelihood. If I couldn't face this fear, I could do anything.

It started with asking the same what if...

What if I let myself fall in love?

The best way to face that fear was let it happen and see what came of it. Although, to be fair, it was a little too late, because as much as I'd tried to stop it, I'd fallen for Declan Kingman. I was irrevocably in love.

I think I might have been since the moment we met.

Declan was kissing me with more passion than I even knew existed and I never wanted him to stop. I pushed one of my hands into his hair and wrapped my legs tighter around his waist. He groaned in a way that I was sure meant he was going to die if he didn't get more of me. Or maybe that was just what I wanted. Right, that was definitely what I wanted.

I broke the kiss just long enough to make sure he knew. "More, Declan. I want more of you."

"You can have all of me, Kelsey." He pushed me up against the base of the enormous tree that smelled like Christmas in July. Sunshine and fresh air and pine and butterscotch. I was about to give myself the best kind of present.

A surge of courage coursed through me. With every breath, I inhaled the scent of possibility, of a love that had the potential to heal all my wounds. My heart raced with anticipation, knowing that this moment was about more than just physical desire. "Yes. I want that. I want all of you. Make love to me. Right here, right now."

Declan's eyes held a deep intensity as he whispered against my lips, "Are you sure, Kelsey? Once we cross this line, there's no going back."

I met his gaze and spoke from my heart. "I've never been more sure about anything. You're everything I need right now."

A smile that was more dirty and naughty than before tugged at the corner of his lips, and he gently brushed a strand of hair away from my face. "I want to be the man who gives you everything you need."

He ground his hips against me and buried his face in the crook of my neck like he had before. I could feel the heat and steel in his jeans and my eyes rolled back in my head. "Don't tease me, Declan."

With one fell swoop he turned and went down to his knees, laying me down on the blanket he'd spread out for our picnic, still between my legs. "I'm going to do a lot more than tease you, babe. But first I need us both very, very naked."

"Woof, woof." Pooh rushed over, her little butt waggling and licked Declan right on the lips, and I think she may have gotten her tongue up his nose.

He shook his head and made a face but laughed too. "Don't think I've forgotten about you, little girl. But it is not your turn for snuggles."

"I think she's jealous I'm getting all your attention." Pooh was cute and adorable and the love of my life, but right at this moment, I wished we'd left her with Penelope. I wasn't sharing his attention. Not now that I knew how much I actually wanted and needed it. But what were we going to do with her?

I was not tying her up. Sigh. I guess we'd have to

postpone until we could get back to the cabin and feed her or something to get a little alone time.

Declan stretched one arm out and flipped open the lid of the picnic basket. He riffled around inside for a minute and then pulled out a ball that looked like it was made out of strips of fabric. "This should keep you occupied for a while, pupperina."

He gave the ball a short toss, so it landed under the next tree over, and Pooh went racing after it as fast as her short little legs could go.

"Not that I doubt your prowess, but it might be hard to get naked and have some fun while also playing fetch. But that might just be me."

"Oh no, that will keep her attention while we... have some fun." He nodded his head toward Pooh, and she was doing her best to tear the fabric apart. After just a second, a treat popped out, and she happily munched on it, then went back to work looking for another one. "There're at least fifty cheese and peanut butter nuggets in there. I expect it will give me enough time for at least two or three orgasms."

Clever man. "Two or three of mine or yours?"

I was teasing, but he got this profoundly serious look on his face and leaned down to nip at my ear. Which had my insides going all squishy and wiggly. Then he whispered, "Sweetheart, when I make love to you, you will always come first, last, and a few times in between."

Was that even possible? Like outside of a spicy

romance novel? I'd been lucky to get to come at all, unless I helped a lot, with other men I'd been with.

"Darlin, I know that look. You think I'm all talk, and I'll bet you whoever else you've slept with couldn't fulfill those kind of promises." He kissed his way from one ear to the other "But I guarantee, I'm going to make you forget every single one of their names. You're going to forget that they existed."

Then he sat up and pulled his shirt over his head. And... oh, god. I didn't just forget the name of every boyfriend I'd ever had, I think I forgot my own name. That chest, those abs, and the expression on his face as he looked down at me like I was the snack, it was all mesmerizing.

"I can make you come with your clothes on, babe, but I think we'll both have more fun if you take them off." He reached for his jeans and pulled the button open and, yeah, sure, I should take my clothes off, but I was a little busy watching him strip for me.

I'd felt the hard length of him when he had me up against that tree, I'd practically seen the outline of it when he'd been wearing those gray sweatpants that day at Rust Rocks. So I had an idea of what he was about to reveal, and I absolutely could not look away.

Declan shucked his jeans, literally tossing them over his shoulder and oh, boy, he wasn't wearing anything else underneath. There had been mere millimeters of fabric between us and that gave me such a thrill that I got goosebumps all up and down my arms and chest.

He knelt before me, completely naked and utterly sublime. My eyes trailed over his rippling muscles, his golden skin bronzed by the sun, and his thick, erect dick that stood tall and bold. Desire pooled deep within me, a primal need to touch him, to taste him, rose up, threatening to consume me whole.

He was big... everywhere. And yet I knew absolutely that we would fit together perfectly.

"You're unbelievably hot," I murmured, my voice barely a whisper as I reached out and ran my fingers over his chest, feeling the hardness of his muscles, the trail of hair that led down below.

He was built like a god, the kind that fought battles, not posed for a camera. He was exactly my vision of perfection, and I was about to be the luckiest girl in the world.

It was definitely my turn, and I slowly pulled my shirt over my head, savoring the sun on my skin. I did the same with my leggings, keeping my eyes locked on his as I slid them down my legs.

I was acutely aware of the fact that I was exposing myself to him, that I was placing myself completely in his hands. And where I might have been afraid with other men, men who were caught up in the trappings of fame and the Hollywood ideal of beauty, I already knew Declan didn't care.

No, it wasn't that he didn't care. He did. But he had already shown me exactly how much he liked what my body had to offer. I didn't question even for a second if my thighs or my ass were too big for him, if the rolls of my skin would turn him off, or if he would want the lights out.

We were baring ourselves to each other in the light of the day and the look he had on his face as I revealed another inch of skin was hotter than the sun shining down on us.

I reached for my bra, but he grabbed my hand. "Stop. Let me."

He gave me a little push, so that I laid back down on the blanket, and then covered my body with his, holding himself above me. His eyes were dark and intense as he looked me over, his fingers trailing over the curve of my hip, down my thigh, and back again.

"You're so fucking beautiful," he whispered, his voice hoarse.

I drew in a sharp breath, my nerves and excitement causing my body to tremble in anticipation. My heart pounded in my chest as Declan lowered himself between my legs, his gaze never leaving mine.

"Tell me you want this, Kelsey. Tell me you want me to finish stripping you bare. Say you want me to fuck you." His voice was low and husky, and god, was there anything sexier than a man who actually asked for consent?

I nodded, my voice unable to form the words. Declan's lips sought mine in a kiss that took my breath away, one filled with promise. Absolute trust and love washed over me, knowing that I was giving myself to him completely, both physically and emotionally.

"Say it, Kelsey. I need to hear that you want me." The words were a demand and at the same time, the barest vulnerability.

"I want you, Declan. I want you to make love to me, to fuck me, to take me and make me yours. I want you." More than I'd ever wanted any man.

He smiled like I'd just lit up the universe with stars. "That's my good girl."

He leaned down and kissed me, his tongue teasing mine in a dance that left me breathless. I could feel his cock grazing against my thigh and cursed that he hadn't let me take off my panties. I could have just spread my thighs and grabbed his ass to guide him into me.

"I've still got too many clothes on. Please take them off. Touch me. Touch all of me."

"You forget that I'm the bossy one here, Kels."

His hands and mouth were everywhere, exploring every inch of my body, leaving a trail of arousal in their wake. He kissed my breasts over the bra, gently biting at my nipples until I was sure they would break through the material they were so hard. I moaned softly, wanting more.

"Please, Declan."

He kissed me again, this time more demanding, his tongue delving deep into my mouth as his body pressed against mine. I could feel the hardness of him against my panties and squirmed, trying to get just a little friction where I needed it most.

"God, Kelsey, you're driving me crazy. But not yet, I want you so badly, and I'm going to make sure you remember this for the rest of your life." Declan smiled, a wicked grin spreading across his face.

"I want to taste you, Kelsey. I want to explore every inch of you, and make sure you're ready for me, exactly the way I want you."

I looked into his eyes and saw the desire there. He wasn't just doing this to get off, he was once again doing everything for me.

And for once in my life I was going to let someone else be in charge, let this man that I trusted with my heart, take care of me.

MY HEART WAS WAITING FOR YOU

DECLAN

Kelsey was a fucking goddess, and I was going to worship every fucking inch of her. Twice. Maybe even three times.

My dick was screaming at me to just part her thighs and give us both what we wanted. But being with her was no quick lay. This wasn't a one-night stand, which was my normal M.O.

I was going to make this first time fucking perfect for her. And I swear to god, she was going to be the last woman I ever touched.

She was my forever.

I snagged one of the straps of her bra with my teeth and drug it down her arm, then the other one. This was meant to tease her, but I was the one about to be impatient. I'd planned to kiss my way across the tops of her breasts, pull one cup down and... so much more, but I couldn't wait to see her bare for me any longer.

"Tell me you want my mouth on you, sucking these tight, hard nipples."

"Declan, I promise I want you to do every single thing you want to me. You don't have to..."

"Yes, I do. This is all about enthusiastic consent, baby. The more I know what you want, what makes you feel good, the better the sex is going to be." I nipped at her bottom lip. "Besides, I love hearing you talk dirty to me."

"Then, for goodness' sake, take off my bra already."

"Dirtier, Kelsey. Tell me exactly what you want. You're the one in charge here."

"I thought you were going to be the bossy one."

"Oh, I am. I'm bossing you into talking dirty to me, aren't I?"

Pink heat bloomed on her chest and cheeks. If she wasn't comfortable saying what she wanted out loud, well, we'd work on that, but I wasn't going to push it.

"I want you to suck on my nipples. I really like that."

"Good girl."

I reached behind her back and undid the clasps and practically yanked her bra off to expose her soft, creamy skin to me.

Fucking hell. Kelsey had the most perfect breasts on the whole fucking planet. I was going to get lost in them for a hundred years, kissing and licking and fucking them. I admit to watching more than a little porn in my time, and it all starred women with big tits and hips and thighs. Just like Kelsey's. I couldn't wait to come all over them. But this time wasn't about me.

Kelsey's chest heaved, her breaths shallow and ragged as I traced my fingers along the delicate lines of her collarbone.

"I want you to taste me. I want to feel your lips on my nipples." Her voice was soft, barely audible.

I leaned in, my eyes locked on her nipples as I began to lick and suck, teasing and building the anticipation. Kelsey let out a soft moan, her hands running through my hair as she arched her back, pressing her breast closer to my mouth.

Her breasts were a feast for my eyes, and I couldn't resist devouring them with my lips. I gently took one nipple into my mouth, sucking and nibbling until Kelsey was panting, her moans growing louder and more desperate.

My mind was consumed with thoughts of her, of the way she tasted and felt in my mouth, of the way she responded to my touch. I wanted to be inside her, to feel her around me, to make her scream my name.

"Declan, I need you," she whispered, her voice shaking with desire.

My eyes locked on hers. "I'm going to make you come so hard for me, Kelsey. I promise you that."

I lowered my mouth to her nipple again, but trailed my fingers down her chest and across the soft swell of her belly until I found the top of her panties. She squirmed and lifted her hips, groaning when I didn't move farther than her waistband.

"Please. Touch me. Put your fingers in my pussy."

I gave her nipple a soft little bite and then let it pop out of my mouth. "That's all I needed to hear."

I slid my fingers under the edge of her panties and felt the warmth of her pussy through the fabric. My heart raced at the thought of finally being able to touch her there. I reached down and gently pulled her panties to the side, reveling in the sight of her plump pussy.

"Is this what you wanted?" I asked, my voice ragged with desire.

Kelsey's eyes were glazed with lust, and she nodded.

I raised one eyebrow at her. "Say it."

She licked her lips and took a ragged breath. "Touch me. Put your fingers inside of me, find my clit. I... I like it when you circle it."

I slid my fingers beneath her panties and felt the heat radiating from her core. Her pussy was wet and ready for me, beckoning me to explore it. I slowly slid my middle finger inside her, feeling her muscles clench and release around me as I moved in and out. Her moans grew louder, and I knew she was getting what she wanted.

"Declan, oh my god, that feels so good. Please don't stop."

I laughed lightly and used my thumb to circle her clit just like she asked me to. Like I could ever stop. I increased the pace of my fingers, thrusting them deeper and finding that spot inside that I knew would drive her wild. Her breaths became rapid, and she panted.

"I'm so close, Declan. I need you. Not just your fingers. Please, I want your cock inside me." She gripped my arm, holding me where she wanted me.

"You're so beautiful when you're like this, sweetheart. Come for me, let me see you come."

Kelsey's eyes were wide with desire, and she nodded eagerly. I crooked my fingers and circled her clit with my thumb faster than before. She gasped as she came, her pussy pulsing around my fingers, her back arching, my name on her lips.

It was the best thing I'd ever seen or experienced in my entire life. Knowing I'd given her this kind of pleasure, and that I planned to do it again and again, for as long as she let me.

I pulled my fingers out of her and licked them clean. Then I leaned in to kiss her, so she could taste her sweet release on my lips. Her body trembled against me, and she glowed with a rosy blush across her skin. I wanted to be inside her so badly, to feel her tight around me.

Today wasn't about me and what I wanted.

She wrapped her arms around my shoulders and sighed against my mouth. "That was amazing. But I want more. I want you inside of me."

I stroked her hair and nibbled her lips. "Not yet.

This is all for you, sweetheart. I'm going to make you come at least a dozen more times first."

Her eyes, that had been lazily closing, popped open and she pushed me back as she sat up.

"I see what you're doing here, mister. I may be on the verge of burn out."

"Maybe?"

She rolled her eyes and shook her head, but she also poked me in the chest, which I found cute as shit. "I'm not admitting to anything."

Since she'd pulled us into a seated position, I pulled her into my lap. "Which is why I'm here to take care of you."

Her eyes went wide and then a big smile crossed her lips. "Mr. Kingman, are those your crown jewels I'm sitting on?"

I chuckled at her adorable flirting, but I wasn't giving in. No matter how much I wanted to. But if I didn't do something soon, I was going to need a cold shower.

Ooh. That gave me a great idea. "Babe, have you ever been chunky dunking?"

"If that's a sex position, I don't know what it is, but I'm down for pretty much anything you wanna do."

"Oh, I think you're going to love it." I reached under her thighs, stood up with her in my arms, and hightailed it to the lake. Pooh chased after us and jumped right into the water, doggy paddling her little heart out.

Kelsey squealed and kicked her feet. "What are you doing?"

"Just trust me, sweetheart. This'll be a moment you'll remember for a long time."

I took about five long strides into the water and then twisted and sank down, dunking us, holding her tightly against me. Her laughter and shock echoed in my ears as we plunged into the lake. With a splash, we rose back up into the sunlight and she giggled and squirmed in my arms. We broke apart laughing and splashing each other as we played in the lake, while her little dog circled around and around us.

"This is chunky dunking?" she asked paddling toward me. When she reached me again, she wrapped both her arms and legs around me, putting our naked bodies together. I was surprised the lake didn't start boiling.

I dipped us down into the water so only our shoulders were exposed. "I have never in my life been skinny, honey. So we certainly aren't skinny dipping."

"Oh, that is going into a song absolutely immediately if not sooner." She laughed again and splashed me. "Declan Kingman... I love you."

For a moment, everything stood still, the water, the sun in the sky, even my own breath. Kelsey's unexpected confession caught me off-guard. She stared at me, her eyes a bit guarded. I think she hadn't meant to blurt that out, but I also thought she meant it.

I traced her jawline with my thumb, gently grazing

the curve of her cheek, my gaze falling down toward her lips and then back up to meet hers. A wave of emotion crashed over me, overwhelming in its intensity. I looked into her eyes, shining with sincerity and vulnerability, and a surge of love so strong it nearly knocked me off my feet roared through me.

I held her closer, my heart pounding so hard, it might be trying to get out of my chest. "I love you too, Kelsey Best. I've never felt this way about anyone, and I think it's because my heart was waiting for you."

Her smile lit up the air around us brighter than the Colorado mountain sun. But it wasn't nearly as hot as the kiss she laid on me. The chill from the lake evaporated with the heat building between us. "Kels, I want nothing more to let you ride my cock right here, right now, but the condoms are in the picnic basket, and I don't think they'd work in the water anyway."

She let her legs down and grabbed my hand, then pulled me toward the shore. Pooh was yards ahead of us, almost at the shoreline already. "I'm pretty sure I'm going to be freezing when we get out of the water. Know any way to warm me up?"

A few steps from the edge of the water, I picked her up into a princess-style carry and took her back to our blanket. Pooh met us along the way, yipping and yapping. "I think she wants me to pick her up too."

"She's a jealous girl and for good reason. But after that swim, I'll bet she'll settle down for a nap."

A pinprick of guilt hit me at that. "She's probably

got the right idea. You should nap too. I'll be just as happy to hold you in my arm all afternoon. We don't have to—"

Kelsey set her feet down and faced me, putting her hand up to my face and cupping my chin. "I know you've decided it's your responsibility to take care of me, and I love that, Declan, I really, really do."

"Don't you dare say that you can take care of yourself." That's always what came next. "I know that, of course you can. But you don't have to."

She smiled so sweetly, and not in the way women did when they thought I was being dumb, or overprotective, or that I simply didn't understand what they wanted. No, Kelsey looked at me like I hung the sun in the sky and she was waiting for nightfall for me to hang the moon and stars too, and it was giving me life.

She put a finger to my lips. "I'm telling you I do love that. But I'm not fragile. You don't have to handle me with kid gloves. I know I gave everyone, including myself, a scare. But I promise, if you make love to me under the shade of a tree, by a mountain lake, on a sunny fall day, I'm not going to break."

She was right, both in that she'd scared me, and that I was worried I was going to hurt her or hinder her recovery. But Kelsey was stronger than I was giving her credit for. I could already see how even a few hours away from the stressors of her tour were good for her psyche. And she did have a whole lot of gorgeous color in her face.

"I will always want to take care of you. Taking care of what's mine, the people who belong to me, is a part of who I am." I pushed my hands into her hair and lowered my lips to hers, brushing my mouth gently over hers. "So let me take care of you now with a whole lot more orgasms."

Kelsey's eyes met mine, her pupils dilated and her breaths shallow. I saw the hunger in her gaze, the need for me just as strong as my own. With a swift movement, I slid her wet panties down her hips, going down on my knees in front of her. The soft blonde curls over her mound were still wet from the water, and neatly trimmed in the shape of a triangle pointing right at my target. I wanted her wet in another way.

I leaned in and kissed the apex of those plump pussy lips, and Kelsey pushed her fingers into my hair. "Tell me what you want, sweetheart."

This time she didn't need more prompting. "Lick me, use your tongue on my clit, and don't be gentle."

I obliged, my mouth watering at the thought of her sweet taste on my tongue. I gripped her thighs and spread them apart, kissing her inner thighs softly before diving in for a long lick. Kelsey's throaty moans filled the air as I dove in with my tongue, licking and sucking at her wet, swollen clit. Her taste exploded in my mouth, sweet and salty, the perfect combination that made me crave her even more.

As I focused on her pleasure, I felt Kelsey's hands gripping my head, her fingers tangling in my hair, pulling me further into her. She moaned softly, and her hips bucked against my face. I reached up and grabbed her ass, holding her against me, letting her thighs tremble against my shoulders.

I continued my assault on her clit, my tongue flickering and pulsating in rhythm with her body, pushing her higher and higher until she reached her peak. Her moans grew louder, urging me on, and I began to suck her clit harder, flicking it with my tongue just how she asked, not gentle at all.

Her hands gripped my hair tightly, her nails digging into my scalp as the pleasure built within her. She was so close, and I could feel it in the tremble of her thighs and the way she got wetter by the second.

Her hands moved from head to my shoulders, and her knees buckled as she cried out my name, coming so hard, I could feel her swollen clit pulsing against my tongue.

I held her up as her body arched and twitched while she cried out in pleasure. Her release burst onto my face, wetness trickling across my mouth and beard, and I reveled in it. I continued to lick her until she begged me to stop, her legs shaking as she caught her breath.

Finally, the spasms of her orgasm subsided, and I slowly lifted my head and then stood up and pulled her into my arms, kissing her deeply, loving the way her eyes sparkled when she tasted herself on me. "You taste so good, Kels. I could eat your pussy all day."

She hummed a satisfied sound that was music to my

ears. "I think I would enjoy that very much. But what I'd like even more is to have you inside of me and getting to hear you moan my name when you come with my pussy gripping you tight."

Oh, how I loved a dirty talking woman who knew what she wanted. Because I was going to give her it all.

I'D LIKE TO TEACH THE WORLD TO SING

KELSEY

*D*eclan pulled me down to the blanket and covered my body with his. The gentle touches he'd used the first time we laid here were long gone. Powerful hands stroked and caressed, tracing a path across every inch of me, making my skin sing.

His lips moved hungrily from my neck to my breasts and down between them. Then he licked the faded stretch marks on either side of my stomach. He didn't stop there. He nibbled the ones on each hip, and then moved back up, running his tongue over the ones on the sides of my breasts. No one had ever done that before, and it had me feeling absolutely worshipped.

He groaned, his breath hot on my skin. "I want you so badly it hurts."

The time for gentle caresses and teasing touches was over and I needed to show him that. I pulled over the picnic basket he'd packed with such care and rummaged through it. Beneath the red-checkered cloth and some sandwiches that we were going to devour later, my fingers closed around the telltale foil squares hidden like treasures. A victorious smile tugged at my lips.

"I need you inside of me." I held up the condoms. I didn't want any more teasing or playing. I just wanted him.

He took them and smiled, his eyes darkened with a mixture of passion and something deeper, something that made my heart skip a beat. "Put it on me. I want you to know exactly what you're getting from me."

I pushed him back onto the blanket, a playful forcefulness in my movements. This was just one more way he was asking for my consent, and I was so fucking here for it. The grass whispered beneath the fabric as his sculpted back met the ground. With deliberate intent, I tore the packet open and sheathed him with a touch that was both delicate and demanding. The world seemed to hold its breath.

Or, uh, that was just me, holding my breath and his cock in my hand. He was no Coke can, but he had some girth and length. He was definitely the biggest I'd ever had, and damn if I wasn't looking forward to it. I wanted him to fill me like no other man had. I had a feeling we were going to fit together perfectly.

"Straddle me, babe. Take exactly how much you want, how much you need." Declan grabbed my hips as I straddled him.

I savored the moment of power he was demanding of me, giving me control because he knew I needed it, before slowly sinking down onto his tip. A shared gasp rippled between us, and for a heartbeat, or perhaps an eternity, we were suspended in perfect unison.

"Kelsey…" His voice was strained, thick with emotion and need. His fingers dug into my hips and tried to hold me where I was. "Slow, babe, slow. I don't want to hurt you."

"No, you feel so good. I need more." I sank down further, and then up just a little, then down again until I had him as deep as he could go. I rocked against him, my hips finding a rhythm better than any song.

"Fu-uck, Kelsey, I—" He cut himself off, and with a fluid motion that spoke of his strength and athleticism, he flipped me beneath him, not breaking our connection for a moment. I found myself gazing up into those fathomless eyes that promised so much more than just pleasure.

He grabbed my right leg and put it over his shoulder, and then he did the other. Good thing I did a lot of yoga and stretching to make sure I stayed in shape for the dance routines and effort it took to put on a show. He thrust forward, sinking even deeper into me, and we both let out guttural moans.

"God, no one has ever fit me like this. We were

made for each other." There was no space for doubt or fear, only the blurring of lines where we ended and again where we began. He withdrew and thrust again, and I watched his eyes roll back in his head. He went so slow that I thought I would scream, except I couldn't because every time he sank into me, I gasped, or whimpered, or moaned his name.

"Kelsey, Kelsey," he murmured my name as if it was a prayer. "I love you, fuck, I love you so much."

"I love you, I need you, please Declan, please." I arched into him, as if I could get even closer to him. His hips met mine in a way that was both primal and achingly tender. With each thrust, he filled me completely, creating a pleasure so deep that words and thought became impossible, until there was only feeling, only Declan, only us.

"Only us," I whispered, the world narrowing to the expanse of his shoulders blocking out the sun, the sheen of sweat on his skin, the palpable love that we created with every shared breath. My thighs began to tremble, and I felt the orgasm building, so close.

"Look at me," he commanded softly, and I did. In those dark eyes, I saw not just the fervor of our lovemaking but something enduring, something infinite. "I'm so fucking close to coming inside of you. Tell me what you need to get there. I want us coming together."

"I just need you." The words barely passed my lips before my release crashed over me in way I'd never experienced before. My whole body clenched and then exploded, the pleasure pouring through every cell. Declan followed me into that bliss with a groan that came from the depths of his soul, his body shuddering with the force of it.

We stayed locked together for a long minute. I didn't want to move, mostly because I didn't want this to be over. This perfect moment was so much more than I ever expected to feel in my entire lifetime, much less an afternoon.

I didn't want that feeling to end.

Declan moved his shoulders so my legs could slip down, but he stayed buried within me. After a few harsh breaths, he leaned down and kissed me just as intensely as he'd made love to me. It made the end of our lovemaking last just that little bit longer, and I realized he wasn't ready for it to end either.

I wrapped my legs around his hips, locking my feet to hold him against me. I knew we couldn't stay wrapped up in each other forever, but just a little longer would mean everything to me. "Don't pull out yet. Stay just a little bit longer."

"Even if I wanted to move, I'm not sure I could. You just rocked my fucking world, Kels." He laughed but dipped his head to rest in the crook of my neck. We laid there for a long time, just basking in the bliss, the dappled sunlight, and each other.

Until Pooh decided she wanted kisses too. And not from me. She came right up to Declan and went straight for his face with her wet and sloppy tongue.

He grabbed her and rolled, making sure to take the condom with him. "You're quite the mood killer, Poopity Pooh. I'll remember to bring a dozen of those treat balls next time."

I loved that he planned on there being a next time.

We rinsed off in the cold water of the lake again and then ate the food he packed. Nothing had ever been so delicious before, and it was just cheese sandwiches, apple slices with peanut butter, which, of course, Pooh devoured, and the cutest box of chocolates from some fancy pants place in Aspen.

It was the perfect day.

"When did you have time to pack this fun-filled picnic basket?" It was too well thought out with dog treats, condoms, and delicious food to have been thrown together last minute.

Declan swallowed a laugh. "Everett and Hayes did it. Hayes is too smart for his own good, and I'm sure he's the one who thought of the treat toy. But Ev is definitely the one who threw in the condoms. He's a horny safety guy."

We dressed and walked back to the cabin. The rustic interior was actually much nicer than I'd noticed in those first few minutes we were here. It was welcoming and warm, promising respite and seclusion. There was definitely a woman's touch. He had said it was his mother's. I wanted to ask about her but didn't want to break the spell of serenity we had right now.

I flopped onto the plush bed, which was the only

place to sit, and sunk into the feather comforter and big fluffy pillows. On the opposite wall was a huge picture window with a gorgeous view of the wilderness beyond. This was a place to breathe, to heal.

It hadn't even been an entire day on this semi-enforced vacation, and I already felt better, mentally lighter, than I had in ages. Declan had been so right to make me take this break. Already today I was finding my way back to the music that pulsed in my veins—a melody not born of obligation but of joy. I was ready to embrace the silence, to listen to the whispers of my own heart, and perhaps in those whispers, discover a song that was mine alone to sing.

"Hand me my guitar?" I wanted to play a little with a tune for the lyrics that were popping into my head for a song about chunky dunkin'.

"Nothing would make me happier, as long as it doesn't feel like work," he chastised, but smiled so big it crinkled the corners of his eyes with genuine affection.

I shook my head. "This isn't work, Deck. It's... something else." My hands strummed idly over the strings, coaxing out a tentative melody that had been simmering in the back of my mind all day. "An idea that you gave me today."

I moved through a couple of chords and the notes grew bolder, more confident. The song was raw, as if it had broken through a dam within me, flooding out without permission. "It's about breaking free from...

insecurities so you don't miss out on life and having fun."

A laugh erupted from Declan's chest, deep and genuine. "Chunky dunkin'?"

"Yup," I replied, my fingers dancing over the strings with newfound vigor. "You know, for those of us who've skipped skinny dipping because we're worried about what others might think of our bodies."

"I love it, babe. I'm going to go start a fire and we can sit outside in a bit." He moved off the bed and Pooh took his place but then realized he was going outside and trailed after him. "Sing it for me when it's ready?"

I normally held my songs close to the chest until I had something a little more solid. But this one felt different from the beginning.

I played with lyrics about sunlit lakes and sun-kissed skin, about the freedom of diving into cool water unashamed and unafraid. I sang of laughter bubbling to the surface, echoing across the water, a celebration of every curve, every line, every imperfection.

With each verse, I felt lighter, as if the song was lifting away the weight of the early years of my own struggles with body image. I did everything I could to show my fans, especially the girls that looked at me as a role model, that all bodies were beautiful and I loved my curves.

But all women had days where they didn't feel great about the way they looked. And the pressure on me to be positive, happy, and confident all the time was... probably part of the problem with this bout of exhaustion. It was a lot of work to be what the world wanted me to be every day.

"Damn, Kels," Declan popped his head in the doorway. "That's beautiful. You're beautiful."

"Thanks," I whispered, suddenly shy under his intense gaze. "It feels good to sing about something so... real."

"Real is good." The way he said that made me think he meant it in a way that was more than just about my song. Was he talking about us? I hoped so.

Later, as darkness settled around us and the stars blinked awake one by one, we sat side by side. His hand found mine, our fingers entwining naturally, as if they were always meant to fit together this way.

The fire crackled, its sparks dancing like tiny stars against the night's canvas, and the warmth of its embrace wrapped around us as we nestled close on the log meant as a bench. Declan's thumb traced idle patterns on the back of my hand, his touch featherlight and not meant to stir up sexual tension, but it was.

"Kelsey," Declan said softly, his fingers tracing patterns on my back, "I've never felt like this before."

"Me neither," I admitted, the vulnerability in his voice echoed in my own. "It's scary, isn't it?"

"Terrifying," he agreed, smiling. "But there's no one else I'd rather face my fears with."

"Same," I replied, sealing our pact with a kiss that spoke of hope, love, and a tomorrow that we'd face together.

He stood and put out the fire, and then in one fluid motion, he lifted me up, his strength on full display. My legs wrapped around his waist instinctively, craving the closeness, the connection that only he could provide. "A girl could get used to being carried around everywhere."

"I could get used to always having you in my arms." He carried me back inside, waited for Pooh to come waggling in after us, and then kicked the door shut before laying me down on the bed.

"Ready to get some sleep?" The glint in his eye suggested other activities might precede rest.

"I'm not a good sleeper, you know that." I stretched and yawned because after our walk to the lake, a couple of swims, and three amazing orgasms, I thought I could actually sleep. "Know anything that could help wear me out a little more?"

"I might have a few ideas." With deft movements, he pulled off my shirt and my bra, exposing the swell of my breasts to the glow of the moonlight streaming in the through the big window. The cool air kissed my skin, but his mouth was warm, worshiping me with each brush of his lips. I gasped as he took my nipple into his mouth, sucking gently, coaxing moans from deep within me. In no time flat, we were naked, he grabbed a condom, and pulled the soft blankets over our bodies.

The world beyond the walls of the cabin faded away. There was only the two of us, wrapped in each other's arms, surrendering to the pull of desires both tender and wild.

"Tell me you want me." His eyes searched mine for any hint of hesitation.

"More than anything," I assured him, reaching down to guide him inside.

He entered me, and the world fell away. It was just Declan and me, moving together in perfect four-four time. His thrusts were deliberate, powerful, yet filled with an emotion that made my heart swell. I arched into him, meeting him stroke for stroke, lost in the sensation, the profound intimacy, of the act.

"Kelsey, you feel incredible," he groaned, his movements growing more urgent.

"Declan, don't stop." The coils of pleasure that I only felt with him tightened within me. The fourth orgasm of the day was already building. No one else had ever done this to me before. I was lucky to get four orgasms a relationship, not a day.

"Never," he vowed, his pace relentless, driving us both toward the edge. "I'll love you forever."

His words ignited something inside of me, and my climax hit me so hard, overwhelming, and all-consuming, and I cried out his name as I shattered around him.

Declan followed, his own release fierce and raw and the sexiest damn thing in the world.

We lay there, entwined under the covers, the little wood stove's warmth cocooning us as we basked in the afterglow. Our hearts beat in sync, and the melody of a yet unwritten love song played in my head.

I closed my eyes and the last thing I noticed was Declan lifting Pooh off the floor and onto the pillow behind my head.

I had the dirtiest of dreams of Declan interspersed with weird visions about my guitar being plucked out of my hands and being replaced by a huge block of cheese. But the cheese turned into a giant cell phone that I had to keep scrolling, scrolling, scrolling, but I didn't know what I was supposed to be looking for.

I jolted awake to find late morning sun shining in through the big window and Declan bare-ass naked trying to quietly teach Pooh how to roll over.

"What time is it?" I turned onto my side and curled up under the blanket, not quite ready to get up. I couldn't remember the last time I slept through the night and also slept in.

"Don't know. No phones, remember?" He grinned at that like he'd just scored a touchdown, or perhaps like he'd just tackled the guy with the ball. Either way, he was damn proud of himself. "But I suppose we'll have to check the clock in the SUV, because if you're up for it, we have an invitation for tonight."

There went the secluded vacation. I supposed one

full day away was as much as I could expect. "From whom? If it's with cameras, I'm going to need to go back to my suite and—"

He held up a hand. "Nope. We're not going anywhere near town for a few more days at least. But it's Sunday, and me and the boys don't have a game on account of our bye week, so that means it's Kingman family game night."

Game night with his family? That sounded way too cute for words. It would be nice and relaxing, and I'd get to know his family a little better.

"Sounds fun. But be prepared to get your butt kicked, because I'm kind of competitive if you hadn't noticed."

Declan laughed so loud that Pooh started barking just to join in. "You're going to fit right in, babe."

KINGMAN FAMILY GAME NIGHT

DECLAN

Kelsey and I walked the path to the Kingman family cabin. It was just down the hill, maybe ten minutes away, and the reason my parents had met in the first place. I'd have to tell Kelsey the story later of how my dad rescued my mom from a snowstorm.

We'd spent a lot of time up here as kids, and it felt like there was a new addition every year. There were six bedrooms, two baths, and just like at home, a big family room, sans television. It was mom's one requirement. All she wanted was one room in the house where we could spend time as family and where there was no football.

The boisterous sounds of the Kingman family warming up for game night echoed through the trees, and Kelsey gave me a wide-eyed look. "Is that just your family?"

Pooh got excited by the noises and raced ahead. Through the trees we could sort of make out the front porch, so I wasn't worried she'd get lost along the way. Plus, there was the squeal of a particular younger sister welcoming the little dog home like she was one of the family. "Wiener the Pooh! Come here, that's right, come here, girl. Yes, you're so cute. Yes, you are."

"Yeah, we get pretty rowdy when we're all together. You tell me if we get to be too much for you. We can head back up whenever you want." She'd met everyone, either with me or when she'd come to my game, but all eight kids, plus Chris's fiancée Trixie, and my dad, well, that was a lot of Kingman cockiness in one room at the same time.

We pushed in the front door and laughter and teasing already filled the large living room, where the game of the night, double decker Uno, was already being set up, ready for an evening of competitive fun.

I glanced at Kelsey, worried that I'd made a mistake by pushing her back into that place where she felt like she had to be perfect in front of other people. My large, loud, crazy-competitive family might be too over-whelming for her. She was an only child and was supposed to be resting after all. But as she looked around, her eyes sparkled with excitement. Okay, maybe she was up for the challenge.

"Good, Declan and Kelsey are here just in time for your team assignments." Dad clapped his hands and used his coach voice to get everyone's attention. "Declan and Hayes, Chris and Gryff, Everett and Isak, me and Flynn, and our newly established ladies alliance of Kelsey, Jules, and Trixie."

Pooh gave a little bark as if to say she wanted to play too. My dad scooped her up and gave her a good ruffle on the head. "Mascotted, of course, by the tiniest dog to ever set foot in this cabin."

I teamed up with Hayes, and we exchanged a competitive grin and fist bumps. "Prepare to lose, ladies and gents. You all don't stand a chance against the meanest player in the league and the genius."

Everett grinned like the cat that ate the canary and nodded at Isak. "Don't count on it, bro. We've got the lucky pillow." He jerked his chin at Isak, who whipped out of thin air the faded green pillow that had been hand stitched with the saying "In this house, we bleed green" on it.

"Lucky pillow?" Kelsey stage whispered to me as we watched Flynn and Gryffen try to tackle Isak for that prized possession.

"Yep. Whoever has the pillow definitely has a distinct advantage over every other team."

"Huh." She blinked a few times and watched the

boys wrestle like they were four and not adults. "I don't think I've ever seen boys fight over an embroidered pillow before."

Despite Isak and Everett's best attempts, Gryff managed to wrestle the pillow away and tried tossing it over everyone's heads to Chris. Kelsey reached up and snagged it right out of the air and the room went silent in awe.

She shrugged and sat down on the couch next to Jules and shrugged. "What? I was feeling lucky."

Everett fell to his knees in front of her and clutched his chest. "I think I'm in love."

Jules smacked him with pillow but so fast that he missed when he tried to snag it from her. "You're always in love. She's taken, butt munch."

"A fact I think at least five out of eight Kingman men are heartbroken over," my dad said, and gave Kelsey a wink. "Now take a seat and let's play."

Kelsey looked up at me and grinned, her cheeks pink with a soft blush. "I like your dad."

Well, at least he didn't scare her away.

Kelsey, Jules, and Trixie huddled together, whispering their strategy. I caught Kelsey's eye, and she narrowed her eyes at me and stuck out her tongue, a clear sign she wasn't going to go easy on me. Hayes and I were definitely going to lose, mostly because I was going to be thinking about what else she could do with that tongue later.

The game kicked off with a roar of laughter and friendly banter. Every draw, skip, and reverse card was met with dramatic groans or triumphant cheers. During one particularly intense round, I played a Draw Four card on Kelsey. She feigned outrage, dramatically throwing those four cards back at me, causing the room to erupt in laughter. "Declan Kingman, how could you?"

"I never knew Kelsey was so competitive," Jules whispered to me as she watched Kelsey plot her next move with a mischievous glint in her eyes.

"Yeah, she fits right in," I replied, pride swelling in my chest.

As the night wore on, the game became more intense. At one point, Chris tried to sneak a card into the pile, but Trixie caught him and made him draw four cards while Gryff groaned.

"I demand a review of the tapes," Chris protested in jest, causing more laughter.

Kelsey was a natural. She strategized with Jules and Trixie like a seasoned pro, her laughter and excitement infectious. Watching her interact with my family, I realized how perfectly she meshed with the Kingman clan. She may have grown up as an only child, but she had no trouble diving into the chaos of my big family.

In the end, it was a close game, but Kelsey's team clinched the victory. She jumped up, high-fiving Jules and Trixie as they did a little victory dance.

"Looks like we have new Uno champions," Dad announced, clapping his hands. "Next time, boys, you'll have to step up your game."

"It was the pillow!" Everett shook his fist at the sky.

Kelsey and I were helping to clean up by putting away the cards in the cabinet where games lived in the kitchen, when her gaze fell on a framed picture on the wall. It was an old photo of my parents, young and radiant, with the unmistakable sparkle of fresh love in their eyes. Beside it, the last all-family portrait caught her attention, showing all of us kids, with baby Jules cradled in my mom's arms.

She turned to me, her eyes wide with surprise. "Declan, is your mother April De la Reine, the plus-size model?"

I nodded, a hint of pride in my voice. "Yeah, that's her. She was beautiful, wasn't she?"

Kelsey's eyes shone with a mixture of admiration and nostalgia. "I can't believe this. Your mom... she was a huge influence on me as a teenager. When I first started performing and was struggling with my own body image, I read an article interviewing her. It changed everything for me."

I leaned in, intrigued and moved by her revelation. "Really?"

She smiled, but it was tinged with a hint of sadness I fully understood. "Yeah. I was a plus-size teen in the public eye, and it was... tough. The music industry can be so fatphobic. But reading about your mom, how she embraced her body and her message of self-acceptance, it gave me the courage I needed."

Kelsey's gaze drifted back to the photos as she continued, her voice growing more passionate. "There was this one moment on *The Choicest Voice*. One of the judges suggested unless I lost weight to fit the typical beauty standards, I wouldn't make it in this business. I remember thinking of your mom and what she stood for. It gave me the strength to stand up for myself. I told the judge I wouldn't change who I was for anyone."

She laughed, but it was a laugh filled with triumph. "That moment, standing up for myself, it resonated with the audience. It was a turning point. I think it played a big part in why I won."

The realization of this connection between her and my mother was mind-blowing. I felt a sense of awe at how lives can intertwine in the most unexpected ways.

"That's incredible. My mom would be so touched to hear that. She always believed in making a difference, in paving the way for others to be themselves, unapologetically."

Kelsey's eyes met mine, and in them, I saw a reflection of the same ideals my mom had fought for. "She did make a difference, Declan. She made a difference in my life. And now, here I am, with her son. That blows my mind."

We shared a moment of silent understanding, a

recognition of the serendipitous threads that had woven our lives together. In that cabin, surrounded by the legacy of my mother's courage and Kelsey's own journey of self-acceptance, I felt an even deeper connection to her. It was as if fate had played its hand, bringing us together not just through our own choices, but through a shared history of resilience and empowerment.

She reached out and touched my hand, but then took it even further and pulled me into her arms. "I'm sorry you lost her so young."

As a family, we'd grieved hard when she died, but as an adult, I didn't talk about her that much. She'd had a profound impact on my life, and sharing her now with Kelsey, and having her understand who she was and what she meant to me, had me feeling a little more emotional than I expected. "Yeah, me too."

If I said any more than that right now, I was going to get choked up about it. Someday soon I'd like to share stories of the good times with my mom, but now, today, it was enough to know that she was someone important in both our lives.

As the night wound down and everyone started to say their goodbyes, I pulled Kelsey aside. "So, what did you think? Too much Kingman for you?"

Kelsey smiled, her eyes shining with happiness. "Are you kidding? I loved every minute of it. Your family is amazing. Way different than mine. My parents are great, but, umm, quieter. Your family really made me feel like I belong here tonight."

Hopefully she'd belong with us for a lot longer than just one night, or week, or month, or year. I wanted her here forever.

Yes. Forever felt just about right.

As Kelsey and I were about to leave, Trixie caught us at the door, her arms filled with a small stack of books. "Wait, Kelsey, I almost forgot. I brought you something."

Kelsey looked surprised as Trixie handed her the books. "What's this?"

"Romance novels," Trixie said with a big grin. "I'm an OG fan from back in your *Choicest Voice* days, and I remember how much you love them, but I saw you say somewhere recently that you never get the time to read."

Kelsey's eyes widened as she flipped through the titles, each a promise of adventure and love. "Trixie, this is so thoughtful. I can't remember the last time I had the time to just sit and lose myself in a good book."

I watched, amused and touched by how a simple gesture meant so much.

Trixie shrugged modestly. "Well, you're taking a break, right? I figured what's a break without a little romance and, you know... dragons?"

Kelsey laughed as Trixie waggled her brows and pointed to one particular book on the top of the stack called *Chase Me*, with just a man's dragon-tattooed chest on the cover. She hugged the books close. "You're absolutely right. And these look like just my kind of escape."

As we said our goodbyes, I noticed the genuine affection in Kelsey's eyes. This small gift from Trixie wasn't just about the books. It was a symbol of the time she could now afford to herself, a luxury she hadn't had in a long while.

Walking back to our cabin, Kelsey clutched the novels like treasures. "I've envied people who could just sit and read for pleasure. I'm really looking forward to this."

I took her hand in mine, feeling a sense of peace. "You deserve this time, Kelsey. Time to relax, to do things you love. I'm glad I get to be a part of it."

She leaned into me as we walked under the starlit sky, the books a reminder of the simple joys we often overlook in our busy lives. In that moment, I knew these small, quiet times were as precious as the loud, exuberant ones. And I was determined to make sure Kelsey got plenty of both.

When we got back to the cabin, I went to work lighting a fire in the little stove to keep us warm, Pooh ever present at my feet. Kelsey set the books on the small bedside table and picked up her guitar. "I'm gonna work on that song for a bit."

Uh-oh. One full day without work and she was already jonesing. I crossed the room in a half a second and had her flat on her back on the bed. "Nope. If that song has become work, sweetheart, I'm going to have to come up with something to distract you."

I grabbed the button on her jeans tugged them and her panties down while she squealed and giggled. We got her naked from the waist down before she could even protest. I knew exactly how to keep her mind off work.

BAGGWIEYPUYCOMF

KELSEY

"*I*t's not work, I swear." That was a lie. The song hadn't started off that way, but old habits die hard, and I'd admit that I was already thinking about whether "Chunky Dunkin'" could be a single on the next album. Maybe even the title song.

He ignored me and slapped one of the books into my hand. "Read your book, Kelsey."

Umm, okay, that was not what I expected when he'd taken my pants off. Naked reading was still fun, I guessed. I opened the book, mostly because he was on top of me and staring at me with a face that said he wasn't backing down. I perused the first couple of lines. It started off in the point of view of the heroine who it seemed was some kind of a wedding planner. Fun.

Although not as fun as having sex with Declan would have been. Maybe I'd read a little just to get to know the characters and then skip ahead to the sex scenes.

"Flip to the sex scene and read it to me."

Oh, I see what he was doing now. Okay, that was a new form of foreplay, but I liked the idea. I grinned at him and flipped the pages to the middle, hoping this wasn't one of those slow-burn romances. I already had bangxiety from Declan's teasing depantsing of me, and then his order that I freaking read a book.

Here was a chapter titled Mine. That looked promising. I began to read. "Ciara's whimpers went on a war path directly from Jakob's ears, down his spine and straight to his cock. Being inside of her wasn't enough. He needed to possess her, body and soul."

As I read, Declan lowered his head and kissed that sensitive spot behind my ear, then sucked my earlobe into his mouth. Gulp. It was going to be hard to concentrate on the words if he was going to keep doing that.

I blinked a few times and kept going. "The skin at her neck was the sweetest thing he'd ever tasted. Addictive. She would be covered with bruises and bite marks, all that he promised himself he would soothe, after he claimed her."

Declan took a cue from the story and pressed his

lips to my neck, right where my pulse beat under the skin. With each sentence I read, he kissed his way further down my body, and I sure wished he'd taken my shirt off too. I bet the heroine in the book was naked. Didn't that mean I should be too?

I skimmed the words on the page to see if I could find another part that I wanted him to do to me. Hell yeah, here was the perfect bit. "Jakob reached one hand between their bodies and slid his fingers into her slick folds. With each thrust into her, he stroked his fingers across her plump clit."

Declan raised his head and smiled. He slid his hand between my legs and his eyes went all dark and sparkly when he found that I was already wet for him. He slipped two fingers into me and circled my clit with his thumb, all while watching my face.

I lowered my hand to set the book down, but he stopped playing with my clit. "Read your book, Kelsey. Be a good girl while I eat your pussy until you come on my face."

I was the one whimpering now.

The next few sentences were about how the heroine was responding to the hero's touches by arching her back and crying out. I could relate, because Declan chose that exact moment to lock his lips around my clit and start sucking on it. Hard.

The words on the page blurred and I stopped reading. He stopped sucking.

Oh no. No, no. There was no way I could do this

until he made me come. But I was going to die trying. The story got even more explicit. I read each sentence very slowly, and Declan put his mouth back on my clit, using his tongue in the same way as he'd been using his thumb earlier. But he added an in and out thrusting of his fingers too.

I'm sure the spice in this story was top tier, but it was all I could do to keep saying the words out loud, much less comprehend them. If I slowed even a little bit, so did he. But I need more, and I needed it now. I took a deep breath and started speed reading.

Declan laughed with his face buried in my pussy, and I'd have to remember to try and make him laugh a lot more because it felt amazing. I turned the page and gasped, both because he did something with his tongue that took my breath away and because the chapter was almost at the end.

The words coming out of my mouth now were more like a keening moan than anything comprehensible, but I was so close, and I needed to come so badly. My legs were already trembling, and I clenched around his fingers.

Declan moved his fingers in a way that made my whole body clench and flicked his tongue over my clit again. My orgasm hit me hard, and the book went flying as I arched my back and gripped the sheets in my fists. He didn't stop, and I came so hard, I forgot how to breathe as my world exploded into darkness and light and fireworks and pleasure.

I sucked in air, gasping and moaning, whimpering and groaning. Declan finally released me and crawled back up my body, pulling me into his arms.

"Wow," I murmured against his chest, tracing the lines of his muscles with my fingertips, savoring the feel of his skin against mine. "That was…"

"Worth giving up some work for?" he offered, his voice a low rumble, vibrating through me.

"Magical." Just like looking up into his eyes, those deep blue mirrors reflecting a myriad of emotions.

He kissed the top of my head, his lips lingering as if he could imprint this moment between us forever. "I'll be sure to buy you more magical dragon books then."

As we lay there, the stars sparkling through the window, the weight of the world felt lifted. There was no scrutiny, no expectations, just Declan and me, in a space where time seemed irrelevant.

Except, in a matter of days, this would all be over, this bubble of joy and simplicity.

Declan's arms tightened around me, as if sensing the shift in my thoughts. He pulled me into his arms, tucking me under his chin. "Hey, what's going on in that beautiful head of yours?"

"Nothing," I lied, my voice muffled against his chest. "Just… feeling lucky, I guess."

"Kelsey," he whispered with a note of chastisement, his breath warm on my hair. "Talk to me."

I sighed, pulling back enough to meet his gaze. The earnestness in his eyes made my heart ache. "It's silly.

I'm just... worried about when this little break ends. When I have to go back to the real world, back to work. What if—"

"Shh." Declan cut me off with a gentle kiss, his lips pressing lightly against mine. "Don't borrow trouble from tomorrow. We're here now, together. That's all that matters."

His kiss deepened, and for a moment, I allowed myself to get lost in him, in the here and now. But I couldn't shake the thoughts and stay in the moment with him. I broke the kiss before either of us were ready, that worry gnawing at me again, a persistent whisper in my mind.

"It's been an amazing couple of days, being separated from the outside world, being part of your family tonight. But once I step back into mine..." My voice trailed off, the unsaid fears hanging there.

He cupped my face with his strong hands, his thumbs caressing my cheeks. "I know this can't last forever. I'm honestly surprised you made it two whole days. Give it just a few more. The world and the work will all still be there next week, but you'll be able to tackle it better for having given yourself some rest. We'll make it work. Together."

"Together?" I asked, needing the reassurance, craving the strength that seemed to pour from him.

"I'm not letting you go anytime soon, sweetheart. Just like the dragon said, you're mine and I'm yours. We belong to each other now." Even though he teased with the line from the book, which I hadn't really comprehended while reading, he meant it.

Was this real love? The kind I'd been searching for? I thought it was, I wanted it to be. My heart was still scared, but that worry had been too loud, and it needed to calm down.

Declan had proved himself as a better boyfriend, lover, and partner than anyone else I'd ever been with. It was about time I believed in him instead of the bums like Jake Jay who'd treated my heart like his own personal bouncy ball.

We laid there, wrapped in each other's arms, letting the silence of the night envelop us. His presence was a soothing balm to my frayed nerves. Yet, even as we clung to the present, cocooned in the serenity of the woods, the tick of an unseen clock grew louder in my ears.

"I really am lucky to have found a love like yours," I murmured against his lips.

I curled into Declan's side, my head resting on his chest. His heartbeat was steady, a comforting rhythm that promised everything would be okay. But even as I surrendered to the warmth of his embrace, I couldn't shake the sense of impending loss—that soon, the distance of our separate lives would stretch out before us like an insurmountable chasm.

"Let's just stay like this forever," I whispered, half-joking yet entirely earnest.

"Forever sounds perfect to me," Declan replied, his voice thick with emotion.

But forever was a fantasy, and reality was waiting just beyond the tree line. For now, though, I'd savor every last drop of us, storing up memories like treasures to sustain me through whatever tomorrow might bring.

What tomorrow brought us was another day of making love, eating campfire breakfast, more song ideas, more sex, and a leisurely walk with Pooh as she chased bugs and even a little bunny rabbit. When the next day was the same, and the next, I slowly felt the worries about the future slip farther away.

There really was something to this taking a break to refill the mental and physical well. I'd always thought taking a vacation like this would mean laying around doing nothing. Like, I could sit and read a book next to a pool or something for a few hours, but doing nothing at all still made me uncomfortable.

Declan had shown me that downtime didn't have to mean doing nothing. It just meant doing things for myself, taking care of myself in a way I'm not sure I ever had. My parents had been trying to get me to do this for years, and I owed my mom an apology for not believing her when she said it would do me good.

I lost all sense of time, but one morning after a some very enthusiastic sex by the lake and some more chunky dunking, Declan broke the news that we'd been here for close to a week. How could that even be?

"It's Thursday, and I've got to get to practice tomorrow, or I won't be able to play in the game on Sunday."

"I can't believe that time didn't stop just because I wanted it to," I joked, but I was having some real mixed emotions about getting back to the real world. Skeeter and Penelope were probably freaking out because they hadn't heard from me. I knew my next show was supposed to already be getting set up. I was scheduled to play some back-to-back shows in several major cities in Texas.

The crew could do the set up and prep without me, I trusted them. But it had been basically never since I hadn't been involved in all of that. It would feel very weird to just show up. And what would it mean for our brand-new relationship to be separated by our jobs already?

"I guess this is good timing, because I think I have a show in Houston on Saturday."

"I'm going to ask you something, and it's not because I doubt you or because I'm trying to be some kind of controlling dick who thinks I can just take over your life just because I'm in your bed, okay?"

Uh-oh. That sounded like he was going to ask me something I either wasn't going to like, or that I wouldn't like the answer too. But I trusted him. He was so much better to me, and for me, than anyone else in the whole world. "Okay."

"I'm asking because I love you, and I don't want to see you exhaust yourself again."

I rolled over and sat up on my knees and took his cheeks between my hands so he had to look me in the eye when I said this. "Declan, I know. I know that you need to take care of me and still you're so careful to make sure I feel like a strong, independent woman. It's a little bit of why I've fallen so hard in love with you. Ask me what you want to ask or say what you need to. I trust you because I know you're not doing anything to hurt me, only to help me. I've needed someone in my life like that for a long time, and I'm so glad that it's you."

He gave me a long, hard kiss that stole more than my breath away, it stole my heart. Then he pulled me onto his lap and wrapped his arms around me. "Are you sure you're ready to go back to work? You can take more time if you need it. Stay with me here, or rather, in Denver for a little while."

How I wanted to that. I just didn't see how to stay here with him and be on the road at the same time. Even if I flew back and forth from my concert venues and Denver every day, eventually it would be too much. "Let's check back in with the real world first and see what kind of magic Skeeter and Penelope have made happen to reschedule my tour dates without upsetting the whole world. Then we can figure out how to make the rest of our lives feel like we have this week."

"I like the rest of our lives part of that."

We spent the afternoon packing up what we needed

and closing up the cabin. This place would forever be special to my heart, no matter what came in this next chapter. Ooh. That gave me an idea for a song. Some kind of a sequel to my hit "Book Boyfriend".

We drove down the mountain, and I'd never had so much fun on a road trip. We stopped in Bear Claw Valley for gas, and I got to pick out crazy gas station snacks for the ride. Who knew Pop Rocks were still a thing? Then we listened to whatever radio station we could get to tune in since we didn't have phones to play our regular music choices. Declan sang along to every single word of so many oldies, including two of my faves, John Denver's "Rocky Mountain High", and Sir Mix-A-Lot's "Baby Got Back".

We hit a little traffic when we got into Denver, so I played with the radio stations as we sat in some bumper-to-bumper traffic right near the stadium downtown. It was good market research to find the ones that played my music, so I could also see who else was getting airtime.

I found some kind of top forties station that was playing a remix of one of my newer tracks. The song faded and the DJ came on. "That was Kelsey Best's most recent number one single, 'Blow Me Down'. You lucky ducks who were at the Aspen music festival last week are probably the last ones to ever get to hear it live now that she's cancelled her tour. We're wishing her a healthy recovery, but word on the street is that record label Big Marine is claiming breach of contract."

My mouth literally fell open and a tinny ringing whooshed through my ears. But it didn't cover the sound of the DJ continuing on. "There's still no news out of Best's camp, but in an interview with The Celeb Scoop, former boyfriend Jake Jay said quote 'I never would have told Kelsey she had to give up her career for me.' referring to the rumors that her new beau, Denver's own Declan Kingman, is bullying Best into these decisions to withdraw from public life after her health scare."

"That's fucking bullshit." Declan pulled the SUV onto the shoulder and zipped up the side of the highway until we made it to the next exit. He pulled off and pulled the car into the closest parking lot, which was a small strip mall that reminded me a lot of the one where my parents had their shop.

He screeched to a stop and threw the car into park and killed the engine, which also cut off the radio. Then he turned to me. "Kels? Are you okay? You haven't said anything. Talk to me, please."

I hadn't said anything because I was just trying not to throw up. Concerts cancelled, breach of contract, give up her career, withdraw from public life. Those phrases just swirled in my mind like a tornado. The only thing tethering me so I didn't get whipped away into the storm of what-the-fuckery was Declan.

I swallowed twice, three times, and when I was sure I wasn't going to spew all over him, I took his hand and squeezed hard. "I don't know what the hell is going on, but the one thing I do know is that you are not some bully. You're the best thing that's ever happened to me."

He let out a long, pent up breath that I think he'd been holding since we'd stopped. "Thank fuck. I know I've got a shitty reputation, but I never cared. I'm sorry it's hurting you right now."

"It's not. Jake is being the gaslighting dick very few people know he is. When this is over, I'll make sure people do know." Add another new song to my to-be-written list. "Let's ignore that part right now. I need to get a hold of Skeeter and Penelope to find out what's really happening."

The lights of a cell phone shop glowed in the parking lot in front of us. Perfect. First, new phones so we could reconnect. Then a smack in the face from the real world.

MZ. BESTIES' BESTIE POSTS

*H*ey Besties,
No, I don't know what's going on either.

I know a lot of you are feeling mad, or sad, or betrayed, or a whole lot of other unhappy emotions about the concerts being cancelled and Kelsey's radio silence about what's going on.

I have a lot of mixed emotions about it too. It's like I've lost my job.

But I have to believe in our girl. I have to believe that she's doing everything in her power to make this right for us all. She's never let us down before, and I have to believe that she isn't going to now.

Something big is definitely happening behind the scenes that we aren't privy too. I know, I know, I'm usually your source for all things Kelsey, but even my insider connections are cut off right now. No one has heard from her, and while that scares me, I one hundo believe that the King's Man is taking care of her. Don't believe any of that chatter that he's a bully and that he's making her do anything. That's just jellies looking for clout or views or clicks.

Kelsey is a strong, independent woman who knows her worth. Declan knows her worth too. I've seen it.

Be the true Besties I know you are and let's send out our love to Kelsey. I think her health scare last week really changed something big for her, and she needs our support more now than ever.

XO

Your BFF,

Mz. Besties' Bestie

KelsCrownJewel: Sending all the love to Kelsey! We trust you, Mz. Besties Bestie, to always keep us updated. Hoping Kelsey is doing okay. #WeBelieveInKelsey

MusicManiaMeg: Totally heartbroken about the concerts but health comes first. Thanks for always giving us the deets, Mz. Besties Bestie! Kelsey's happiness is all that matters.

Mz. Besties Bestie (replying to MusicManiaMeg): Absolutely, Meg! Kelsey's well-being is our number one priority. Thanks for the love and support!

DeclanDefenseSquad: Anyone who thinks Declan's a bully clearly doesn't know him. He's Kelsey's rock! #TeamDeclan

ConcernedCarol: I'm just worried about Kelsey... Declan seems nice, but he's known for being tough on the field. Hope he's gentle with our girl.

Mz. Besties Bestie (replying to ConcernedCarol): Hey, Carol, I get your concern. But rest assured, Declan's on-field persona is totally different from how he is with Kelsey. He's a total softie around her.

HarmonyHarp: Anyone else feeling anxious about this silence? Kelsey, if you're reading this, we're here for you, always!

MustangFanatic: Declan's a great guy! He wouldn't hurt a fly. Unless you're playing for the other team. Kelsey's in safe hands. #KingmanForTheWin

Mz. Besties Bestie (replying to MustangFanatic): Couldn't agree more! Declan is a gem and they're amazing together.

KingmanPrincess (replying to MustangFanatic): Couldn't agree more. For anyone who knows him, these accusations are total bullsh*t, and they're hurting his family with them too.

PopCultureQueen: Still can't believe Kelsey's tour is cancelled. Sure I can get my money back for the tix, but I prepaid for a hotel, and they are not being cool about it. Mz. Besties Bestie, keep us posted if you hear anything! You're our lifeline!

SkepticalSam: Not sure what to think anymore... I

agree about so many of the posts floating around being for clout. Just hope Kelsey knows we're all rooting for her!

Mz. Besties Bestie (replying to SkepticalSam): That's the spirit, Sam! Let's keep the positive vibes flowing for Kelsey. She needs us now more than ever.

THE REAL DEAL

DECLAN

*W*e pulled into the driveway of my house, and I felt a mixture of relief and apprehension. The familiar surroundings were a welcome sight, but I knew the real world was about to come crashing back into our lives. Pooh bounded out of the car, sniffing around the lawn with the enthusiasm of a pup on new turf.

Kelsey followed suit, stepping out and gazing around. "This feels so... normal. Not exactly where I thought a star football player would live."

I placed a reassuring hand on her shoulder. "Everything we need is right here. My family are all in those houses, Trixie too, and they'll all be here in a flash if we need them."

I pointed to the houses on either side of mine, and the two across the street. Everyone's lights were on, and I was tempted to call them all over now just so Kelsey knew we had her back.

"Wait, all of them?" She glanced at the houses surrounding us and she made a face of surprise. "Your whole family lives in the same neighborhood?"

"Yep. That's Chris's doing. He uses his money to invest in real estate. Owns most of the neighborhood. Including all of our houses. Except Everett's, who won his in a bet." That was a story for another time.

"That's so... Kingman of you. I kind of love it." She almost smiled. Almost.

Thank goodness she was here with me and not in some isolated apartment in New York or L.A. where she probably didn't even know her neighbors. This was the time to circle the wagons and rally the troops.

We went inside and I set our bags at the foot of the steps to the upstairs. I'd take them up later when we went to bed. I already was itching to hold her and love on her, help her forget what was happening. But there was no escaping this bullshit yet.

"I really don't like that I still haven't heard from Penelope. Her messages aren't even showing as read or anything." She glanced down at her new iPhone. After the woman at the store had gotten over the initial shock that Kelsey Best really was standing in her shop trying to replace a, uh, lost phone, she'd been able to set us both up and port our contacts and apps from the cloud. "It worries me more than Skeeter telling me she needed to get to her office and call me from there."

Just then, her phone rang, the sharp buzzing slicing through the quiet inside my kitchen. She answered, putting it on speaker. "Hello?"

Skeeter's voice, sharp and reprimanding, filled the room. "Kelsey, where have you been? You can't just disappear for almost a week with no contact. We're in a huge mess because of your utter disappearance from the world."

I watched Kelsey's shoulders slump under the verbal onslaught. It pained me to see her like this, so strong, yet so vulnerable. And I wasn't going to stand for it.

"Kelsey needed time to recover," I interjected, unable to hold back. "You should've been able to manage whatever was going on. Everyone would understand her not being available because of medical reasons."

It took all I had in me to keep the twelve instances of the adjective fucking out of my warning to Skeeter. I hadn't liked this woman from the beginning, but I wasn't the one who had to deal with her, so I'd done my best to ignore her. But nobody berated my girl. Nobody.

I could practically hear Skeeter bristling at my words. "And who are you to—wait, am I on speaker? Kelsey, you're letting him be part of this conversation?"

Kelsey straightened up, her voice firmer now. "Yes,

Skeeter, Declan is a crucial part of my life now. I'm comfortable having him involved because he genuinely cares about my wellbeing."

The tension in the room was palpable. Skeeter's silence spoke volumes, and I could almost feel the shift in power dynamics happening over the phone line.

Kelsey continued, her newfound strength evident in her tone. "Declan wants to protect me and my interests, Skeeter. It's something I'm starting to question whether you truly have at heart."

I squeezed her hand, a silent message of support and solidarity. The look she gave me was one of gratitude mixed with determination. It was clear that Kelsey was taking control of her life, her career, and who she trusted.

Skeeter huffed, the sound one of frustration and resignation. "I am acting in your best interest, but you're making it very hard."

"How about you tell me what's going on?"

"Fine." Skeeter's voice was grating and grave. "Big Marine has decided that you've breached your contract. They're citing that you cancelled shows without their permission, add that to being past due on the date for your next album, and they're done. I told you they were pissed, but you didn't listen. You had to go to a football game."

An icy dread seeped into my psyche. She was trying to blame this on me. Kelsey was going to need another new phone because I was about to smash this one.

Except she looked like she was on the verge of fainting again. She'd gone pale and her pupils were like little pinpricks. "What does this mean for the tour and my contract with them?"

"They're pulling the plug, Kelsey. The rest of the tour's canceled and so is your next album. You're done."

"But I thought they understood I needed more time to work on the songs for the next album." Her voice was barely a whisper. "And the shows were sold out arenas. I was going to do them. I was going to leave for Texas tomorrow morning."

She looked at me, and my heart sank clear through my stomach, dropped down to the floor, and rolled away. This was my fault. I was the one who'd made her take the week off. I'd thrown our phones in the lake and insisted we ignore the world for a few days. But what really hurt me was not how much I'd fucked up her career. It was the tears threatening to overwhelm her.

"It's too late. Maybe if I'd been able to get a hold of you a few days ago, but now? We're all screwed."

The call ended, leaving us in a heavy silence. Kelsey exhaled deeply, the burden of what had just happened still lingering in the air.

After Skeeter's call, a heavy cloud seemed to hang over us. Kelsey, with tears threatening to spill over, nodded at my suggestion to call it a night. The weight of the day's revelations was too much, and we needed some respite, however brief.

Pooh, sensing the somber mood, whined until I picked her up as we made our way upstairs. I could tell Kelsey was lost in her thoughts, her shoulders slumped, a stark contrast to the vibrant woman I knew. I hated seeing her like this, but I had to respect her need to process everything in her own time.

We went to bed in silence, the usual comfort of being in each other's arms overshadowed by the day's events. I held her close, hoping to offer some solace through my presence, but the tension in her body was palpable. I stroked her hair until she fell asleep, but she slept fitfully and shallow.

The morning sun brought no relief. We woke to the sound of my family congregated downstairs, their voices a cacophony of concern and confusion.

"Looks like we've got company," I muttered, rubbing the sleep from my eyes.

Kelsey groaned softly, burying her face in the pillow. "I'm not ready for this."

I kissed the top of her head. "I know, but we can't hide up here forever. Let's face this together."

Hand in hand, with Pooh trotting along behind us, we descended the stairs to find my entire family in my living room. Dad, all my brothers, Jules, and Trixie, their expressions a mix of worry and support.

"What's going on?" I asked, bracing myself for more unwelcome news. The entire family only showed up if we were celebrating or something bad had happened.

Otherwise, we were just in and out and around each other's lives like normal.

Dad stepped forward, his face serious. "Tell us straight, right here, right now. Is this relationship fake?"

Oh shit. Pooh growled at him, but he just scooped the little dog up and held her like a baby, giving her belly scratches. If this wasn't such a serious question I had to answer, I'd be worried I'd just been usurped as Wiener the Pooh's favorite Kingman. "No, Dad."

But at the same time as I said that, Kelsey blurted out, "It started out that way, but it isn't now."

Every eye in the room flicked back and forth between the two of us. Then the room erupted with everyone asking a different question. My dad whistled and everyone shut up. Then he raised one eyebrow and said, "Explain."

Jules tossed her phone to me. She was the only one who knew about the NDA. Her screen showed a page with a big headline in red that said "Romance or Showmance? An insider in Kelsey Best's camp reveals an agreement between the couple to engage in a fake relationship!"

Kelsey looked at the phone and then up at me. "I think we'd better come clean."

I shook my head. "No, you're the one I need to come clean with Kels."

"What?" She took the tiniest step back. Fuck. First, I fucked up her career, and now I was about to fuck up our relationship. In front of my entire family. I was ready to beat myself up just like I did when I screwed up playing ball or didn't get a shoe sponsorship, but this wasn't a game or any other kind of competition. And it was time to step up.

Because that's what Kingmans did.

"I never signed that agreement. I never even read it. My agent told me your people wanted to do that whole showmance thing, have us go out on a few dates or whatever, to get the press off your back about your ex, or whatever, but I never agreed to it, Kelsey."

"But then, how, why did you come to the concert, and then to Aspen, and all the other appearances we made?" She frowned and got a little wrinkle in the middle of her brows. "I don't understand."

But what killed me is the way she wrapped her arms around herself, shielding herself from what she thought was coming, that our relationship was a lie. She was protecting herself from my dumb-fuckery. I should be the one to protect her from the rest of the world. She shook her head and took another step away.

Double fuck. I gave her that space even though all I wanted to do was throw her over my shoulder and drag her away from all of this. I had to pray that my words would be enough, which I wasn't even close to sure about, because what I knew how to do best was use my body to make my way in the world.

I took a deep breath and spilled out the truth. "I took advantage of the fact that you gave me those tickets to get to talk to you again. I know you only called me because you thought I'd agreed to the fake relationship thing, and I thought if I showed you that I was falling for you for real that it wouldn't matter. I should have told you right from the beginning, and I fucked up, and—"

Kelsey put her finger on my mouth to shut up my blathering. "What do you mean 'for real'? That first kiss at my hotel? The trips up to Aspen to hang out with me, the... everything?"

I pulled her hand from my mouth and kissed the inside of her wrist. "It was all very real. I think I fell in love with you the first moment I saw you."

I was about to make a huge fool out of myself, and I didn't care. I'd held this all in for too long and now was not the time to let her have any doubts about how I felt about her. "I'm sure there are a million other men and probably a lot of women, and non-binary folks too, that feel the same, because frankly, you're spectacular and how could everyone not be in love with you?"

Kelsey shook her head and looked down at the floor, but she knew what I was saying was true, she was just too sweet and humble to acknowledge it. "But you've let me see the real you, and I don't just love the pop star part of you that you put out there for the whole world. I love the way your hair is always in your eyes so I get to brush it away from your face, and the way you love your dog, and the deep sense of responsibility you have to your fans to be authentic for them, and the way you want to conquer the world, but with joy and kindness. That's what I fell in love with, Kelsey."

One of my brothers, probably one of the twins, whispered loud enough for everyone to hear, "Is he proposing?"

Jules replied, "Shut up, you're going to ruin it."

Kelsey's eyes went wide, and I brushed the hair out of them and behind her ear. "Make no mistake, I would love to spend the rest of my life with you and have every intention of making that happen, but I'm not asking you to marry me right now. I just wanted you to know before we go out there to fight these dragons that I love you, and always have, so you don't have any doubts that I am here for you through this. Okay?"

She stood there, absorbing the words I'd just poured out of my soul. Her expressions moved through shock, vulnerability, and a dawning realization. If she wanted, she could break up with me. I would have to accept her decision. But it would kill me.

For a long moment, she didn't speak, and I wasn't the only one in the room holding my breath.

Finally, she took a step closer to me and my stomach did a touchdown dance to rival Everett and Hayes. But my brain said there was a flag on the play.

Her eyes searched mine, and with everything in me, I hoped she saw the sincerity in all I said there.

"You had a million chances to tell me the truth, Declan," she said, her voice laced with a mix of hurt and understanding. "But you know what? I'm glad you didn't."

Umm. What?

She reached up, touching my face gently. "I don't think I would have let you in without that safety net. I was scared. Scared of getting hurt, scared of falling for someone again when I'd had my heart broken so many times. I let you in because I thought what we were doing was for show until life, the universe, and everything else forced me to admit that I was falling for you too."

I cupped my hand over hers and fuck if I didn't have to blink back some tears I couldn't keep in. I was definitely about to blow my mean, tough-guy image by crying in front of everyone most important to me.

"But you..." Her voice cracked, but she steadied it with a deep breath. "You're the most real person I've ever known. How can I not love you?"

Those tears spilled over, and I wasn't for one second ashamed of showing her the emotions that were quite literally pouring out of me. She believed what we had was real.

She wiped a tear that had slipped out with her thumb, and then pulled me down for a kiss. A kiss that refilled my soul.

I didn't know if everything was going to be alright, because it sure sounded like she was getting fucked by her record label. But if she and I were solid, nothing else mattered.

KING AND QUEEN OF THE BESTIES

KELSEY

I was well known to be a bit of a crier. I'd cried on stage when I got really emotional about the way a song made me feel or how the fans responded to something. I cried at movies and great TV shows, and I definitely cried reading books. But nothing tugged at my heart strings more than seeing a grown man show his true emotions and fight back tears.

It was a miracle I wasn't bawling my eyes out right now. But somewhere deep inside, my soul was satisfied to let him shed the tears for both of us. I wiped away Declan's tear and pressed my lips to his. We were in love for real and no one could take that away from us.

A sense of clarity washed over me. The raw honesty in his eyes, the vulnerability of his confession, resonated within me, igniting a fire I hadn't realized was smoldering. His love, so genuine and profound, gave me the courage I needed to face every challenge being thrown at me.

Pulling back, I gazed into his eyes, a mix of emotions swirling inside me. "I love you, and I'm incredibly grateful that I've got you on my side, because I don't think I can face everything I have coming at me on my own."

"I'm so ready to tackle this head-on with you," Declan said, then he winked. "I've got you, Bestie."

That made me smile, and I needed that right now.

Declan turned to his family. "I'm sure everyone else here does too. What do you want us to do, Kels?"

I looked at the enormous family I somehow found myself a part of, and it filled me with joy. "I have to find out what's happening with Big Marine and this supposed breach first. Get some answers. But I'd really love some breakfast, and Pooh needs a walk, and I need a space to sit and make calls."

Mr. Kingman swirled his finger in the air. "You heard the lady. I'm on doggie duty, boys, hit the kitchen, and Jules, go to school."

Jules fake coughed into her hand. "Hech, ech. I'm sick. Can't go today."

Mr. Kingman gave her the evil eye, and I remembered seeing my own dad give me a similar look when I tried to get out of school for an audition or concert. "Good try."

"Mental health day," she countered. "I haven't taken one yet this year."

That was apparently the trump card, because while he scowled, he gave her the head nod of approval.

"Yes." She looked over at me. Declan's den is the perfect place to set up shop. He never uses it, but it's got the best Wi-Fi in the house, and it's quiet."

Declan looked at her sideways. "How do you know that?"

Jules shrugged but motioned for us to follow her down the hall. She was right. It was perfect. There was a desk, but also two easy chairs, and the walls were decorated with his awards, along with a bookshelf. I was sure I spied a first edition *Winnie the Pooh* on there. I'd explore all of that later.

I reached for my phone. "It's time to call Skeeter and figure out where we stand. And then, we need to plan our next move."

I clicked on her number, surprised she hadn't already called me this morning. This time, weirdly, I was sent to voicemail after one ring. Frowning, I dialed Penelope, but it was like her phone had been disconnected. I hadn't even seen her active on social media for days. Something was off, and it was gnawing at me.

"I've relied entirely on Skeeter and Pen for almost

all of my communications for so long that I don't even know how to get a hold of anyone at Big Marine. I suppose I could just Google their number?"

I did and found a general number that got me to some kind of switchboard or receptionist or something. A woman answered with a generic greeting.

"Hi, this is Kelsey Best, I need to—"

"Ms. Best. I've been instructed to tell you that all further communication with Big Marine needs to go through your lawyer."

"My lawyer?" I swallowed down something awful tasting.

"Yes. Thank you." The line went dead. She hung up on me. What the hell?

Jules, flipping through her phone, chimed in, "There's a statement online from Big Marine. They're saying they've parted ways with you, claiming you've become volatile and unpredictable. They're accusing you of negotiating for more money while not fulfilling your obligations."

Her words hit me like a ton of bricks. Me, volatile? Asking for more money? That was the last thing on my mind. I felt Declan's hand squeeze mine, a silent gesture of support amidst the chaos.

"Could it be something Skeeter's done behind your back? I have never trusted her," Declan questioned, his brow furrowed.

I paused, thinking back on Skeeter's increasing

pressure during the tour. "I know I have a lawyer, but again, Skeeter always handles all of that for me. I need to talk to my dad. He handles my money, so maybe he knows something."

Without concrete information, I felt utterly stuck. Lost in a sea of confusion and betrayal with no land in sight. I called my dad but got his voicemail. I'd have to call the shop.

My mom answered on the first ring just like she always did. "Best Christmas Ever, this is Marilyn, how can I help you?"

"Hi, Mom."

"Kelsey, how nice to hear from you. How are you, sweetheart?"

Declan gave me a funny look. I'd have to explain later how my mom refused to treat me other than just an ordinary girl, including completely ignoring any sort of news, social media, or any other information about the pop star I was.

"I'm okay, but I need to ask dad something, is he around?"

"Sorry, sweetie, he's golfing. When are you coming home for a visit?"

Declan reached over and pushed the mute button. "Your parents are in the San Diego area? Our game is there on Sunday. Tell her you can come for a visit in a few days. I'd love to meet them, if that's okay?"

I guess since I wasn't going to Texas for a concert, I

could go to his game, and he could meet my parents too. I'd never brought any of my other famous boyfriends home to them. It just hadn't ever felt right, especially with the way my mother pretended fame didn't exist. Except, of course, for the celebrity of jolly old St. Nick.

I unmuted and gave her the good news. "I was thinking this weekend actually. I have someone I want you to meet. Could we do dinner on Sunday?"

"Oh, yes, lovely. I'll tell your dad. Does your someone for us to meet like roast chicken dinner? Ooh, I'll make a pie."

"That sounds great. Ask dad to call me as soon as he can though, okay? It's important."

"Yes, of course. Just as soon as he gets home. Oh, gotta go, customers. Love you, sweetheart. Bu-bye."

I hung up and Declan blinked at me like I'd grown three heads. "Your parents have a store called Best Christmas Ever and didn't care that you were in the hospital or that your concerts are cancelled?"

"My people are on strict orders not to let my mom know anything unless it's a real emergency. It's just too stressful for her. She's a good mom, but all of this, well, it's not for her."

It was clear that the concept of a family member not being all up in your business was a very foreign concept to him. We'd both need a little getting used to for each other's families. Even thinking about a future where we get to combine his family and mine gave me warm and fuzzies.

Yes, I was thinking about a happy ever after with him.

Trixie walked into the office with a laptop and suggested a bold move. "How would you feel about a press conference? Lay it all out in the open. It worked for Chris and me."

Declan made a face, and I knew there was a story there.

Jules proposed a more modern approach. "I think you should take to social media. Let your fans hear it from you."

"Penelope usually takes care of that kind of stuff. I honestly don't even know my own logins." I sure thought I was in charge of all of my business, but the past two days was showing me what a joke that was. I'd been relying on others for years, thinking I was always on my own. "I'm really worried that I can't get a hold of Pen."

A parade of Kingman men streamed into the office with plates loaded with scrambled eggs, toast, tomato slices, avocado, a whole pot of coffee and two full pitchers of some kind of pink smoothie. These guys knew how to cook and feast. Declan served me and poured me a cup of coffee and it was the cutest thing I'd ever seen that everyone waited for him to do that. Especially since the second he was done, they pounced on the rest like they were starved hyenas.

Hayes chugged a smoothie and then said, "Jules says you can't get on your socials, but we can use our accounts to get you online. Maybe Penelope will see it and reach out. We can stream it from our gaming studio setup at my house."

Flynn and Gryffen high fived. "Remember how the internet broke when Declan joined on our stream? We'll get you a massive audience on the Tube."

Everett added, "I'll live stream it on FlipFlop. I've got a few million followers, and to be honest, it's mostly women, and they love you. They'll tune in for sure."

Isak held up his phone. "I got you on InstaSnap. The more channels you go live on, the better."

"And I can stream it on the Besties' Bestie Face-Space group," Jules offered, her fingers already dancing over her phone. "I'm a mod."

Mr. Kingman, still cuddling Pooh, gave her a stern look. "You're not supposed to be on social media."

She shrugged. "I tried, but the whole world is online. I'm careful, super incognito. No pics, no personal details."

"We will talk about that later." He gave her a look that would have withered a normal human. Not Jules. She had every man in this family wrapped around her little finger. "Right now, let's use your super-secret, sneaky spy knowledge to help Kelsey."

Declan looked overwhelmed but resolute. "I've

never been a friend to the media, but for you, Kels, I'll do anything. Say anything you need me to."

Their suggestions swirled around me, a lifeline in the storm. My heart swelled with gratitude and determination. I had a voice, and it was time to use it for myself. It was time to walk tall.

"Okay," I said, my voice steady. "Let's do this. Let's tell the world my side of the story."

Yes, I was facing a career crisis, but I wasn't alone. Declan and his family were with me, ready to help in any way they could.

"We need to get the truth out there," I declared, feeling the weight of the situation but also a sense of empowerment. "Before any more rumors and lies take hold."

Declan nodded, his expression serious yet supportive. "Whatever you need, Kelsey. I'm here for you."

I took a deep breath, gathering my thoughts. "First, I need to clear the air about the contract situation with Big Marine. It's important for my fans to know I didn't abandon them."

Trixie, who had been quietly observing, spoke up. "You should also address the stuff about the relationship being fake. Show them the truth. With you both on camera, it will be obvious."

I nodded, appreciating her insight. "Yes, and I need to let everyone know I'm safe and recovering. That my health scare was real, not some publicity stunt to hide away from some kind of drama with the label."

The Kingman men, now finished with their breakfast feast, gathered around, each one offering their support in their own way. It was heartwarming to see such a tight-knit family rally around someone they barely knew. Oh, song idea. I made a quick note in my phone about it.

I didn't even think about the fact that I didn't have a label and had no idea if I was ever going to get to produce another record in my life. It didn't matter. Music was still deeply rooted in me, and I'd never let it go, even if I couldn't make my living from it anymore.

Declan squeezed my hand. "It would help me if we could draft up some talking points. I'm not natural in front of the camera unless I'm allowed to just glare at it."

I smiled at his honest request. "That sounds like a plan."

The rest of the morning was a whirlwind of activity. Declan and I, with the help of his family, crafted a statement that addressed everything from my health to the contract breach and the true nature of our relationship. It was honest, heartfelt, and transparent. Everything I stood for as an artist and a human.

We moved over to Hayes's house, and geez, these guys could be on my roadie crew, or even on the stage. Their set up was pro. It took them a few minutes to get everything ready to stream. I had so much experience being in front of a camera, but as the time approached to go live, my nerves kicked in. Declan wrapped his arms around me. "You've got this, Kels. Just speak from the heart."

I nodded, taking strength from his embrace. As the lights went on and streams went live, I took a deep breath and began to speak. My voice was steady, my message clear. I spoke of my gratitude for my fans, my commitment to my music, and the truth about my relationship with Declan.

The response was immediate and overwhelming. Messages of support flooded in, fans rallying behind me, expressing their relief and admiration. It was a reminder of the power of honesty and the bond I shared with those who believed in me.

There were some people who were unhappy, a fair number of trolls, and that was expected. But overwhelmingly, the people who I wanted this message to reach, namely my fans, were understanding and supportive. I expected there would be some backlash afterwards, but I said what I needed to and showed the world my truth.

And so did Declan. Near the end of what I'd prepared, he pulled me into his arms and gave me a soft kiss in front of the millions of people watching. His presence sitting beside me had been a silent show of solidarity. But this spontaneous public display of affection got me right in the feels.

After, he looked straight into the camera and said, "We're in this together, but don't doubt the power Kelsey wields all on her own. Mess with Kelsey, and the

Besties will have her back, and I'm King of the Besties, baby."

He was better on camera than he thought he was. Hearts were breaking all over the world tonight because he was mine and everyone knew it.

WHEN SANTA MET FROSTY

DECLAN

*T*he stadium was a cacophony of noise, the competition intense, and both the players and our fans emotions riding high with each play. The Denver Mustangs and the San Diego Thunder were longtime rivals, and today we were locked in a fierce battle.

The score was tied fourteen all with less than two minutes left in the game. Tensions were skyrocketing, and I was fucking living for it. The anticipation, the collective breath of the crowd held in suspense, the hot tempers of exhausted players on both sides puffing into the air just waiting to explode. This was it, this moment that could make or break the game.

I was on the field, muscles tense, every sense

heightened and ready for this one play. The safety snapped the ball and the Thunder's quarterback, a known sharpshooter, dropped back into the pocket, scanned the field, and hesitated just a millisecond too long. I almost always went in for a sack, but I read the play, watching him lock onto his receiver, and I was in exactly the right position.

The ball soared through the air, a perfect spiral, aimed at the Thunder's wide receiver. It was now or never. I lunged forward, intercepting the pass with a leap that felt like flying, and still somehow landed on my feet. The stadium erupted in a roar as I landed, the ball securely in my hands.

Holy shit. I had the ball, and the play was still live.

Adrenaline pumped through my veins, and I charged forward. Offensive linemen from the Thunder tried to tackle me, but I was a force unstoppable. One by one, I knocked them down, a juggernaut on the field, driven by a singular goal. The endzone.

The crowd's cheers fueled me, and I almost felt like I could hear Kelsey yelling, "Run, Declan, run!"

Each step pounded over the turf, bringing me closer to victory. The endzone was just a few more yards away and there wasn't anyone standing between me and those six points.

With a final push, I crossed the line, securing the touchdown. The Mustangs had taken the lead, and the visitors in the stadium went into a frenzy of euphoria. I could hardly believe it. I hadn't scored a touchdown since fucking pee wee. This was my first score in the pros.

I looked up at the big screen, and, of course, the stadium cameras were on her. She was jumping up and down screaming and pounding the window of the box. That was my girl.

With the football in my hand, I pointed up at the box for a full ten seconds until the rest of my team caught up with me, their faces alight with excitement and disbelief. They joined me in pointing up to Kelsey, acknowledging that she was our brand new good-luck charm. The cameras panned back to us on the field, and in a moment of uncharacteristic flair, I launched into a dance, mimicking one of Kelsey's iconic concert numbers.

The crowd went wild, cheering and laughing as I embraced the ridiculousness of the moment. It was a celebration of not just the score, but of something more, a tribute to the woman who had captured my heart, a playful acknowledgment of our journey together. Any troll who still thought this was fake could suck on this.

As I jogged back to the sidelines, my teammates clapped me on the back, their laughter mingling with the still thunderous applause from the stands. Chris, Everett, and Hayes just about tackled me when I got to the sidelines. Hayes literally jumped up on me and like a little kid climbing a tree, holding his hand in the air, with a number one finger pointed to the sky, stirring the crowd up even more.

After the game, the atmosphere was electric with excitement. Kelsey and I, still buzzing from the win and my unexpected touchdown dance, were making our way through the throng of fans and press towards our car. We had plans for that dinner with her parents, a meeting I was both nervous and excited about.

Pooh was trotting happily beside us, soaking in the excitement and getting just as many people taking her picture as me and Kelsey. Suddenly, her ears perked up, and she let out a series of excited barks. Before we could react, she wriggled free from her leash and darted into the crowd.

"Pooh!" Kelsey called out, worry etching her face. She moved to chase after but there were too many people surrounding us, and I waved the security detail over. They were on it right away and dove into the crowd on the other side of the barrier to try and find the dog. Enough of the people there were either pet owners themselves and recognized a freaked out owner, or they were Kelsey's fans, because the sea of people parted as we watched Pooh weaving through their legs. She knew exactly where she was going and made a beeline towards a familiar figure.

"Is that... Penelope?" The woman was squatting, and Pooh jumped right into her arms.

Kelsey grabbed my arm. "Oh my god, it is." She waved and yelled out her assistant's name.

Security swiftly retrieved both Pooh and Penelope, bringing them over to us. Kelsey immediately enveloped Penelope and Pooh in a tight hug, relief and happiness squealing out in her voice. "Pen, I've been so worried about you."

Penelope, looking equally relieved and a bit over-whelmed, hugged her back. "Kelsey, I saw your livestream, and I had to come in person. Skeeter, she... she fired me, told me it was what you wanted."

Kelsey pulled back, shock written all over her face. "Fired you? But why? I never said anything like that. You're my rock, my life's blood. I've been lost without you."

Penelope's eyes were filled with a mixture of hurt and determination. "She took my phone, my tablet... everything. Said I was too close to you, that it was clouding my judgment, and I was probably the reason you'd worked yourself so hard that you almost died."

I could see the pieces falling into place in Kelsey's mind, the betrayal and manipulation becoming more apparent. She pulled Penelope in for another hug. "Never. That's all a pack of lies."

I looked around, not liking that there were so many eyes and ears on us, and I ushered the ladies toward the car. When we got inside with the doors closed, Kelsey whispered, a hint of anger lacing her voice, "What else has she done?"

I put my arm around Kelsey, feeling a protective rage boiling inside me against Skeeter. This was more than just a simple misunderstanding or mismanagement. It was sabotage.

Penelope looked down, then met Kelsey's eyes. "I don't know. But I've figured out she's been making deals and promises on your behalf, things you'd never agree to."

"We're going to get to the bottom of this," I assured them both, resolve hardening within me.

"But first, you're coming to dinner with us, Pen." Kelsey took both of Pen's hands in hers. "You're basically a part of my family, so it's about time you actually met my parents."

Penelope's eyes misted over, and she gave a small, grateful nod. "What? Are you sure? Your mom won't freak out?"

Kelsey shrugged and smiled, and I could see how much relief having Penelope back in her life was to her. "I'm just bringing home some friends for dinner. She'll love you."

"Wow, I don't know what to say. Thank you, Kelsey. That means the world to me." Pooh happily settled in Penelope's lap. Clearly, she'd missed her too.

Dinner with Kelsey's parents was going to be more than just a meet and greet now. It was going to be a gathering of allies.

Stepping into Kelsey's parents' home was like walking into a perpetual Christmas wonderland. The walls were decked with holly, twinkling lights adorned every surface, and a gentle chorus of carols played softly in the background. Marilyn, Kelsey's mom, was the epitome of holiday cheer, and I swear she was a slightly younger version of Mrs. Claus, with blonde hair instead of white. But her eyes twinkled as brightly as the decorations surrounding us, and she even had rosy, red cheeks and smelled like hot chocolate and cookies.

"Welcome, welcome," she greeted us, enveloping Kelsey in a warm embrace and giving Pooh a good scratch on the head. Then she turned to me with an outstretched hand. "You must be Declan. We've heard absolutely nothing about you, but my husband says you come from good people."

I shook her hand, a little overwhelmed by the festive atmosphere and feeling like I'd just been transported to the North Pole. "It's great to meet you, Mrs. Best."

"Oh, please, call me Marilyn." She beamed like she'd just won a lifetime supply of candy canes. "And this is the infamous Penelope. Come here, sweetheart."

Pen's eyes went wide as Mrs. Best enveloped her into a huge hug and gave her a little squeeze, rocking back and forth.

As if all of this was normal and every day, she led us into the dining room where a feast awaited us. The table was a vision of yuletide splendor, complete with a centerpiece of pinecones and red berries. In October.

I leaned over and whispered in Kelsey's ear. "I think

I see where you get your ability to put on a spectacular show."

"You have no idea. My first performances were all Christmas carols." She gave me a smile but made those big eyes like she knew how strange this all must be. "And now you know why my second album was a holiday one."

It was adorable to me, and growing up like this must have absolutely given Kelsey her joyful outlook on life.

A tall man stood at the head of the table. He was built like a linebacker, and I saw where Kelsey got her height and her eyes. I put out my hand and shook his. "Mr. Best, nice to meet you."

"Xavier, but you can call me Zav, Declan. Good game today."

"You watched, sir?" Kelsey hadn't mentioned her father was a fan. I'd have brought him a jersey or a hat or something.

"I'm a long time Thunder fan." Uh-oh. "Played a little ball in college myself. I'd be mad at you if that hadn't been one of the greatest interceptions I've ever seen."

Yikes. "It was pretty fun to run that ball in. Sorry it lost you the game."

"No you're not." He smiled at me and those eggshells I'd been prepared to walk on disappeared.

"No, sir, I'm not."

Dinner was quite the affair, filled with laughter and

light-hearted conversation. There was enough food to feed an army, and her mom even prepared a special doggie bowl for Pooh. Kelsey's dad was smart as a whip, and I could see why Kelsey had entrusted her money management to him.

As Marilyn excused herself to get the pie, she motioned for Kelsey and Penelope to join her in the kitchen. "Girl talk," she said with a wink. It was obvious she wanted the lowdown on our relationship.

Left alone with Zav, I took a deep breath, bracing myself for the inevitable fatherly interrogation.

"So, Declan," Zav began, his tone casual but his gaze piercing. "What are your intentions with my daughter?"

Yep, there it was. There was something comforting in knowing that huge mega-star Kelsey came from such a normal... okay, slightly weird, but normal family. I met his gaze squarely, my answer ready and sincere. "I intend to love her, sir. For the rest of our lives."

Zav studied me for a long moment, then nodded slowly, a smile breaking across his face. "That's what I wanted to hear. She's a special girl, our Kelsey. Deserves someone who sees that. Not like that Jake boy she was seeing. He was all about his ego and couldn't accept that my girl was a bigger star than he was. How are you going to be at dealing with her fame, son? She's only going to become a bigger and brighter star in the future. Could probably buy your whole team if she wanted to."

"My ego isn't fragile," I assured him. "And neither is my love for her."

Zav clapped me on the shoulder. "Glad to hear it. You're a good man, Declan. I can tell."

The moment was interrupted by the return of the ladies, Marilyn carrying a pie that smelled like heaven. Kelsey stood in the doorway smiling, and I was guessing she'd overheard the end of that conversation. But she already knew exactly how I felt about her.

The rest of the evening passed in a blur of warmth and familial bonding, leaving me feeling more connected to Kelsey than ever. Her family might be small and quirky, but I saw so much of her in them, and it made me happy that I'd gotten to see yet another layer of her.

Following dinner, after we helped with the dishes, Kelsey's dad gestured discreetly to the two of us to follow him. It was time to talk business.

"Hey, Pen, why don't you show my mom that video of my favorite Christmas song." Kelsey handed Penelope her phone. "I don't think she's heard it yet."

Mrs. Best smiled like it was... well, Christmas morning. "Oh, sweetie, did you write a Christmas song? If I'd known, I would have been playing it in the shop."

Penelope nodded at Kelsey, totally understanding the assignment. "Oh, you're going to love it Mrs. Best. It's called 'When Santa met Frosty.'"

Penelope dragged Pooh and Marilyn to the living

room, engaging her with videos of Kelsey's Christmas performances, leaving us free to accompany Xavier to his den.

The den was a contrast to the rest of the house, more subdued, lined with bookshelves and the air heavy with the scent of aged paper and leather instead of Christmas lights and holiday spice. A large desk sat in the center, flanked by plush chairs. Xavier motioned for us to sit.

As we settled, Kelsey leaned forward, her hands clasped tightly. "Dad, Big Marine canceled my contract and the rest of the tour. I'm... I'm scared this might be the end of my career."

Xavier's expression was unreadable for a moment, and then a small smile played at the corners of his lips. He leaned back in his chair, folding his hands in front of him. "Kelsey, my dear, sometimes what seems like an ending is just the beginning."

Kelsey and I exchanged glances, a mix of confusion and curiosity mirrored in our expressions. Xavier's eyes twinkled with a hint of mystery, a man holding a secret just waiting to be revealed.

"I talked to Chet a couple of months ago, we played golf." His voice was steady yet filled with an undertone of excitement. He looked over at me. "He's the founder of Big Marine."

Whoa. That was an interesting development I didn't see coming. Kelsey's breath hitched, and I could feel the tension in the room thicken with anticipation. Xavier's next words promised to unravel the uncertainty that had been looming over us, potentially altering the trajectory of Kelsey's career.

"Seems they've been having some cash flow problems, and me being a money manager, he wanted to see if I knew of any way that they might get flush again."

"Dad, what are you saying?" Kelsey leaned in closer and folded her hands on her dad's desk. "Does this have something to do with why my contract with them was cancelled?"

"No." He shook his head and frowned. "He didn't mention anything about that. Their announcement the other day surprised me just as much as I think it did you. I put in a call to him, but it's the weekend, and for being a music guy, he sure does like to keep banker's hours."

"So what was your meeting with him about?" I think Kelsey was about to crawl across the desk and shake her dad if he didn't reveal his insider information in the next ten seconds.

He leaned back in his chair and folded his hands behind his head as if lounging. "You know, a lot of deals are made on the golf course."

"Dad, you're killing me here." Kelsey threw her hands up in the air.

"I take it back," I stage whispered to her. "You get your showmanship from your dad. For sure."

He winked at me. Good news was coming, I could feel it, and I already felt better. Whatever he was about to tell her was good. Really good. But if it wasn't about her contract, I didn't have a clue what he was going to say.

"Well, let's just say I helped Chet with their little cash flow problem to the tune of about three-hundred and thirty million dollars. Or rather, you did."

Holy shit. I knew Kelsey was a gazillionaire, but to just lend some music company founder that kind of money was... she really could afford to buy the Mustangs, or at least several of our top players. That was more than my five-year contract extension, plus Chris's, and maybe even Everett's and Hayes's too.

"Are you saying Big Marine owes me money or something? I mean, royalties sure, but Skeeter implied I was going to owe them over this breach of contract thing."

"No, no. Kels." Her dad finally leaned forward in his chair and looked like he was the cat who'd eaten the partridge in the pear tree. "We bought your masters."

MASTERS OF THE UNIVERSE

KELSEY

My dad's words bounced around in my mind, a surreal symphony of disbelief and elation. "You bought my masters?"

The concept felt too grand, too empowering, to fully grasp in the moment.

"Yes, kiddo," my dad confirmed, his eyes twinkling with a mix of pride and mischief. "When I saw how the industry was treating artists, I knew I had to protect your interests. So, when the chance to secure your masters presented itself, I pounced. They're all yours."

I sat there, stunned, the magnitude of his revelation sinking in. Owning my masters meant control over my music, my legacy. It was a game-changer. "This... this changes everything," I managed to say, my voice a mix of awe and excitement.

Declan gave me a puzzled look. "I'm sure I'm happy for you, Kels, but I don't quite get it. What does owning your masters actually mean for you?"

I laughed, giddy with this knowledge. "Owning my masters means I own the original recordings of all my songs. It's a big deal because it gives me complete control over them. I can decide how they're used, reissued, or licensed. Most artists don't get to own theirs, record labels do. It's pretty standard to sign away the rights to masters in a recording contract. It was a part of mine, and I never imagined I'd have the chance to own them myself."

His eyes widened in realization. "So, you're saying you have full control over your music? Like, everything?"

"Exactly." I could hardly believe I was saying this. "I can release them how I want, when I want. It's the ultimate freedom as an artist."

Declan whistled, impressed. "Wow, that's huge. You can basically be your own boss now, can't you? Screw your label. Who cares if they want to cancel your contract. It sounds like it's better for you if they do."

A laugh escaped me, a release of tension and disbelief. For years, I had danced to the tune of Big Marine, but now, I could compose my own life. "Yeah, it is."

"We need to figure out what to do about Skeeter,"

my dad said, his tone serious now. "There's something hinky going on there."

"Yes. Very hinky, Scooby Doo." I had a feeling when we pulled off the bad guy's mask, Skeeter would be the old man inside. "I need to confront her. She's been avoiding my calls, and I have a feeling she's behind all this mess with Big Marine."

My dad nodded, his expression hardening. "Skeeter has been too quiet through all this. Let me call your lawyer and get her involved now."

"You have no idea how glad I am to have you, Dad. I really let a lot of my business slip through the cracks because I thought I had the right people working for me. But this has been a learning experience in who I can trust and what I should allow to be handled for me and what I shouldn't." It was time to take control, to face the challenges head-on.

He smiled, a warm, fatherly smile that filled the room with comfort. "We've always got your back, pumpkin. Always."

Armed with the knowledge that my career was going to not only be fine, but that I could take it even farther than I ever imagined, I was ready to reclaim my power. And it was all going to be even more delicious with Declan by my side.

On the jet ride back to Denver, the tension was palpable as Penelope, Declan, and I brainstormed ways to track down Skeeter. We were a team on a mission, united by a common goal, bringing Skeeter to justice for her deceit.

Penelope tapped away on her tablet and turned to me. "Your live streams were really impactful. We could harness the power of social media again, but this time to find Skeeter."

I nodded thoughtfully. "But I don't want to make it too public. We don't need a witch hunt or to put Skeeter in any danger. Is there a way to keep it just within a group of dedicated fans?"

"How about the Bestie's Besties FaceSpace group?" Penelope suggested. "They're incredibly active and loyal, and the admin team has their own chat. We can ask them for help discreetly."

"Does that group include my little sister?" Declan asked.

"Umm…" Penelope looked between the two of us. I gave her a nod. "If I tell you KingmanPrincess has been a mod in the group for several years, is that going to get her in trouble?"

Declan put his head in his hand and groaned. "I knew that screen name felt a little too familiar. She's probably already grounded for being on social media when she wasn't supposed to be, so I don't think I'll add to her trials. But do me a favor and tell her King-man98 knows, and she'd better watch her step."

Pen made a grimace and nodded.

"That group has been amazing," I mused. "Actually, if I'm going to start my own label, I'd love to have someone like that Mz. Bestie's Bestie on my team. Pen, could we try to reach out to them personally? I'd love to meet them and maybe do something special for being such an amazing fan all this time. I'm pretty sure they've been with me since the beginning."

Penelope hesitated for a moment, then took a deep breath. "Kelsey, there's something I need to tell you, and I'm not sure how you're going to react, but I want you know anyway."

Ooph. I didn't know if I was ready for more big revelations. "Okay. We're living in a new age of openness and honestly like never before. No secrets between us, okay?"

She nodded and set her tablet down. Something I'd never seen her do before. Like, ever. She even had it when I was in the hospital. She was eternally taking pictures and videos of me, for me, for social media.

"Okay, here's goes." She swallowed hard and then looked me straight in the eye. "I'm Mz. Bestie's Bestie."

I stared at her, my mouth agape. "You? What? But how? Why didn't you tell me?"

I stopped myself and took her hand. "I'm not in any way mad. Just surprised. I always assumed Mz. Bestie's Bestie was just a huge fan."

"I am a huge fan. Have been since forever. I voted for you when you were on *The Choicest Voice*," Penelope admitted, a sheepish smile on her face. "When I started working for you, I wanted to do more, be more than just an assistant. But Skeeter told me that without a degree, that's all I'd ever be."

Anger and sadness mingled within me. "Skeeter had no right to limit your potential. I don't have a degree, why would you need one? Pen, if I'd known, I would have confronted her ages ago."

One more mark against Skeeter. If I had any question in my mind whether I was going to fire her ass, that doubt was eviscerated now. I was going to need to find a new agent, a new manager, and actually, if I was going to start my own label, because yeah, that was a real possibility now, I was going to need a whole lot of staff. Might as well start from scratch with the whole she-bang.

With Penelope's identity revealed, we put our plan into action. We crafted a careful message to the Besties' Besties mod group, asking for their discreet assistance in locating Skeeter. They were excited about getting to help me, and I promised the group something special coming up from me if they could keep all of this quiet.

When we got back to Denver, Declan set Pen up in his guest room, and she and I took over his home office to start our plans for world domination. The first step was a team of lawyers.

Turned out Big Marine was in some serious trouble with the IRS, and they were going down, fast. The lawyers worked to ensure that I was at no fault with Big Marine and while it would take a lot of billable hours, they'd get all of that settled. Which meant, I could launch a whole new career.

Every day, Declan would go off to football practice and Penelope and I would get to work on all the first steps to setting up my own label and rescheduling concerts in the cities that had been cancelled. It was a lot of work, and while I was excited about most of it, I didn't love the nitty gritty details and mountains of paperwork.

Penelope did though. She had quite the eye for detail, and she was maybe as big of a workaholic as me. She was definitely getting a huge raise and a promotion. Probably to vice president of my whole-ass company.

But I'd learned my lesson and built in downtime for the piles of work for us both. Each day when Declan got home from work, we had to close up shop. I think he came home extra early a few days in a row just to test if I really would quit working for the day.

When he threw me over his shoulder and up the stairs to make love to me five ways to Sunday, I did not protest one single bit. The one caveat I got in the new world order of work and rest was that songwriting didn't count as work.

Mostly because it didn't feel like work anymore. For the first time in years, the music brought me joy again. I was already planning an album with a bunch of my locked-away-in-the-vault music the label hadn't let me release before. And I had the basics of a whole new album too.

After the tour was over, I'd need to get back in the studio and the songs would become magic. The *Chunky Dunkin'* album would be a reality by next summer, and I was definitely releasing a new Christmas song. Something about a Rocky Mountain white Christmas, I thought.

At first, Pen didn't know what to do with herself if we weren't working twenty-four-seven. I introduced her to Declan's younger brothers and suggested she learn how to play video games with them, and after hanging out with them just a couple of times, she was talking about enrolling at DSU next fall.

Maybe I would too. I'd had excellent tutors to help me finish high school after I'd won *The Choicest Voice*, but college was never something I thought I could fit into my life. But being my own boss, and one who was working really hard to balance work and life better, I think it was high time I matriculated.

About a week after we asked the Bestie's for help finding Skeeter, they did. It was amazing. The FBI should seriously consider hiring this team of women as investigators. They were sharp.

They traced her to the hotel I stayed in in Aspen, still charging to my account. Time to pull some vigilante shit.

Armed with a whole team of lawyers that had uncovered just how much she'd both screwed up my contract, and embezzled money from me, we were going to take Skeeter down, and make sure she could never do this to another artist ever again.

With the army of lawyers and a pack of Kingmans at my back, we headed to Aspen.

I was so ready to confront the snake.

We found her lounging by the hot tub on the concierge level taking up two deck chairs like the greedy bitch she was. It was sure going to be cold getting kicked out on her ass in only a swimsuit.

"Hello, Skeeter." I stood right in her sun, throwing shade her way.

She looked up in surprise, but it took her only a second to put her familiar mask back on. "Kelsey, what an interesting surprise. I see you brought your himbo and your ditzy-ass assistant. Still can't fight your own battles, hmm?"

Declan, standing right next to me, just crossed his arms and glared. He knew I got this, and I loved him for it.

"You're fired, Skeeter," I said firmly. "I am done with your manipulations and lies."

She scoffed, dismissing my words with a wave of her hand. "Please, like it even matters now that you're pop music's dud of a one hit wonder. I have plenty of other clients who will actually make me money."

"But not for long," I retorted, meeting her scoff with a determined gaze. "My lawyers have forwarded the information we've gathered about the way you portrayed me to my label, and your embezzlement to your other clients, Big Marine, and the law. Expect some calls."

Skeeter's confident demeanor faltered, a hint of panic flashing in her eyes. She stood up, trying to regain her composure. "You can't do this to me, Kelsey. I made you."

"You didn't make me, Skeeter," I countered, my voice steady. "You just rode along on my talent and hard work. I'm taking control now."

Penelope stepped forward, her expression resolute. "And I'm not just an assistant, Skeeter. I've been the voice behind Mz. Bestie's Besties for years. I've supported Kelsey more than you ever did."

Skeeter's face turned a shade paler, the realization that her empire was crumbling evident in her eyes. She glanced at the third person I'd brought along with me. My lawyer, dressed in a staid black suit that belied her profession, then back at me. "You'll regret this."

"I don't think so," I replied. "I'm looking forward to a fresh start, working with people who actually care about me, the music, and my fans, more than the money."

My lawyer stepped in, handing Skeeter the termination documents. "Everything is in order here. Please review and sign."

As Skeeter begrudgingly took the papers, a sense of liberation washed over me. This was more than just firing a deceitful agent and manager, it was a declaration of my independence, a step towards a future where I called the shots.

Turning to Declan and Penelope, I smiled, grateful for their unwavering support. "Let's get out of here. We have a new chapter to begin."

But one more ugly chapter from my pre-boss-bitch days opened up right before me.

"Skeets, babe, what's going on here? Kelsey, is that you? I hardly recognized you. I've been trying to call you for ages." Jake, yes, that Jake, my ex-boyfriend and Hollywood's current trending bad boy, leaned forward and kissed each of my cheeks before I even knew what he was doing. He crossed to Skeeter and handed her a drink, and then bent to give her a kiss. But not the European kiss-kiss greeting he'd given me. He kissed her full on the mouth and with a wink at me, slipped her some tongue.

Gross.

UNSTOPPABLE

DECLAN

I recognized Jake Jay. He was in some shitty action movies. A month ago, I couldn't have told you that Kelsey had dated him. But I was a full-blown Bestie now, and even if I didn't know, I would be able to tell from Kelsey's shocked reaction that this guy was her gaslighting ex.

When her people originally approached me to act like her new boyfriend, it was to get the press off her back about her breakup with this douchepotato. I'd been engaged to do a job, and I was going to do it right now.

I stepped between Kelsey and Jake, putting my size to good use as a shield. I knew exactly how to block, and my initial instinct was to tackle him, shielding

Kelsey from whatever drama he might stir up. But I'd learned from being with her that she was strong and capable, and my role wasn't to fight her battles, but to support her in them.

It wasn't that I didn't think she could destroy this guy if she wanted to. It's just that she shouldn't have to do the dirty work that I was very happy to do for her. Kelsey stuck her head out from behind me. "What are you doing here, Jake?"

"Just Netflix and chilling with the Incognito Mosquito here. Didn't realize we'd see you." He tried to move so he could actually see Kelsey. I subtly shifted my stance to maintain the barrier. "This wall's your new beau I've been hearing about, I guess."

"Yeah, I am," I said, keeping my tone even but firm. Nobody was accusing me of being a bully or mean today. But that didn't mean I was backing down.

"At least I fucking took her out in public. I wasn't ashamed to be seen with her. Are you?" Jake verbally lashed out at me and tried to side-step again despite Skeeter trying to grab him to pull him away. "You looked real good on my arm on the red carpet, baby. That look you got going on in the baseball jerseys ain't it though. Who's your stylist because they should be fired AF."

"Watch what you say to my girl, Jay. She's a whole lot nicer than I am." I'd been bothered that the league, the press, and even the stupid gossip rags thought I was mean. I knew I wasn't, and I was just doing my job, but it still bothered me that I was perceived that way. Kelsey had never once made me think for a second that she saw me like that. In fact, she'd recognized the real me from the get-go.

Her opinion was the only one that mattered to me.

"Your girl, huh? It sure as shit seems like you're real good at hiding her from the world. Biggest star outside of Hollywood, and she disappears from public view for a week? Is it because you don't want to be seen dating a—"

I held up my hand in the universal stop signal. "I'm going to stop you right there, before you say something you'll regret."

"Yeah." Penelope held up her phone and showed that she was recording the whole thing. I did not envy his agent or publicist's job right now.

Kelsey stepped forward, moving beside me not behind me. "That's enough, Jake. What happened between us is in the past. I've moved on to, uh, bigger and better things."

Jake's face tightened, a hint of genuine regret crossing his features. "Kelsey, I—"

But Kelsey cut him off, her voice steady. "No, Jake. We're done here. Don't call me or text me anymore. Not even drunk dials. Take my number out of your phone. Or better yet, I can just block you. I wish you well, but there's nothing left to say."

Skeeter, who had been watching silently and very uncomfortably, finally spoke. "Jake, let's just go."

As they turned to leave, Jake looked back, a mix of emotions on his face. "You're a lucky guy," he said to me, his voice lacking its earlier bravado. "Take care of her."

I nodded, acknowledging his words with a newfound sense of maturity. "I plan to."

We headed to the car so we could make the drive back home, and while we were waiting for the valet, my phone buzzed. Alexis's name flashed on the screen. I owed her the time. Her calls to me had gone unanswered for a bit.

The valet was going to be a minute, and the girls were deep in discussion dissecting what had just gone down. So I took a step away and answered the call.

"Alexis, what's up?" I asked, bracing for a chastisement.

"Declan, you've been a busy man," her voice was laced with excitement. "Swoosh is on board. They love how you've been supporting Kelsey, and it's done wonders for your image. We're talking more than just a shoe deal now."

I leaned against the wall, a sense of rightness with the world washing over me. I might not have even entertained the idea of Kelsey in the first place back then if it wasn't for the Swoosh deal being in jeopardy, so I figured I sort of owed them for hooking me up with the love of my life. "That's great to hear. What else are they thinking?"

"They're interested in aligning you with some of

their women's sports initiatives. It's a big step, Declan. You're not just a football player in their eyes now, you're a role model."

The words hit me with a mixture of pride and surprise. I'd never seen myself as a role model, especially for women's sports. But with Kelsey in my life, my perspective on a lot of things had changed.

"That sounds perfect, Alexis. Let's do it. And hey, while I have you, do you guys have connections with music agents? I know someone looking for new representation."

There was a brief pause. "Music agents, huh? I can make a few calls. Someone specific in mind?"

"Just a talented artist who deserves the best," I replied, a smile spreading across my face as I hinted at exactly who we were talking about. The De le Rein agency was older than dirt and had repped a lot of people over the years. But Kelsey would be a star among their stars.

"Consider it done. I'll get back to you with some options," Alexis assured me.

Life was really fucking good right now. Not just because of the Swoosh deal, but for being able to help Kelsey too.

I walked back to Kelsey, and her eyes were filled with curiosity. "Everything good?"

"Better than. That was my agent. Swoosh is on board with a bigger deal, and they want to align me with women's sports initiatives."

Her eyes lit up. "That's amazing, Declan. You're a great role model for men and women. A lot of little boys and girls would benefit from seeing how you treat the people you care about."

I shrugged, feeling a bit sheepish at the praise. "And I might have mentioned to Alexis about someone needing a new music agent."

Kelsey raised an eyebrow. "Alexis?"

"De le Rein. She's my agent."

"Is she related to your mom? I mean I've heard of the De le Rein agency, but are you related to them?"

"Yep, Alexis is my cousin. The agency was actually started by my grandfather. It's been the other family business, you know, besides football, for a while," I explained, watching Kelsey's expression change from surprise to realization.

Kelsey reached out, taking my hand. "That's incredible, Declan. Your family continues to surprise me. I'd love to be represented by De le Rein. Their music arm is really powerful."

"We tend to keep a low profile about it. But I think it's time we used that influence for good, especially for someone as talented and deserving as you."

Her eyes softened, and she squeezed my hand. "Thank you, Declan. That means a lot to me. To have your support, and your family's too... it's more than I could have asked for."

"I got you, babe." I winked at her.

"Did you just quote Sonny and Cher?" She started

humming the song. "Maybe it's time for a remake of that classic."

"Who are you going to get to be the Sonny to your Cher, babe?"

"You, of course. I've heard you sing, Kingman. You've definitely got a future in pop music."

I snuggled her into my arms and whispered in her ear, "What I have is a future inside of a pop music star."

"Ooh. I have been paying for a fancy hotel room here for weeks, maybe we should go see if we can use it one more time."

"You two are disgustingly cute. Blech."

Oops. I maybe had forgotten that Penelope was even here. I only had eyes for Kelsey. "Let's just get home. I'd rather see your hair spread across my pillows than a bougie hotel any day."

After our successful confrontation with Skeeter and Jake in Aspen, the drive back to Denver was quiet. That is until we got close enough to Denver to pick up the radio stations. I tuned to the top forties, but Kelsey turned the dial until she found an oldies station. The three of us sang along to a bunch of songs that my dad would probably be really upset to know were considered old, since they were all from when he was in college.

Our first stop once we got back into my neighborhood in Thornminster was to pop across the street and pick up Wiener the Pooh from my dad's place. Penelope excused herself and headed down the street to play video games with the boys. She was becoming a popular player on their streaming channel. Turned out a lot of Besties were gamer girls and the boys' subscription numbers had skyrocketed once she started playing with them.

I didn't see dad inside the house, so we went into the back yard. What we found was one of the strangest things I'd ever seen. Chris, Trixie, my dad, and Jules were sitting on the patio watching Luke Skycocker ride around on Wiener the Pooh's back.

Oh man. So many dick jokes, so little time.

Kelsey chuckled softly and walked over to Pooh to grab her so we could go home. Pooh had other ideas. When she saw her coming, she bucked Trixie's rooster off her back and made a beeline for my dad, nuzzling into him as if she'd found her long-lost friend.

"Looks like Pooh's got a new favorite," Kelsey said, her eyes sparkling with amusement.

I shook my head with a grin. "I guess I've been replaced. Pooh's heart is fickle. But then again, she's got good taste. Dad's always been a dog whisperer."

My dad, playing along, picked up Pooh, who wriggled in delight. "Looks like you've got some competition, son. I think Pooh's figured out she'll never win your heart, since it belongs to another."

I wrapped my arm around Kelsey, pulling her close. "She's right about that. Pooh's smart, but even she knows Kelsey's got my heart forever."

We thanked Dad and headed back to my place with

Pooh trotting alongside us. Once we were finally home, I dragged Kelsey upstairs to bed. I'd been fantasizing about all the things I wanted to do to her for most of the ride home and had been half-mast for hours.

The world outside faded away as I stripped her naked and licked every inch of her body. After I made her come a couple of times, she surprised me with a scene out of one of her now tall stack of smutty romance novels she'd taken over the bedside table with. Wolf shifter smut was top tier, and when she was done reading a mating scene to me, I flipped her over and took her from behind, just like the dirty wolf did. I even gave her a little bite right as she was coming with my dick buried deep inside of her.

Afterwards, we savored the peace we found in each other's arms after days of emotional turmoil. Kelsey snuggled into me. "I think we should get your dad a dog for Christmas. He clearly loves them, and you said he's a dog whisperer. You said you had dogs growing up, right?"

"Our first one was my dad's dog, and he was pretty old when we were little. When I was three and Chris was four, Ev was just a baby, our parents didn't want to tell us that their Bear had died. That was his name. He was some kind of a big Newfie mix that really did look a lot like a big bear. So mom made dad go out to every shelter in town until he found another enormous, brown, fluffy dog, and brought it home and started calling it Bear."

Kelsey popped her head up and her smile dazzled me. "And you guys didn't notice? I guess you were really little."

"No, I totally noticed, but I think at that age, I just thought all dogs were called Bear." I enjoyed the little dachshund that Kelsey loved, but there was nothing like a big dog. "I didn't figure it out until I was like eleven or twelve, I guess, and we got Bear number three. She was a good dog. Could fit a whole-ass football in her mouth."

"Football family through and through. We'll have to either teach Pooh to catch a ball or maybe just dress her up like one for Halloween. No Bear four?" She snuggled back into my chest, and I wrapped her tighter into my arms.

"Since Jules is the last kid living at home full-time, dad decided he wasn't going to get a Bear four. We've talked about getting him one after Jules flies the coop for college. He's not going to know what to do with himself with no more kids to raise."

If any Kingman was going to buck the system and not get their degree from Denver State University, it would be Jules. She had a mind of her own and we all knew it.

As we lay there, Kelsey's head resting on my chest, she broached the subject we'd both been ignoring for a little while. "We've got a lot of traveling coming up. My make-up tour and your games. It's going to be crazy."

I brushed a strand of hair from her face, pondering

over our schedules. "It is going to be hectic. But I promise you, Kels, I'll be at as many of your concerts as I can. I don't want to miss watching you shine on stage."

"I really enjoy watching you smack other guys into the grass. Which is not something I ever thought I'd say. I'll be at your games, cheering you on."

We lay there in silence for a moment, each lost in thoughts about our future together, a future filled with music, football, and shared dreams.

Kelsey lifted her head, meeting my gaze. "No matter where we are, whether on the road or on stage, we'll always find our way back to each other, right?"

I nodded, sealing the promise with a kiss. "Always, Kels. No distance can keep us apart. We're a team in everything we do now."

She smiled, a beautiful, genuine smile that reached her eyes. "I love you, Declan Kingman."

"I love you too, Kelsey Best, from the moment I first saw you until forever."

Holding each other like this, the challenges ahead seemed less daunting. We had each other, and that was all that mattered. Our careers might take us to different corners of the country, but our hearts were tethered in a bond that wouldn't be broken by distance or time.

My life had changed so much since meeting her. I wasn't just a football player anymore, I was part of something bigger. A partnership built on mutual respect and love. The realization filled me with a sense of purpose and excitement for what lay ahead.

This was just the beginning for both of us, a new chapter where we could not only pursue our dreams but also support each other in ways we never thought possible. I would always be there for Kelsey, supporting her, cheering for her, and loving her. She was my partner, my confidante, my love. And together, we were unstoppable.

That gave me an idea for a song. I wondered if she'd teach me how to play the guitar.

BESTIES FACESPACE GROUP

[Pic of Penelope Quinn, Wiener the Pooh, and Kelsey Best]

*H*ey Besties,
Exciting things are happening in Bestlandia!

And I am here to be your insider for all things Kelsey Best in her new upcoming era. The era of girl power.

You know I've been here reporting from behind the scenes with all kinds of videos, lives, photos, and deets for you on our very favorite and talented pop star.

But today I'm here to make a few announcements. Lots of exciting things are coming your way, and you're going to be the first to know.

First, I've been your anonymous friend, Mz. Besties'

Bestie, for a long time, but today, I'd like to let you get to know the real me.

Hi, my name is Penelope Quinn, and it's been my privilege to work as Kelsey's personal assistant for the past four years. Yep, that's how I had so much insider knowledge. I have literally been in the Best camp, doing everything from walking the precious Wiener the Pooh to helping set up Kelsey's brand new record label, Simply The Best.

You read that right. Kelsey is launching her own record label! More deets to come about all of that.

We all know the debacle that's come out on social media, news media, and you know, court reports, about what went down with Big Marine, and she who shall never be named.

(P.S. Should you ever notice a screen name of Incognito Mosquito hanging around Bestlandia, be sure to swat it.)

But what's come out of all that drama are some really exciting things. Stay tuned right here in Besties Bestie FaceSpace group, because in the coming days, Kelsey herself is going to go live to answer your questions and make some ah-mazing announcement regarding rescheduled tour dates. Can you say stadiums?

Commence the squealing!

(and please be kind, the pic is a selfie #nofilter #all-bodiesarebeautiful #therealme)

XO
Your BFF,
Penelope

EPILOGUE: KING OF MY HEART

KELSEY

*I*n the midst of my makeup tour, bigger and better in stadiums across the country, the energy and excitement of performing for my fans filled me with an indescribable joy. Even with as much fun as I was having, amidst the cheers and the adrenaline, on this particular night, a great big part of me yearned for Declan, who was on the opposite coast for a game and a subsequent photoshoot.

This was the first concert since the tour began that he had to miss. We attended each other's events whenever possible, our schedules often intertwining like a well-orchestrated dance. But this leg of the tour had us separated for longer than usual, and I couldn't help but miss him terribly.

I was sitting in my hotel room post-concert, staring at the city lights outside my window, knowing I really needed to get to sleep. But I had so much on my mind. My new album, releasing in just a few months under my label, was already a massive success with three number one singles. And the songs resonated with fans in ways I never imagined. I was finally making music that was entirely me, unfiltered and bold.

New song ideas were everywhere now, like someone—someone named Declan—had found the tap to my dried up creativity well and turned it back on.

I picked up my phone to work on a few lyrics but ended up scrolling through the photos from our last weekend together. A smile spread across my face as I recalled the laughter, the shared looks, and the quiet moments that had become our haven. Our love had grown stronger with each passing day, each challenge faced together.

But my scrolling was interrupted with a call from the one and only person I wanted to talk to, even though it was well past midnight and I had a show tomorrow.

"You were supposed to try and get some rest." His chastising tone was a little too sexy. "Can't sleep again?"

"I'm wide awake." Even more so now that he'd called. I always slept best in his arms. Not so much in a lonely hotel room without him.

He chuckled. "I am too."

I really wished he was here so we could be wide awake together.

"I had a feeling this might happen, and I've been thinking about a bedtime story for you. I know what will help you relax."

Did I detect a hint of naughtiness in that suggestion? Or was that just wishful thinking?

"Do you now?" I decided this would be a good time to go crawl into bed. I got under the big, fluffy duvet and snuggled into my pillow. I mentally crossed my fingers that he was going where I hoped he was. "And what's that?"

"You tell me if this isn't what you want, or if I'm going too far, okay?"

No matter how many times he did this, a consent convo was always sexy with him. "Okay."

"Anytime, I mean it. You can say stop and I will."

This man held my heart so hard.

I doubted I was going to ever tell him to stop, not for the rest of our lives. "I want whatever it is you're about to say, Declan."

He made a low, sexy humming sound. "Then tell me what you're wearing."

He was going to go there. I felt like I should say I was in some kind of sexy lingerie, but with him, I didn't feel like I had to lie. "A long t-shirt."

"Panties?"

Ones that were starting to get a little damp. "Yes."

"Take them off."

Oh. He was really, really going there. And I wasn't lying even a little bit when I said I wanted him to. I set the phone on my pillow, reached under the covers, and yanked off my undies, then tossed them aside. I'd have to pick them up in the morning before the underpants thief known as Wiener the Pooh got a hold of them. But even if she did, I had a feeling this was going to be worth it.

"Are they off?" His pitch had gone lower and rumbly.

"Yes." Mine had gone breathy and soft.

"Good girl." Boom. My brain exploded. "The next time I see you, I don't want you to be wearing any."

Double boom. Other places south of my brain were going to explode too if he kept this up.

That tickle that had been floating around my belly took an express straight shot between my legs. Did I like being called a good girl? Yes. Yes, I did. Those two little words went straight to the pleasure centers of my brain. They were the holy grail of smut talk in all the romances I read. Especially the ones I read out loud to him.

"I won't, if you don't."

"Deal." He agreed to that awfully fast. I was holding him to that. Commando was going to look good on him. Except in football pants. He needed to keep his family jewels protected on that field. I had plans for them. "Now take the t-shirt off too."

"Are you going to get naked as well?"

"I already am. I have been since well before I called you. Now take off the t-shirt, Kelsey."

I was so caught up in this little game, like a really good song that swept you away. A really good stripper lap dance kind of song.

I slid out of the t-shirt, and where I expected cool sheets to caress my body, there were none. My body heat was on the rise, and I'd turned my bed into a furnace. Or rather, Declan Kingman had.

"Tell me what kind of foreplay you want, sweetheart. What's going to turn you on tonight?"

"This, Declan." What I really meant was the way he was romancing me even when he didn't have to. He'd already won my heart, and yet he still flirted with me every day. "Words are my jam, make me some sexy new lyrics."

"Dirty talk I can do." If we weren't both dog people, I would have said he purred those words.

Was I in a romance novel right now? Because it sure as hell felt like it.

"Close your eyes, Kels, and put your hand between your legs. Unless you tell me to stop, I'm going to talk you through what I wish I was doing for you right now."

For me. Not to me. "I'm not telling you to stop."

"Let's get you warmed up and wet for me."

Did I mention how much I'd been missing him while I was on the road? "I... I'm already wet."

"Mmm. Then imagine I'm spreading your legs,

looking my fill at your lush thighs and your plump pussy. I'd push my fingers between those lips and give you a nice long lick."

I moved my own hand to match the words he was saying. This wasn't going to take very long. I was already too keyed up.

"One taste of you will never be enough. I'd push your legs open wider, needing to lose myself between your thighs."

I spread my knees farther apart, imagining his big shoulders between them. "And?"

"And I'd tease you, swirling my tongue around and around your pretty little clit, not giving you want you want yet."

My fingers emulated exactly what he said and I didn't mean to, but a moan escaped my throat.

"Fuck, that's a beautiful sound. I want to hear more of it. I'd flick my tongue over your clit, over and over just to hear you moan my name. Do it, Kelsey, tease your clit and say my name."

God, this was too much. My pussy was already throbbing. I meant to give him what he wanted and say his name, but it came out a whimper. I'd been touching myself for all of about a minute, and I was already on the edge.

"That's it. Do you feel me sucking your clit into my mouth, lashing at that sensitive tip with my tongue over and over?"

I could. God, I could.

"Faster, sweetness, rub your clit harder and let go." His voice was so low, it was barely audible, but I heard every word as if he was in the room with me, whispering in my ear. "Let me taste you, I want you to come on my tongue."

"Mmm, I... oh yes." Swirls of colors and stars exploded behind my eyes, and my back arched up off the bed as I came on my own hand. The pulsing of my orgasm flashed through me like the beat of sensual song, and I gasped at how incredibly good it felt.

"Don't stop. I'm still licking and tasting and sucking on that clit. Make it last, give me all of it." His words were so damn demanding and hot as hell.

I was barely able to move, but I swirled my fingers over my clit one more time, absolutely imagining it was his tongue, and my body clenched again, just as hard, drawing my orgasm out.

"Again, Kelsey. I want more."

I groaned and slid my fingers across myself once more and this time, the sound I made wasn't even something I recognized.

"That's a good girl. Just like that."

The contentment of a really great orgasm washed over me, and I laid there just breathing, panting, for a few moments.

"Ready to go to sleep now?"

"I wish you were here."

"I am."

I sat straight up in bed, and Declan stood there, leaning against the frame of the door, butt naked.

"Declan," I exclaimed, rushing into his arms. "What are you doing here? I thought you had a photoshoot."

He chuckled, wrapping me in a warm embrace, a warm, naked embrace. "I did, but I moved some things around. I couldn't stay away any longer. I wanted to surprise you."

The feeling of his arms around me, the familiar scent of his skin, and the sound of his heartbeat felt like coming home.

"You have no idea how much I needed this," I murmured, my heart swelling with love.

"Hey, I got something for you," Declan said, snagging his bag. He pulled out a Mustangs jersey with 'Kingman's Bestie' emblazoned on the back, along with his number. "Thought you might like your own official gear."

I laughed, touched by the gesture. "I love it. And I can't wait to wear it at your next game."

As we snuggled under the covers, I realized Pooh hadn't alerted me to Declan coming into the hotel room. "Where's Pooh?"

"I bought her silence with a treat ball filled with peanut butter and bacon flavored treats." Oh, what a smart, smart man.

Falling asleep in Declan's arms, I realized that no matter where our careers took us, we would always find our way back to each other. Our love was the constant in the ever-changing landscape of our lives, the melody that would always play in harmony.

This was just the beginning. There were more tours, more games, more challenges, and more triumphs to come. But with Declan by my side, I felt like Wonder Woman. The world was ours to explore, our love the guiding light through any darkness.

In those quiet moments before sleep claimed me, I thought about our journey. The doubts, the fears, the uncertainties we had faced and conquered. Declan's love had been a balm to my past wounds, healing me in ways I never thought possible. He had shown me that love wasn't just about grand gestures, but also the small, everyday acts of kindness and understanding.

I thought about our families, now interwoven in this beautiful tapestry of support and love. Our lives were a blend of music and sports, stages and fields, but at the core, it was about us, our dreams, and the future we were building together.

There would be more days when we'd be apart, chasing our individual goals, but the strength of our bond, the trust and respect we shared, made every goodbye temporary and every reunion sweeter.

As I nestled closer to Declan, his heartbeat a steady rhythm in the quiet room, I felt a profound sense of peace. This was more than a happy ending. It was a happy continuation. Our story wasn't just a romance followed by millions on social media, it was a testament to the power of love, resilience, and the magic that happens when two people are brave enough to march to their own drum, write their own song.

This wasn't just a love story. It wasn't just a love song. He was my lover and belonged with me. Everything had changed, and I knew one thing that I'd whisper on a soft tune every single one of our midnights. "You are the king of my heart."

NEED MORE DECLAN AND KELSEY? Grab their bonus chapter when you join my Swoon Zone email newsletter!

READY FOR MORE KINGMANS? Read The Next Book in the Cocky Kingman series now.

A NOTE FROM THE AUTHOR

AMY AWARD

THICK THIGHS & YUMMY GUYS

Wanna hear story about how I was *almost* (a.k.a never) a country, pop, and/or rock star? *pats chair* *hands you glass of tasty beverage of choice*

cue Taylor Swift playlist

A LONG TIME AGO, IN AN ERA FAR, FAR AWAY~

When I was younger, I didn't know that not everyone in the entire world did not have a song stuck in their head ALL THE TIME. I thought everyone did. Seriously. Do you have a song stuck in your head right now? How about two? Do you ALWAYS have a song stuck in your head or is it just the occasional earworm?

(FYI - I will never be able to hear or even think the term earworm without thinking of those horrible earwig alien bug things in Star Trek II: The Wrath of Khan - *shivers*)

There is not an hour, minute, or second of the day

that I don't have a song stuck in my head. It's usually set off by something I've heard, although not always a song. Even a single word can set off an earworm for me if it happens to be the lyric of a song I once heard. Or rhyme with a lyric of a song.

Like... seriously, you could shake me awake in the middle of the night and ask me what song was stuck in my head, and if you give me a second to realize what's happening, it will be there, and I can probably sing part of it for you.

I've learned much later in life, from TikTok, that that is often a signifier of some kind of neurodivergence, like ADHD.

shrug I've always known my brain was different.

As a result of this, music has always been an important part of my life.

I loved to sing the songs at Girls Scout camp. (Interestingly, my mom was often our troop leader, or a camp counselor, and would be in charge of making the song books, and lead the songs. She was also mostly tone deaf, and still she found joy in singing those silly songs, and so did we, singing right along with her.)

When I was in Junior High and High School, I was always in choir. Sometimes two at the same time. I took private voice lessons and developed my whistle voice (aka that super high squeaky thing that Mariah Carey does), even though I'm a natural alto.

In college, I was in my sorority's singing group called the Cat's Meow, took choir as an elective every single semester, and even went on a choir tour of Spain and France, where we got to sing in great big, really old churches and cathedrals.

But I always knew that I could never be more than a choir girl. Nashville, New York, or L.A. weren't for girls like me.

Why? Because I was chubby. And chubby girls don't become country stars, or pop stars, or rock stars, or even get cast in the school musical… not in a lead roll anyway. I did be the understudy for Violet Beauregaurde, you know the girl who turns into a giant blueberry.

Chubby girls aren't stars. Or so I thought. That's what society told me.

I remember watching one of those audition episodes of *America's Got Talent*, where this girl blew the judges away with her incredibly powerful voice. But good old Simon Cowell told her it would be hard for her to become a star because she needed to lose a lot of weight. She just stood there, looking at the floor, looking completely defeated and said, "I know."

Ugh. I'm crying now.

But then came along *American Idol* and Kelly Clarkson.

Now look, Kelly Clarkson is not what I would call fat, or even chubby. She just wasn't a skinny mini girl, and I was LIVING for it. But I also watched her throughout her career try to conform to the ideal body and get brutally shamed in the media when she didn't.

Then we got Jennifer Hudson. But... didn't she end up doing Jenny Craig or Nutri-slim or Weight Watcher commercials?

Then we go Adele! But she decided to go on a health journey (which she's allowed to do, I'm not shaming her for doing what she thinks is best for herself), got some kind of weight loss surgery, and lost a lot of weight.

Then we got Lizzo. Oh, my god, LIZZO. She was large and loud, and unapologetic, and she was so damn talented. We'll see how things continue for Lizzo. (At the time of writing, she's just coming out of a bit of a scandal with reports of fat-shaming some of her dancers, and she started a shapewear company. At least its size inclusive. *Shrug*)

What I'm saying is ALL MY LIFE, I've been looking for a female role model in the music world who had a body like mine.

Representation matters.

And it's hard to find good fat rep in the music world.

So, with Kelsey, I set out to make her a curvy, beautiful, TALL, plus-size MEGASTAR, with an ass that does. not. quit.

It's MY WORLD, I CAN DO WHAT I WANT.

*knock glass off the counter

Now if you've been around for a while, you also know I'm an OG Swiftie. I love me some *Teardrops On My Guitar*, *Love Story*, *Blank Space*, and *You Belong With*

Me is literally part of the inspiration for the first book in this series, *The C*ck Down the Block*.

And, at the time of this writing, I am having a BLAST watching the romance between Tay Tay and her new beau, football player Travis Kelce. (God, I hope I look back on this in twenty years and get to say "Oh, look, they made it! How nice!).

I pull my inspiration for my stories from all kinds of facets of my life, and since music runs through all of them, I knew from the get go, that I wanted to write a football player and musician romance.

It just so happened that a real life football player and musician romance was playing out before my very eyes -aka social media feeds. Which always feels very "Lady Whistledown" to me.

So..., is this Taylor-Trav fanfic?

Not exactly.

Kelsey and Deck's story is what I imagine could have been if a pop star that's a little bit Taylor, a little bit Kelly, a little bit Adele, a little bit Jennifer, and a little bit Lizzo, had met a kind, caring, cinnamon roll golden retriever of a football player, right before her career exploded.

Can you imagine how any of those ladies' careers might have been different if they'd had a super supportive partner backing them up all the damn time?

Well, we'd have a lot less really bad-ass break up songs. And who doesn't need a *Since You've Been Gone*, or a *We Are Never Ever Getting Back Together*?

We all do. It's the human condition.

But in MY WORLD I DO WHAT I WANT!

*knocks another glass off the counter. Don't worry, they're actually plastic cups and Uno thinks this is the best game ever.

You or I may never be a millionaire pop-star, but it doesn't mean we can't have positive female role models who can show us that there are great men out there who love us just the way we are, if we just let go of some of our fears, and jump in the water when they ask us to go skinny dipping.

(Now forever known as chunky dunkin'.)

The Wiener Across the Way is my love letter to everyone who loves to sing, but maybe you don't because you're uncomfortable when people look at you. The ones who tried out for the musical and always ended up in the chorus, or the stage crew instead. The ones who were told you needed to lose weight before you could do…anything.

I hope you sing.

This story is for you.

This book is also a celebration of the mountains. I've lived in a mountain state almost all my life, and I would LITERALLY be lost without them. (Mountains are WEST - IFKYK *waves to the Front Range*)

I NEVER even imagined setting a book here. But do you have any idea how pretty it is in the mountains in the fall? If you ever get a chance to have that picnic in the aspens, Do It. But probably don't jump right into that mountain lake. They're really cold IRL.

Just in case you were wondering, the dragon romance novel that Kelsey reads out loud in the BAGGWIEYPUYCOMF chapter is real. It's called *Chase Me by Aidy Award* (which is also me, writing paranormal romance.) If you like paranormal romance with shifters who fall for curvy girls, have I got a whole binge read for you.

Finally, you should know that a portion of the proceeds of this book will go to the Denver Dumb Friends League (don't worry Pooh, nobody thinks you're dumb!) who are a more than 100-year-old independent, local, nonprofit organization that helps to rescue all kinds of animals, including cute little wiener dogs in my home town.

Together, we're gonna save puppies just like how Kelsey rescued Pooh!

Extra Hugs from me to you,

—Amy

ACKNOWLEDGMENTS

OMG. I literally pulled an all nighter to finish this book (which… as a GenXer was both fun and painful). I ignored my friends and family to get this story done, so I need a special shout out to them, especially my Cook-iePie, Katie. Thanks for always understanding when I can't come out and play.

Special thanks goes to my Bring It On Mastermind group who kept telling me I could do it. JL Madore, Krystal Shannan, Claudia Burgoa, and Bri Blackwood. I would go crazy without you. And to the Zoom writing Crew - I see you Kaci Rose and Dylann Crush and I love that you're always there.

I so appreciate the author talks and days away from the computer at rando coffee shops around the Denver metro area with M. Guida, Holly Roberds, Parker Finch, and Nikki Hall. Y'all are my tribe.

Thanks to my Amazeballs Writers: Danielle Hart, Davina Storm, and Stephanie Harrell for always thinking I'm Amazeballs, even when I don't. You bring joy to my life.

Extra hugs to my curvy girl author friends, Molly O'Hare, Kelsie Stelting Hoss, Mary Warren, and Kayla

Grosse. We're changing the world one fat-bottomed woman at a time, and I'm so grateful you're here fighting the good fight with me. I will ALWAYS continue to rec your books when anyone asks for romance with plus-size heroines, because I KNOW readers can trust their hearts with your positive fat rep!

Part of why I wanted to write Kelsey's story of creative burn out is because I've been there, done that, got the tears and frustration. If Becca Syme hadn't been there to coach me through that, challenged me to be the best recover-er, and taught me to answer the what if questions when they plague me, I would definitely not still be writing today. Burn out is real, real shitty. I'm so grateful you're there for me and all the other authors who need help to pull ourselves out of those dark places. Extra hugs for you.

I am ever grateful to my editor Chrisandra who I must SMOOCH IN THE FACE when we get to actually meet in person someday. I'm sorry I still suck at commas and deadlines.

Thank you to Ellie at Love Notes PR for (still) not firing my 'deadlines-schmedlines' dumb ass. So much of the BANANAS would not have happened if it weren't for you and the way you believed in my books. Forever, SLAY.

Huge thanks to Leni Kaufmann for giving us that amazing ass on Kelsey. I wasn't sure the world would like it, and yet everyone literally gasps at how gorgeous this piece of art is. Thank you for helping me change the world one book cover at a time.

So many hugs to my friend and PA Michelle Ziegler. My author life would be such a tangled mess with out. I appreciate you more than you know.

And to my Patreon Book Dragons - you are the reason I write books. I hope I continue to entertain you and make you proud. Your continual support means so incredibly much to me. You make me smile and happy cry when I read your comments on the chapters.

For my VIP Fans, signed books are coming your way!

- Amanda R.
- Amie N.
- Anette R.
- Angie K
- Ashley B.
- Barbara B
- Jenn P
- Kerrie M
- Sandra B
- Sara W
- Tracy L

For my Swoonies, Deck and Kelsey's box with some fun swag is coming your way!

- Alyssa T.

- Becky B
- Belinda M.
- Cara-Lee D.
- Dana R.
- Erin G.
- Ilona T.
- Irehne A.
- Jen N.
- Johnna A.
- Judy R.
- JW
- Kathryn B.
- Kaylee B
- Kiarra C.
- Kristin
- Maria
- McKaylee E.
- Montse
- Nanci C.
- Nicole P.
- Nicole C.
- Rebecca C.
- Sami M.
- Sophie H.
- Stacey M.
- Tiffany L.

For my Biggest Fans Ever, book boxes with so much hilarious wiener dog and football stuff and signed book are on their way. Thank you so much for believing in me.

- Alida H
- Cherie S
- Danielle T
- Daphine G
- Elisha B
- Jessica W
- Katherine M
- Kelli W
- Mari G
- Marilyn C
- Melissa L
- Orma M
- Rosa D
- Sara S.
- Shannon B
- Stephanie H
- Stephanie F
- Corinne A

ABOUT THE AUTHOR

Amy Award is a curvy girl who has a thing for football players, fuzzy-butt pets, and spicy romance novels. She believes that all bodies are beautiful and deserve their own love stories with Happy Ever Afters. Find her at AuthorAmyAward.com

Amy also write curvy girl paranormal romances with dragons, wolves, demons, and vampires, as Aidy Award. If that's your jam, check those books out at AidyAward.com

Made in United States
North Haven, CT
20 May 2024

52730947R00253